Finding Us

S.K. Hartley

For permission requests, write to the author, addressed "Attention: Permissions Coordinator," at
s.k.hartley@hotmail.co.uk

Praise for The Bad Boy Series

"S.K. knows how to pull my heart right out of my chest, then puts it back together whole and soundly beating."

– NYT & USA Today Bestselling Author, Katy Evans.

"S.K. Hartley takes you by the hand and straps you in for a rollercoaster ride."

– USA Today Bestselling Author, Belle Aurora.

"S.K. Hartley will have you rooting for one side, then throw you for a loop so you're cheering for the other and will turn everything upside down by the end."

– NYT, USA Today & Wall Street Journal Bestselling Author, Tijan.

Finding Us Playlist

"Brand New Day" – Ryan Star

"No Lies" – Jason Reeves ft. Colbie Caillat

"Home" – Birdy

"Words As Weapons" – Birdy

"Paradise" – Coldplay

"Love Will Tear Us Apart" – Broken Social Scene

"In My Blood" – Black Stone Cherry

"Castle Of Glass" – Linkin Park

"Smoke & Mirrors" – Gotye

"Jar of Hearts" – Christina Perri

"Dark Horse" – Katy Perry

"Figure.09" – Linkin Park

"Faint" – Linkin Park

"Breaking the Habit" – Linkin Park

"Wrecking Ball" – Miley Cyrus

"Crying For No Reason" – Katy B

'Finding'

– The action to find someone or something.

Even the dictionary can't deny the need to find love.

Prologue

6 Years Ago…

My right hand flexed around the 9mm Glock, my body instantly recognizing the weight against my palm. Slowly, I pulled it out from underneath my pillow, my hand tightening around the grip as I swiftly turned over in my bed, the sheets falling away from my body. Cold air greeted my legs as the tops of my thighs were exposed. I pointed the Glock at my bedroom door, where I was sure I could hear noises from the other side. I could hear my heart beating in my ears, distorting the sounds that were putting me on edge in the first place. Slowing my breathing, I tentatively pulled myself up from the bed, keeping my aim on the door as I moved to the middle of my room.

I waited.

My apple-scented shampoo hung in the air as my hair stuck to my face and neck, dropping my body temperature to new lows. My bedroom was small, only a single bed and a bedside table fit into the tiny box room. It was a far cry from what I was used to, the Manor seeming so far away. My breathing accelerated as the sounds became more audible, raising my heart rate to levels I had become accustomed to since I was a child.

I could hear footsteps, the floorboards in the hallway creaking under the intruder's feet as they moved closer. My eyes were concentrated on the slab of wood that separated me from the bullet waiting on the other side, my mind running through every possible escape route if I needed to take one.

Someone was going to die today; it wasn't going to be me.

The chill of the room cooled my skin as I stood in nothing but an oversized shirt and boy shorts, my skin prickling as my chest heaved with every breath. My breathing became sporadic; one minute it was calm, the next it was as if I couldn't catch my breath. I tried to take some control over my breathing, but my lungs felt like a lead weight in my chest.

Shit.

The creaking of the floorboards suddenly stopped: the silence in the house deafening. The chill had picked up, and I noticed I had left my window wide open. Rookie mistake? Or my saving grace? I could get out of that window and climb down from the second floor easily, but I knew as soon as I took a step towards the window, my intruder would be alerted to my movements. I had to face it—I had to face the possibility of my own death.

My trained ear listened for movement, but I heard nothing. Not a single damn thing. Had the intruder fled? Was that just wishful thinking? I held my breath and waited, then exhaling as I felt my heart becoming steadier. I slowly moved my finger to the trigger, ready to squeeze gently if I needed to. Suddenly, I heard the distinct sound of a cylinder from a revolver click back into place: a sound no one wants to hear in the middle of the night.

I braced myself, relaxing each and every muscle as I watched the handle of my door turn and click quietly. I could no longer control my breathing as the door opened inch by painful inch, accelerating my heartbeat tenfold. I couldn't see my intruder, just a silhouette as their arm came into focus.

I breathed in hard, exhaling as I took aim, counting back from three in my head. This could go so painfully wrong if I didn't time it just right.

Three…

Two…

One…

The second I was about the squeeze the trigger, I instantly recognized my intruder. My heartbeat quickened and I was no longer aiming my Glock. My hand loosened around the grip, and I stumbled from the weakness in my knees. My body was suddenly limp from the adrenaline that had been coursing through my veins, and even though I was weak, I smiled.

I was alive.

My knees were about to give out; I could feel them slowly buckling underneath my weight. My intruder was instantly by my side, snaking his hand around my waist and taking my weight like I was a child. My skin prickled, but this time it wasn't from the chill in the room; it was my body recognizing his rough voice, the familiarity.

"Come on, little Willow. Let's get you out of here."

Chapter One

"Oh, sweet Christ," I grumbled, squinting as the light filtered through the window and burned my sensitive eyes. I quickly forced them shut.

Ouch.

Pulling the pillow over my head, I groaned in protest as the side effects of drinking a stupid amount of tequila took hold of my poor, delicate brain. My tongue was dry as sandpaper against the disgustingly foul taste in my mouth as I clicked my tongue against the back of my bottom teeth. Fucking tequila and its stupid ideas.

Slowly, and with trepidation, I pried open my eyes. The harsh light sent a jolt of nausea right through to my unsteady gut. Oh shit, it was a bad one. My vision blurred for a couple of seconds before finally evening out, but it seemed my stomach was having other ideas. The sudden roll of my stomach had me bolting upright on the bed, praying the tequila gods would be kind to me.

Not likely.

My stomach rolled for a second time, but this time it was accompanied by a burning ache in my already dry throat. I sighed; it was more than likely I was spending the day with my head in the toilet bowl and cursing the idiot who thought it was a good idea to make the shit that put me in this state in the first place.

I was quickly on my feet when the third stomach roll bounded through my gut. I was going to throw up and it wasn't going to be pretty. My hands instantly went to my mouth as I made the dash to the en-suite bathroom. I was unsteady on my feet, crashing into a pile of books on the desk that sat against the wall beside the bathroom door.

"Fuck!" I hissed, causing ringing pain to jump through my skull. "Shit."

I made it just in time to pour my guts, and no doubt my dignity, straight into the toilet bowl. Minutes, hours, days ticked by. Slightly over-dramatic, but it felt like days with the never ending bile that erupted from my throat like a damn volcano. Sweat lined my body like a second skin as I peeled my head from the toilet seat, the foul taste of vomit taking over the musky aftertaste of tequila, each as disgusting as the other.

When I thought I couldn't possibly vomit anymore, I pulled off my sweat pants and Rolling Stones shirt. Stepping into the shower, I cranked up the heat to scalding levels, trying to rid myself of the gross smell of bars and booze. The heat from the spray awoke my mind and body, prickling at the sensitive nerves that rested just below my skin. Washing my hair, I was aware of the pulsing pain from my scar at the back of my scalp—it happened from time to time, a reminder—no doubt this time it probably had everything to do with the copious amount of tequila I had ingested the night before. The scar was something I carried and wore with pride, a reminder of my past: a past I was never going back to.

As I rinsed out the apple-scented shampoo from my hair, my head rang out in pain from the constant headache I was now sporting.

Courtesy of Mr. Jose Cuervo.

Thanks, Jose. Thank you very much.

"Stupid woman. Soooo smart drinking that much tequila, huh?" I grumbled to myself in a mocking tone.

The hangover hadn't lost any of its power over my weak body as I stepped out of the shower; if anything it was growing more and more determined to piss me off further. Grumbling, I managed to wrap a towel around my body and hair without any hangover related mishaps. In the past, there had been a few times where I had to peel myself from the slippery floor, and it hurt like a bitch. Standing in front of the mirror on the cabinet above the sink, I took in my appearance. Dark circles hung beneath my eyes; they were always there, consequences of being a light sleeper, even in my inebriated state. Then there were the scars—minute scars that lined small areas of my skin on my face. One just below my lip where my tooth had punctured my skin, another just above my left brow where my skin split. Scars and imperfections I would never allow anyone to see, not to mention the scar on my scalp that was still throbbing painfully.

Makeup, to most people, is a way of enhancing beauty, subtly showcasing beautiful features that, without it, dulled beneath their uneven skin tone. To me, makeup was much more than that; it was my way of hiding the ugliness that lurked within, hiding my scars and becoming my mask. I took pride in my makeup. It helped me through the times when I couldn't even look in the mirror to see the ugliness that had set in so deep. I had scars, not just the ones that sat on my skin; they were deeply engrained, a stark reminder of my hidden past.

Opening my makeup bag from beside the sink, I noticed my hands shaking as I pulled out a small jar of moisturizing cream. I sighed to myself. I needed coffee and some greasy food; tequila always had this effect on me; the trouble of wanting to drown out my past, I had no control or understanding of when to stop drinking the foul shit.

Shaking my head, I slowly applied the cream to my skin, ensuring I worked out every pore to its limit, concentrating on the big, gaping dark circles below my eyes. Once I had polished my skin with the cream, I set about applying the first and most important layer of my mask: foundation. People underestimate foundation; whether it be in powder or liquid form, it's exactly what it says it is: a foundation. You wouldn't try to build a home without putting down the foundation, it holds up everything that's built above it, making it stronger and more resilient to forces beyond our control.

It took half an hour to finally perfect the mask that would hide everything, to hide the person lurking in the background. Now I was Low Parker, the girl that didn't take shit from anyone, the girl who knew her identity and embraced it. We're all masked in one way or another, trying to hide something, or someone. No one's perfect. I had the scars the prove it.

The headache from my ridiculous hangover raged as I pulled on some black skinny jeans, bouncing around my skull like a tennis ball as I pulled on a cream tank top that read "Walking Disaster" in a thick black font. Ironic, considering my life and my current dark mood. Stepping into a pair of black cowboy boots, I was nearly ready to go. Picking up my phone from my bedside cabinet, I fired over a text to Neva, checking in on how she was doing, before throwing it into my purse along with all the other useless shit I needed.

The time read seven-thirty as I made my way out from the dorm and onto campus grounds, my hangover still ever present and kicking my brain's ass in the skull department. My mask may have been on, but deep down I was still the same person, no mask could ever truly hide the demons of our past, no matter how flawless the mask may be.

Taking a lung full of crisp, cool air, I made my way to the small coffee shop that sat on the corner just off campus. It was still early, only a few students passing me by, too worried about their own lives to take notice of the girl hiding in plain sight.

To my friends, I was the girl with the bubbly attitude and a fiery temper to boot. I was the girl who had the unenhanced blonde hair, ice blue eyes, and flawless makeup. But, I was more, so much more than anyone could ever imagine.

Shaking my head as if to rid my thoughts, I sped up my step, arriving at the Black Bean Coffee Shop in no time. The place was small, sitting right on the corner of the block of stores that lined the street. I loved this place: it was vintage, homely, and intimate. The exterior was painted in a pastel mint green, black lace stencils adorned the bottom half of the brick walls, while large bay windows showcased the vintage style further. A small scattering of black iron tables and chairs sat outside in the morning air, two spots already filled with students as they sipped their morning coffee, checking their Facebook pages no doubt.

Making my way into the shop, I smiled as the scent of coffee hit my nostrils. Since arriving at college, coffee has become my addiction, my weakness. I'll take it any way I can get it, as long as it's a double shot and piping hot. Thankfully, at this time of morning, the shop's pretty quiet. Stepping up to the counter, a wide smile broke my face as I noticed

Jared Spencer prancing around listening to *Roar* by Katy Perry as he made an espresso for the customer standing to the right of me.

"'Cause I am a champion and you're gonna hear me roar!" Jared sang cheerily as he slid the coffee to the woman chuckling beside me.

I rolled my eyes as he smiled, flashing me a wink.

"Usual?" he asked, pulling out two takeout cups.

"Do bears shit in the woods?" I said on a groan, the throb of my head reminding me I was still hung over.

It wasn't hard to notice the small sadistic smile Jared flashed as he went to work on my double shot espresso. Moments later he slid my espresso across the counter to my waiting hands.

"Ahh, liquid heaven." I sighed, inhaling the rich aroma from my coffee cup. The scent alone loosened my tense muscles, taking the edge off the monstrous hangover.

"Two skinny lattes!" Jared hollered to absolutely no one, the glint in his eyes told me he knew I was dealing with a hangover from hell. His voice sounded like a high pitch shrill, ringing into my ears and playing my brain like a freaking drum kit. I really should lay off the tequila… and kill Jared.

"Jared, dude, lower the freaking volume, would ya?!" I groaned, slowly rubbing my temples, trying to alleviate the throb that had decided to come back full force.

Jared's laughing eyes meet mine as he slid the lattes across the counter in a drink carrier to the customer who had stepped behind me. "Late night?" He chuckled.

Now if my head didn't feel like it was about to roll off my shoulders and land into a poor, unassuming stranger's lap, I would've probably slapped that stupid smile off his face. Jared Spencer was the hottest piece of ass on campus; dirty blond hair that was long in the front and short at the back, deep blue eyes that instantly pulled you in, and let's not forget the rocking hot body underneath his apron. But, there was a downside… he's gay. I'm not talking a little gay; I mean thrust your hip out, pout like a model gay. Such a shame.

"Just because you can swallow margaritas like water doesn't mean the rest of us can, you know," I said, raising my brow.

Placing his hand on his hip, he thrust it out to the side dramatically. "Girl, that's not the only thing I can swallow like wat-"

"La la la la! I can't hear you!" I shouted, cutting him off as I made a run for the door.

"Don't hate the player, girlfriend!" he called after me, leaning over the counter and sporting his gleaming smile.

I chuckled as I used my back to open the door. Stepping out on to the sidewalk, I took a lung full of air, hoping it would take the edge off this damn hangover. Nope, still felt like someone was pounding my head like a bongo drum. Sighing, I made my way back towards campus, with every step like pure torture to my painful head. My phone suddenly chimed in my purse and I groaned.

"Fuck," I muttered.

Trying to juggle my coffee, I pulled out my phone from my purse, taking a look at the screen I smiled. Tate. Sliding my finger across the screen, I put the phone to my ear using my shoulder.

"Mornin'!" I cheered into the phone.

"Hey baby," he huffed. He must be running, I thought; he ran every morning, no matter the weather. "I'm just on the last leg of my run, meet me at the coffee shop?"

"Way ahead of you, babe."

"Okay, I'll be there in a couple of minutes. You didn't harass Jared again, did you?"

"Would I?"

"Yes, yes, you would. Now, tell me what you're wearing." He chuckled huskily into my ear.

"Why do you want to know what I'm wearing?"

"Because I need to make sure that the woman I am about to throw over my shoulder is my girl."

"Arghhh!" I screamed as Tate flung me over his shoulder, my phone still attached to my ear and my coffee wobbling in my hand. "Tate, I'm going to drop the fucking coffee! Put me down!"

He laughed at my outburst, sliding me down the front of his sweaty body, making sure I felt every single muscle ripple underneath me. "What I have I told you about that filthy mouth of yours?" he husked into my ear.

I rolled my eyes as he took the coffee from my hand. "The only time I should be saying 'fuck' is when I'm underneath you."

Arrogant ass.

"You're finally learning," he whispered, leaning in and pressing his sweat-lined forehead against mine. His right arm snaked around my waist, pulling me towards his deliciously hot body. "Kiss me, Low."

His lips were so close to mine, holding me captive with every breath. This was what he did to me, holding me prisoner with his close proximity, rendering me completely stupid. I can't get my bearings around him, I never could. My control had left the building. Poof. Gone. Sliding my hand around his neck, I pulled him in the last couple of inches and crashed his lips to mine. My phone dangled from my fingertips as I moaned against his mouth. His lips were plump but soft, his bottom lip a little bigger than the top, fitting against mine perfectly. He was warm, so warm that I almost couldn't take the heat that radiated from him.

"I missed you last night," he growled against my lips, and I melted instantly.

No one has ever made me feel like Tate does, and it scared the shit out of me.

I slowly broke the kiss, stopping before we went further than a PG rating on the sidewalk. I needed to regain my focus: this is what happened anytime he was near. I was completely and utterly vulnerable when it came to him.

I lifted my gaze to his, trying hard not to lose myself in those deep green irises which held so many secrets, wisdom, and fear. We all have secrets; some are small but others can be big enough to break dreams and shatter futures. Everyone is hiding something: I was one of them.

"Hey, what's wrong?" he asked, holding my chin between his thumb and finger as his eyes inspected every inch of my face.

"I need to get over to Logan's, I need to give Neva the research she asked for," I dismissed, trying my hardest to break out the smile that told him I'm fine. For a minute I was sure he had found me out, his eyes stared into mine and for a fleeting second I couldn't help but hold my breath.

"Okay. I'm headed back to grab a shower, meet me after class?" he asked, seemingly unaware of my internal battle.

I nodded. Swiftly, he pressed a feather-light kiss to my lips before pulling back and turning to walk away.

"Oh, and remind that jackass that Coach wants a quiet word with him. And if he starts giving you crap about it, a swift punch in the nuts should suffice." He smiled over his shoulder before setting off at a brisk jog.

I chuckled before taking a sip of my searing hot coffee, the burn numbing my tongue – just the way I liked it. With my free hand, I pulled out my cell. Sliding my finger across the screen, I punched in Neva's cell and hit call. When there was no answer, I threw my phone back into my purse and made my way over to Logan's apartment. I shrugged: she was probably in the shower.

I took three flights of stairs to Logan's apartment, my hangover still in full force as every step felt like pure torture to every inch of my weak muscles. Slipping my copy of Neva's key into the door, I heard a click before I swung it wide open.

"S'appening, bitches!" I shouted, quickly regretting my dramatic entrance. "Oh. Dear. God!" I yelled, throwing my hands over my eyes. "I saw vagina… penis… ah, shit. My eyes, my eyes!"

"Get out, Low!" Neva shouted from the direction of the sofa.

"Oooof!" I grunted, taking something to the gut. Probably a cushion. "Okay, I'm going!" I turned, my hands still over my eyes, as I tried to navigate back out of the door.

"Ouch. Fuck!" I groaned as I walked into what felt like a wall. "Shit, my damn toe! The fuck's lying on the floor? It's a death trap for the currently sex blinded best friend in here!" I cursed, hopping on one foot.

"The door, Low!" Logan grunted from… somewhere in the room.

"Hey, don't get all snarky with me. I didn't come over here to see your wang and her cooter!"

"Low!" they shouted in unison.

"Okay, okay!" With my hands still over my eyes, I finally navigated my way out the door. Peering through my fingers, I sighed with relief as

I spotted the hallway wall opposite me.

Hangover—gone. Gross images of my best friend and her boyfriend bumping uglies on the sofa—ever fucking present. I looked down at my feet as a niggling sensation told me I'd forgotten something.

Clean panties? Check.

Matching shoes? Check.

Clean teeth? Check.

Huh. What was I missing? Then I looked down at my hands. Oops!

With the surprise of walking in on my friends, I must have dropped my damn coffee in the living room. Great.

"Ever heard of knocking?"

The sound of Neva's voice broke me out of my missing coffee induced thoughts. Turning, I couldn't help but laugh as she pulled down the hem of her oversized t-shirt.

"Trust me, I don't want to see..." I waved in her general direction, "*that* ever again." I cringed.

"Shut your face and come inside." She smirked, turning and walking back into Logan's apartment.

Walking through the door and into the living room, I suddenly let out a large belly laugh, throwing my head back as I noticed Logan on his knees, grumbling as he cleaned up what looked like a puddle of my coffee.

"You've domesticated him? Nice call," I said, flicking my gaze to my best friend, who only rolled her eyes at me.

"It's a good thing I have hardwood flooring, Low. Otherwise I would make you suck every drop of coffee out of the carpet." Logan grunted as he soaked up more of the coffee with a towel.

"Whatever you say, man whore." I smiled, producing a fake gasp. "I mean, reformed man whore." I smiled sweetly.

"I might change my major to forensics," he muttered under his breath.

"Whatever, you love me, really. Anyway, Tate told me to tell you that Coach wants a quiet word with you," I said with a wave of my hand.

"The fuck? Why?" he asked, standing from his position on the floor and wiping his hands on his unzipped jeans.

Rolling my eyes, I stepped towards him, quickly slamming my fist into his crotch.

"Oooof!" He gasped. "The fuck was that for?"

"For being a jackass." I laughed as he bent over, rubbing his nuts.

"Low, please leave my boyfriend's nuts alone, I need those," Neva shouted from the bedroom.

"Oh, that's just gross," I moaned mockingly, flashing a wink at Logan before walking to the bedroom.

Stepping into the room, I noticed how homely it had become. The last time I was here, I was dragging a pitiful Logan from his bed by his ankles, making him realize he had to fight for the love of his life. Fight for Neva. Now, a month later, it seemed as though things were good for them.

I let my gaze drift, taking in the room around me. The walls were painted an off-cream, a stark difference to the dark hardwood flooring. The furniture was minimal: two large dressers stood against the wall to my right, while a large queen size bed stood against the wall opposite. There were small trinkets here and there, but what caught my eye was the picture frame on the bedside table, with a picture of our little group. The picture must have been three years old, everyone looking a little less mature and innocent. There was me, Tate, Neva, Logan, Ace, and the twins.

"I miss those days," Neva said, standing by my side, now dressed in jeans and a fitted Goo Goo Dolls top.

"Yeah, we look so young," I whispered, staring into my own icy blue eyes.

"Tate had a thing for you even then." She laughed.

My eyes darted to hers, disbelief clogging my throat as she smiled.

"You really didn't know, did you?" she asked, taking the frame from my hands. "Look at his eyes, Low, they're solely focused on you."

She placed the frame back into my hands, shaking her head as she threw her hair up into a messy bun.

I took in the picture once more, my eyes trained on Tate as he stared at my younger self. I gulp hard: a lot had changed since then. Except me; I hadn't changed, just merely understood far more than I should.

“Do you think Ace had his wang pierced by then?” I laughed, swiftly changing the subject.

“Oh, god. I hope not.” She cringed, wrinkling her nose and shaking her head. Grabbing her jacket and purse, she flashed me a smile.

I chuckled, placing the frame back on the bedside cabinet and leaving the room.

Walking back into the living room, I watched with a smile as my best friend embraced the love of her life, holding on as he kissed her fiercely. He held her like she was strong, like she could hold her own. Unlike how fragile and breakable she had been only a couple of months ago. She had come a long way, facing the demons of her past head on, kicking their proverbial asses in the process. There were times where she still lacked the strength she needed, but now she had Logan, the man who had been with her through the rough and the smooth. He was her rock, and she damn well deserved it. They deserved each other, finally.

“For the love of all things holy, can you please stop sucking face? I already have a delicate stomach and I have a class to get to.” I groaned.

Pulling away, they both laughed. Neva rolled her eyes before placing another kiss on Logan’s lips.

“I love you,” she whispered.

“I love you too,” Logan replied with a show-stopping smile.

“Gag. I’m leaving the USB drive on the coffee table, I can’t stand around here much longer and watch your little love fest,” I said, placing the drive on the coffee table to my right.

Turning, Neva smiled and replied, “Thank you. You’re coming over to Bones tonight, right?”

“It’s a date!” I said over my shoulder as I made my way out of the apartment.

A warm March breeze danced over my neck as I finally made it out of the love shack that was Logan’s apartment, the smell of spring very much in the air. The scent of fresh lavender and blooming daisies hit my nostrils as I made it campus within ten minutes. Checking my watch, I had twenty minutes to get to Dr. Voxen’s criminology class. Criminology was my major; I loved trying to understand the mindset of crime in different situations in life and what could cause a person to turn to the crime world.

Pulling my purse higher on my shoulder, I slipped through the throng of students who were making their own way to classes. After finally navigating my way through the narrow corridor filled with bustling students, I made it to my criminology class with five minutes to spare. Opening the door and stepping in, I took my usual seat on the middle row.

The room was like every other in Spring Water College; white-washed walls filled with subject related articles in black frames, row after row of blue seating facing a dry erase board and desk.

The room slowly started to fill up as I pulled out my notepad and pen, ready to take notes on the subject I was most dreading: Organized Crime and the Psychological Implications. Criminology was a subject I was passionate about, and understanding just what made a criminal tick intrigued me. Dr. Voxen was a well-received expert within the field, a psychologist who had based most of his twenty year research on the most explosive of criminal minds behind bars: organized crime lords.

"Okay, settle down," Dr. Voxen announced as he made his way to his desk, throwing his briefcase down and taking out a projector pen. "Organized crime 101."

The light in the room suddenly eclipsed, placing a blanket of darkness over the entire room.

"Organized crime, in basic terms, is defined by a group of criminals engaging in illegal activity for monetary profit," he began, pressing a button on his projection clicker.

The first blood curdling image appeared before my eyes: six bodies laying underneath white sheets on the sidewalk. The black and white image itself an illusion to mask some of the distress within the image.

"However, this basic definition isn't categorically correct." He pressed the clicker to show another image. This time, it was an image of a young ethnic male. "Some organized crime is also politically motivated. This gentleman is Ali Saed Bin Ali El-Hoorie, one of the FBI's most wanted. Suspected of conspiracy to kill US nationals, amongst other charges."

Bowing my head, I quickly took down notes, not registering the click of the projection monitor as it moved to the next image.

"This is Julius Rowe." I inwardly gasped as I kept my head bowed down to my notepad. "Suspected of running one of the biggest mob families within the United States. The charges are anything from conspiracy to sell illegal firearms, to conspiracy to commit murder. He has never been arrested for these suspected crimes due to lack of evidence."

"You think they could come up with something more original," Ace's voice whispered into my ear.

"Fuck. Are you trying to give me a god damn heart attack?" I whisper-spat at Ace as he took his seat next to mine.

"Good of you to join us, Mr. Matthews; pressing engagement, was it?" the professor asked.

"Something like that, Doc." He smiled, leaning back into his chair, crossing his legs at his ankles in a defiant manner.

"Take notes, Mr. Matthews, I expect an eighty-thousand word essay on what we discuss today," Dr. Voxen said, rolling his eyes as he moved on to another image.

"Where have you really been, Ace?" I asked, my attention no longer on the professor.

"I don't think you want to know, darlin'." He winked, throwing me a cocky smile before wiggling his brows.

"No, I don't think I do." I laughed, turning back to my notes. "You headed to Bones with us later?"

"Depends." He shrugged nonchalantly.

"On what?" I asked, gently rubbing my temple, trying to alleviate the remaining dregs of my hangover.

"On whether my pressing engagement is still tied to my bed."

Chapter Two

Dr. Voxen's criminology class lasted a good three hours, discussing everything from the drug cartels to sex traffickers, arguing whether the criminals who ran them were certified sociopaths. I had taken at least ten pages of notes, hoping I had everything I needed to form the eighty-thousand word essay the professor required.

"It's a stupid question and you know it," Ace said, flicking through the first couple of pages of my notes as we sat in the college library.

I had needed extra notes on previous research from other medical journals, and of course Ace had to tag his whiney ass along.

"No, you think it's a stupid question because you're a Mr. Know-It-All who is only taking this class because you need to minor in it to get picked up by the top legal firms in the country," I said, raising my brow and turning the page of the book labelled 'Criminal Sociopaths and the Psychological Impact on the Human Brain.'

"Explain the differences between the social…" Ace said, waving his hand in the air.

"… and political impact of organized crime," I finished for him.

"Yeah, that. That's a pile of BS and you know it," he countered, trying to put his point across. "I mean, who cares what the impact is? Shouldn't we be concentrating on how to rid the problem in the first place before we study the impact of it?"

"Ace, I'm not even going to argue with you on this one. You're a law student; I don't stand a chance of even explaining my side of the argument." I laughed, watching as his lips curled into an over-dramatic pout.

"Spoil sport." He winked before pulling out his phone and focusing on the screen. "Lover boy is on his way here."

I rolled my eyes as he tried to hide his deep chuckle under a mocking cough.

"You drive me fucking nuts, you know that?" I said, giving him a right hook to his bicep.

"That all you got?" He laughed, pointing to the knuckles on the hand I had just punched him with. "Really?"

Ace was an underground cage fighter, and built for it too. His biceps and triceps weren't just unreal, they were like a work of art; each definition a show of just how many hours he had put into training. Underneath the hard exterior was an even harder inner shell, the other side to Ace: his legal side. Ace wasn't just one of the best underground fighters within the circuit, he was a rising law student who pretty much had the pick of the top firms in the US.

An animal in the cage, a viper in the court room.

A law student by day, wearing smart, crisp suits without a slither of metal on his body. A cage fighter by night, wearing semi-tight board shorts and showing off every single inch of inked and pierced skin. He was a certified bad boy with the grades of a first class nerd – he was a walking contradiction.

"Shut up, douche bag," I said, slapping him upside the head. "Anyway, Bones. Or have you still got some poor girl tied to that bed of yours?"

"Wouldn't you like to know."

"No, no, actually, I really wouldn't." I cringed, wrinkling my nose and shaking my head. "Seriously, are you coming or are you just going to avoid my question?"

"Oh, I'll definitely be coming."

"Do you have just the smallest hint of a filter? You know, that thing in your brain that tells you to shut the fuck up?"

"No, he doesn't and I wonder where yours goes too." Tate chuckled as he walked over to our table. "You ready? We have a couple of hours before we need to meet Neva."

Flickering my gaze to my watch, I noticed the time. Shit, I'm going to be late. Tonight Neva was singing at the bar just outside of Spring Water called Bones. It was a rock bar where she sang and also worked part-time behind the bar.

"You going to need my notes for the essay, dude?" I asked as I started packing the books into my overly large purse.

"No, I'm good," Ace said, rubbing the muscles on the back of his neck. "I have some shit to do. I'll text you if I can make it over to the bar."

With that, he gave Tate a slap on the shoulder and made his way out of the library. Smiling at Tate, I packed away the last of my things before placing a small kiss on his lips.

"What was that for?" he asked, grabbing at my hips and pulling me closer.

"No reason." I chuckled, wrapping my arms around his neck and pulling him flush to my body.

The laughter soon died on my lips as he swept in and crashed his lips to mine, sending spine-numbing tingles throughout my entire body. The hot, wet heat from his mouth captivated me, keeping me frozen to the spot. His tongue expertly slid along my bottom lip, seeking the entry he desperately craved. I shouldn't cave into his domineering mouth, but my body betrayed me; it betrayed me at every turn when it came to him. I opened for him, allowing him to slip his tongue inside my mouth. His tongue slid against mine like he was hungry, like a man starved of oxygen and I was the only source for miles.

A low groan escaped him as his sucked on my bottom lip. Fire ignited everywhere, sending my head into a tailspin and causing my panties to instantly combust. His hands moved to my face, cupping me gently, but felt as though he was leaving his mark. A mark only I knew was there. I moaned deep into his mouth as he slid his tongue back against mine, fighting for domination of my mouth. My hands tangled in his hair, my nails scraping along his scalp as I held on for dear life. When he kissed me like this, I was a goner. No one else mattered; the world would fall away at my feet while he held me up, floating into nothingness and taking my breath away with every stroke of his tongue.

"You drive me crazy," he whispered as he pulled back from the kiss, resting his forehead against mine.

I was speechless, completely speechless. Tate undoubtedly takes my breath away, stealing it like a thief, keeping it until I begged for it back.

"I can't think straight when you do that," I said breathlessly.

"Good," he growled. "Ready to go?"

"Uh, yeah." I smiled, trying my hardest to hide how much of an effect Tate really had on me.

"Did I make you all weak at the knees, baby?" He chuckled, taking my hand in his as we made our way out from the library.

"I'm pleading the fifth," I joked.

It was anything but a joke, but I couldn't even admit that to myself, never mind Tate.

The warmth of the June air heated my cheeks as we stepped out onto campus grounds, making our way back to our dorm building. The temperature had picked up several degrees since being inside, and I couldn't help but inhale the sweet, crisp air. The morning mishaps had quickly been forgotten as we rolled into the early afternoon, although the imprint of Logan and Neva would be something I wouldn't forget in a hurry. Ugh.

Our little group had been together for six years, ever since I stepped foot in Spring Water with my mom. Neva James was the first person who spoke to me; she was the only one with the balls to back then. I hadn't been the most gracious teenager when I had gotten here, rebelling was my thing, flipping the bird at as many adults as I possibly could, pissing off every available weak girl in high school. I was young, dumb, and unforgiving, but Neva was the one person who could see past my shit and call me out on my defense tactics.

When you grow up in the deep, dark depths of social deprivation, making friends isn't at the top of the list when you move to a new town. But friends were exactly what I made; it wasn't at all easy, but I got there in the end. Once I had become friends with Neva, the friends kept on coming. Neva introduced me to her brother, Tate, and once we were friends, I soon met the rest of the group. Next came Logan White, the self-confessed man whore who would screw anything with a vagina and a great pair of legs: his words, not mine. Then there were the twins, the gruesome twosome – Zane and Colt. They fought over everything: who was the best looking, who picked up the hottest girls, who had the better arm. But most of the time we referred to them as Asshat One and Asshat Two. Last but not least was Ace, the one who scared the ever loving shit out of students and most teachers: top law student by day, and prized underground cage fighter by night.

The overpowering scent of far too much cologne pulled me out of my thoughts, as I noticed we had made it to the dorm. The smell of Old Spice mixed with sweat burned at my nostrils as Tate and I made our way up the staircase.

"I'm going to get ready in my room," I said as we made it to the second floor.

"Okay, I'll get ready and meet you at Logan's. You take forever in the damn shower," he said, rolling his eyes before placing a lingering kiss on my lips.

"Don't take long. You're staying with me tonight," he whispered against my lips.

It wasn't a threat but a sweet, delicious promise of what was yet to come. My knees knocked for the second time that day, all fueled by the one man who could instantly bring me to my knees with just a single sentence.

"Tate," I moaned, the sudden inability to sound like anything but a quivering mess of hormones struck me like a baseball bat to the head.

"Tonight, Low. I want you in my bed."

I gasped as I felt Tate's thumb graze the apex of my right thigh, his hand shielded from the rest of the students by his muscular frame. I couldn't form a single word, or produce a comeback that would pull us out of the lust filled moment. I was a prisoner, and he was my captor, keeping me silent and still with the smallest of touch from just the pad of his thumb.

"Wear something that's easily removable." He groaned, moving his thumb an inch higher. "Or I'll rip apart anything that gets in my way."

"Okay," I whispered, the husk of my voice surprising even myself.

"Be quick," he said before quickly crashing his lips to mine, only to pull away the second a low moan escaped my mouth.

With a quick wink over his shoulder, Tate made his way up to the third floor. I couldn't help but stare at his ass as it moved deliciously with every step he took. Dammit.

It took me a couple of minutes to finally get my bearings and stop the gush of hormones that had pooled in my panties. Once I could finally think without Tate's ass imprinted at the forefront of my mind, I made my way down the second floor corridor to my dorm room that I shared with Neva. She hadn't stayed with me in over three weeks now; most of her time was spent at Logan's place. Even though she outright refused to move in with Logan, it was only going to be a matter of time before the rest of her stuff moved in with him.

Stepping into the room, I scanned my surroundings. Not a single thing out of place. Everything was where I left it: the six pairs of jeans on Neva's bed, the pairs of shoes scattered across the room, and the books I had knocked off the desk on my hasty dash to the toilet. What can I say? I'm a slob. Sighing, I shut the door and slung my purse onto my desk, pulling out the notes I needed to write my essay tomorrow. Tonight the group's going to Bones, since Neva was singing in between working her shift. Every Friday night we would all meet up at the bar. It'd become some sort of ritual within the group, and we were all there to support Neva.

Once I had sorted through my purse and cleared up my desk, I went to work on cleaning the room. The six pairs of jeans went back into the closet, along with the shoes that I had unceremoniously tripped over in my hangover coma that morning. Soon after, I finally stripped bare and stepped into the shower, washing away the muggy warmth that had attached to my skin from the spring weather. Lathering up my hair with usual shampoo, I washed my blonde locks before quickly shaving and pampering my body with coconut milk.

Ten minutes later, I was stepping out from the shower feeling re-refreshed and smelling rather delicious. Wrapping a towel around my body and my hair, I quickly brushed my teeth and pulled out my makeup bag for the second time today. Padding back into the room, I dumped the bag on my bed, and sat down in the middle of my comforter.

Tonight, I was Low Parker: blonde locks, blue eyes, and no visible scars.

After thirty minutes, my makeup was in place, masking the scars that haunted me daily. Dark coal lined my eyes, enhancing the icy blue tones of my irises. A small amount of blush coated my cheeks, and grape flavored gloss shined against my full lips.

Unraveling my hair from the confines of its toweling prison, I soon went to work, turning my hair from a wet and limp texture to a soft and full bodied look. I quickly curled the ends with my hot iron before throwing on a dress that I had kept away for a special occasion.

The dress was a pastel pink, tight and sleek from the shoulders straight down to the very top of my calves. It was fitted against every inch of flesh it covered, the deep set v-neck enhancing my ample sized chest. Matching the dress with my nude heels, I was ready. It was simple, yet pretty.

It was Low.

I grabbed a cab to Logan's, the air still crisp and warm as I made my way up to his apartment. Ensuring I didn't walk in on anymore sexcapades, I knocked loudly on the door. Seconds later, a very wide eyed Tate greeted me.

"Christ." He groaned, raking his eyes down the length of my body.

I could feel his gaze everywhere: my eyes, my chest, my legs. Heat pooled between my thighs as his gaze lingered on my nude heels. When I was around Tate, I was vulnerable, exposed, and completely under his control. He hadn't even touched me and I was an internal mess.

"Tate, we need to go man!" Logan hollered from inside the apartment. "Is that Low?"

"Yeah!" Tate yelled, his gaze never leaving mine.

Slowly, Tate's arms crossed at his chest, his right shoulder resting against the door frame. He was just… watching me. His gaze was like tiny little pin pricks against my exposed flesh, bringing goosebumps to rise to the surface.

"Is everyone ready?" I asked, fumbling with my purse in my right hand, trying to focus on something other than the man who turned me into a puddle of mush.

"Yes," he paused, standing at full height before pulling the door closed behind him as he stepped forward. "But we can't go yet."

"What?" I asked, snapping my gaze to his.

His deep green eyes were filled with hunger, smoldering under my gaze as he took another step towards me. It was only when he stepped further into the light that I could really take in his appearance. My god. He was six feet three of purebred male. His legs—my god, his legs—thick and strong at the thigh, as his tight black jeans hugged them as if desperately clinging on. His abdomen, shielded by the white button-down shirt, was solid muscle, each individual abdominal muscle a treasure trove to explore. His shoulders, thick and full, caused the fabric of his shirt to stretch to full capacity. His forearms, masculine and bare, were exposed by his shirt rolled up to his elbows.

He was walking criminal sex, and I was his willing victim.

But what I couldn't take my eyes off were his lips. Pink. Full. Sexy. His strong jaw line only accentuating them more. Then there was his nose, a small scar glinting against the harsh light of the apartment building corridor; it had been broken a few times over the years. Then there was the five o'clock shadow that lined his jaw. Jesus.

"Baby, are you with me?" he whispered, taking the last step between us, cupping my face with his strong hands.

"Y … yes," I stuttered, trying hard to stop the stupid flutter that had taken over my stomach.

"You look beautiful," he said before slowly dipping his head, pressing his lips against mine.

He lingered, pressing just a little bit harder, enough for me to want to push back against him. But, the moment I did, he quickly broke away, sucking on the corner of his bottom lip.

"Grape." He smiled as he sucked away the gloss that had transferred from my lips to his.

"Step away from the goods, dude, we need to go!"

Chuckling, I peered my head around Tate's large frame, spotting the twins, Zane and Colt, behind him. I couldn't tell who had made the comment, but judging by Colt's sneaky wink, it must have been him.

"Did you really just refer to her as 'the goods'?" Zane laughed, shaking his head at his twin.

"What? She has goods, lots of goods in that damn dress too!" Colt said, flashing me a cocky grin. Asshat.

Before I knew what had happened, Tate's hand suddenly came out, landing with a loud smack against the back of Colt's head.

"Oooof! What the hell, man? It was a joke, a joke, I swear!" he said, holding his hands up in mock surrender as he shook his head from side to side.

"You," Zane said, pushing his index finger into his twin's chest, "are a first class idiot."

"Me?" Colt scoffed, swatting Zane's finger away. "It was a joke. Fuck, are you all on the rag or some shit? I'm sure there's some Midol in the apartment, maybe some damn chocolate too."

"You're a douche," Zane muttered, throwing on his jacket as he quickly made his way down the staircase.

"Fucking PMS-ing and shit…" Colt muttered as he followed closely behind his brother.

Moments later, out walked a clearly stressed Logan.

"Having those two here is like having fucking kids! They should be on an ad for the next condom commercial. What happens if you don't wrap that shit up," he said, shaking his head before descending the stairs, joining the rest of the group.

Looking back at Tate I couldn't help but let out a full belly laugh; the instant the sound broke through my lips, Tate joined me. He threw back his head and let out the sexiest noise I'd ever heard. His laugh was deep and husky, the sound instantly heating my cheeks… and my panties.

Tonight, Tate was going to take me: he was going to stake his claim on me. He was going to make me his without fear or thought. He was going to ruin me, and what scared me the most was… I wanted him to.

Chapter Three

Bones was filled with a sea of people from wall to wall, all fighting for a spot at the bar to order their drinks. We had been lucky, our table was clear and ready for us when we walked in only fifteen minutes ago, thanks to the awesome Dex and Trix that worked behind the bar with Neva.

"I'll have Cowgirl bring over your drink order, it's fucking suffocating in here tonight!" Dex hollered into my ear.

I couldn't help but laugh at Dex's nickname for Neva; he had dubbed her Cowgirl the day she dropped by the bar and subsequently got a job. He said it's because she would look hot in a checkered shirt and cowboy boots. I rolled my eyes.

"Okay. How is she?" I asked, my voice louder to compensate for the harsh bass of the speakers pouring out some rock music I had never heard before.

"She's good, but I might need to call in some more staff, damn rednecks are crazy tonight!" Dex said, pointing to the never ending sea of people shouting their drink orders at the bar.

Bones was a large bar on the outskirts of Spring Water. It was seen as a biker bar due to all the bikers that stopped by Saturday night for their drinks, but for the rest of the week, it was a chance for students in the area to hang out.

The bar was pretty large, the deep mahogany wood spanning the back wall, opposite of the heavy double doors that you walked in through. The floors were lined with vintage style black and white tiles, while the walls were a deep crimson, holding vintage rock artwork. To the left of the doors stood a small stage, the large speakers covering most of its floor room, and a microphone stand up front. Tonight was open mic night, and Neva was the regular singer with her guitar.

"I'll lend a hand if you need it," I said to Dex. My voice strained as I tried to project it over the loud bass.

"You will?" he asked, clearly shocked at my statement.

"Yeah, of course." I smiled, scanning the excitable crowd.

"I knew there was a reason why I loved Cowgirl." He chuckled, flicking his head in Neva's direction behind the bar. "Have a drink first, and if we're still at capacity, I'll holler. Cowgirl's on in an hour."

With that, Dex started making his way through the crowd, leaping over the bar before he got mobbed for some alcohol.

"Calm the fuck down or no one is getting served!" he shouted, quickly taking orders and sliding them down the bar to the greedy hands of his customers.

Turning back to our group I couldn't help but chuckle as Zane punched Colt in the shoulder. Colt was clearly in the mood to drive everyone nuts tonight, and it seemed as though he was getting on his twin's last nerve.

"Dude, seriously! Get your grubby hands off me, I don't know where that shit has been!" Colt said, throwing a wad of tissue at his twin.

"Will you stop being such a penis, Colt, you're driving me freaking nuts when we should be scouting for hot women!" Zane fired back.

"I don't need to scout, the women come to me. They can't resist the charm that pours from my lips," Colt said, flashing a smirk towards me.

"The only thing that pours from your lips is a boatload of BS. Please, for the love of God, shut the fuck up. I haven't had enough alcohol to even think about dealing with you two tonight," Tate said, scraping his chair against the tiled floor, leaving his seat as he made his way over to the bar.

"Y'all are cramping my style. I love y'all but you're doing nothing for the Colt-myster!" Colt said, standing from his seat and thrusting out his hips.

I couldn't help but snort. "Wait, Colt-myster? What the hell is that?"

I shouldn't have asked, it would only encourage him, but I did…

"Do you need a diagram, Low?" Zane said, jumping in. "Penis, wang, cock, dick, pickle, wiener, baby maker… whatever you call the male genitals. Colt over here calls it the Colt-myster. But don't worry, I don't call mine anything weird."

"Thank god." I laughed as Tate brought over our drinks, taking his seat next to me. "So, I'm curious, what do you call it then, Zane?"

He shrugged his shoulders before smirking at his brother, "The Zane-inator."

"Oh. Dear. God." I laughed, throwing my head back.

"Christ." Logan groaned, while Tate just shook his head.

Flashing their mega-watt smiles, Zane and Colt grabbed their beers from the table before making their way into the throng of people near the bar. I was under no illusion that some poor girls were about to be Zane-inated and Colt-mystered. Cringe.

"Wow," I muttered before taking a long pull of my Corona.

"Wow doesn't even cover… that." Logan groaned, nodding his head towards the twins.

Turning in my seat, I couldn't help but laugh. The guys had found their latest victims, two blonde students who didn't look like they had a hope in hell. Poor girls.

"They must have something, I've never seen them go home alone after a night out," Logan said, picking at the label on his beer bottle.

"Whatever it is, it's working," Tate muttered, turning towards the twins.

"Yo, blondie!" Dex hollered from behind the bar, sliding three bottles of beer effortlessly down the bar to the waiting customers' hands. "I'm going to need your hot ass behind this bar!"

I'm sure I heard Tate growl at Dex's comment, but thankfully he knew it was all in good fun. Dex is pretty much Ace's twin… no filter. Speaking of Ace, I wondered where he was and if he had untied his latest conquest from his bed.

"Don't be long, baby, that hot ass is mine," Tate grunted into my ear, placing a feather-light kiss on the soft flesh just behind my ear.

The simple act made my whole body shudder in absolute want. He knew what he was doing. No matter how much we questioned what it was that the twins had, I knew Tate had it in abundance. Patience, desire, passion—rolled into one slow and delicious race to mutual satisfaction.

It was anticipation.

I nodded to Tate before standing on shaky legs. Pausing for a moment, I regained my balance; knowing full well it wasn't from the small amount of alcohol I'd consumed, or how high my heels were. It was him. Tate could turn my body into jello with just the mere promise of what was yet to come.

Once I could finally move, I made my way to the door to the side of the bar. Walking into the back, I spotted Neva grabbing a couple of bottles of spirits.

"I didn't peg you for a vodka drinker," I said, sneaking up behind my best friend.

"Holy shit!" she squealed, all but jumping out of her skin as she tried to keep hold of the bottles rattling around in her hands.

"I'm so sorry, I couldn't help it." I laughed, taking two bottles from her hands.

"Are you trying to give me a heart attack before I'm twenty-five?! Jesus, Low!" She chuckled, pressing her now free hand against her chest. "What are you doing back here anyway?"

"Dex asked me to help out." I shrugged.

"Really?" She questioned, eyeing my dress. "Dude, how the hell are you going to serve drinks in that dress… and, Jesus, those damn heels? You're going to fall flat on your face!"

As if on cue, my right heel pinched against the flesh of my ankle. She was probably right.

"I'll be fine," I said, waving her off. "I have a very particular set of skills, skills I have acquired over a very long career."

"Did you… did you just quote Liam Neeson?"

"Skills that make me a nightmare for people like you," I said in a monotone voice.

"Yep, she's quoting Liam Neeson," Neva said, shaking her head as she looked up to the ceiling.

"If you let my vodka go now, that'll be the end of it. I will not look for you, I will not pursue you. But if you don't, I will look for you, I will find you, and I will kill you," I finished.

"Are you high?"

"No, why?" I scoffed.

"You freaking should be," she said, letting out a deep laugh. "Of all the people you could have quoted, you picked Liam Neeson?"

"What the hell is wrong with Liam? His voice is all husky and sexy."

"He's old enough to be your dad," she countered. She did have a point.

"So's George Clooney," I argued.

"You think George Clooney is hot?! What's wrong with you?" She laughed, shaking her head at me for a second time.

"There'll be a lot wrong with both of you if you don't get your asses out here! I'm drowning in pushed up tits and angry fists!" Dex shouted from the bar.

"Like he doesn't love pushed up tits," Neva said, rolling her eyes. "Come on, we need to get through some of these drink orders, Mrs. Neeson."

"Har har! You're a comedian," I said, tightening my grip on the vodka bottles as we pushed our way through the bar door to Dex.

As I stepped behind the bar, I was hit with a sea of people, all of them shouting drink orders and waving money in my face. Damn idiots.

"Hey, doll face. Four Jack and Cokes and whatever your pretty self is drinking."

Oh yeah. It was going to be a long night.

It took two hours, two hours to clear the bar of the raging rednecks mingled between the students, all desperate for a drink of alcohol. The balls of my feet ached as I slumped back against the wall of the bar. Neva was right; these damn shoes would be the death of me.

The bar had quieted a bit, some leaving to find more alcohol at another bar while others found seats and were enjoying the company and drinks. Surveying the room, my eyes landed on Tate, who was now stalking his way towards the bar.

"What can I get for you, kind sir?" I said in a Southern drawl, placing my elbows on top of the bar, leaning towards him.

"My girlfriend," he said with a smirk. "She has these incredible legs I've been staring at all night, imagining them wrapped around my shoulders while I feast on her. Would you be a doll and go fetch her for me? Oh, and another bottle of Corona?"

"You're too much, Tate James." I laughed, grabbing a bottle, pulling the top off it and shoving a lime slice down the neck before handing it to Tate.

"You're forgetting something," he said, taking long pull of his drink. "I have my beer, now I want my woman."

Before I could even blink, Tate was over the bar, wrapping his hands around my waist before hiking me up onto his shoulder, smacking my ass hard. Throwing a wink over his shoulder to his sister and Trix, he marched his way into the back room of the bar.

"Now that you have your woman, what do you plan on doing with her?" I asked playfully.

Tate slowly slid me down the front of his body, stopping only when his hands cradled my ass. I threw my legs around his waist as he pushed me against one of the walls in the room.

"I'm going to do exactly as I imagined with these damn legs." He groaned before swiftly thrusting my ass into the air, my legs wrapping around his shoulders.

"Jesus," I whispered as Tate ran his nose down the apex of my right thigh. "Tate, not in here."

Was he crazy? He wanted to do this now? We were in a darkened room attached to the bar, not an ideal place to be doing anything!

Tate groaned, his fingers digging into the flesh of my exposed thighs, hard enough to leave bruises.

"Thirty minutes, baby, that's how long it will take to get back to my place. Can you wait that long?" he asked, his voice sending vibrations from my thighs straight to my core.

"What about Neva's set?" I panted, his nose only inches away from my panties.

"Her set was an hour ago, baby. She couldn't leave the bar," he moaned as he inhaled hard against the soft lace.

"Tate," I moaned as he bit the skin of my left thigh.

"You have a choice, Low. Either I take you right here, right now or… you come home with me so I can make you scream over and over. Pick, and be damn quick about it. Otherwise I'll just take you any way I can damn well have you."

I groaned as my head fell back against the hard surface of the wall that supported me, the promise in Tate's voice making me quiver and writhe against him. There was no doubt in my mind I wanted Tate to take me, to completely unravel me, but I knew if he did, I could become exposed.

Three months, three months of no sex felt like a damn eternity. I wasn't a virgin by any means but I put a halt on my and Tate's sexual relationship; it just wasn't a good idea. Explaining to Tate why I couldn't let him take me, own me or completely ruin me was hard; he didn't understand. Instead, I lied. I told him I was innocent, that I just wasn't ready. It was another lie I had concocted to keep him safe, and it seemed to work. Until now.

Do I risk exposing myself? Do I risk putting Tate in the firing line? Do I go with my heart, not my head? My head was screaming, "Don't be a fucking fool!" While my heart was begging for me just to let the fractures of my mask crack a little bit more.

"Baby, I need an answer. Now," Tate growled as he swiped his tongue up the seam of my panties.

Hormones, want, need, and complete lust wrapped around my mind like a thick blanket, suffocating all rational thought, including the voice telling me to back the hell away. The only thing I could hear was my heart, begging, pleading, wanting to be understood and taken by the man who could ultimately destroy me.

"Take me home, Tate," I moaned as I felt him smile against my sensitive flesh.

My heart's a fucking moron.

Hands fumbled.

Teeth clattered.

Moans erupted.

We crashed into his dorm room, the lust completely over taking my body as his fingers delved into the slick flesh between my legs. I had no idea what happened to my panties, but when my gaze flickered to the floor I spotted them, completely fucking ruined. I shuddered and panted as I realized the panties represented exactly what Tate could do: rip me apart, right down the seam.

My breathing hitched as fingers probed, teeth nibbled, and moans escalated. I couldn't work out which way was up, whether I was standing or floating, or even work out if any of this was real. The out of body experience was a surprise to me. This was something I should've been preventing, but was I strong enough to stop it? Right now, no way in hell.

I moaned into Tate's neck as he lifted me from the ground, my legs instantly wrapping around his waist as I quickly realized this *was* real. I wasn't floating, and the only thing that was up was Tate, whose hardness was pressing against my pubic bone. I was in big trouble.

Once again my back slammed into the hard concrete of a wall, only this time we were in Tate's dorm room, and not some seedy back room of a bar. My dress was now three quarters of the way up my thighs, and with my panties completely disintegrated, I was exposed in far many more ways than one.

Tate's lips quickly came crashing down to mine as he rolled his hips against me; opening for him I lost any conscious thought as his eager tongue danced with my own, pulling every ounce of pleasure from my lips. Tate's fingers threaded in my hair as his left hand cupped my right breast with only his waist supporting me against the wall. A moan ripped from my lips as Tate carried on rolling his hips against my sex, the sensation awakening every delicate nerve ending in my body. He knew what he was doing, and my god he was good at it.

"You like that?" Tate growled, adding pressure to the roll of his hips.

I could only moan in response. All coherent thought had flown right out of the window the minute he pinned me against the wall in the back room of the bar. I should put a stop to it, I should tell him I'm not ready for this, but with every roll of his delicious hips, I could barely remember my own name.

Suddenly I was crying out, his fingers sliding against the slick, wet heat between my thighs. I was panting, holding on for dear life as my body took over my mind, my tongue fighting for control against his. We were suddenly in a battle: a battle for control, domination and pleasure. Our lips broke apart, only enough to pull my dress and his shirt from our bodies.

Tate's bare chest pressed against my still covered breasts as he rolled his hips against me once more, his lips coming back down to my own as his fingers still worked my sex. I could feel the orgasm building from deep within, filling out the hollow recesses of my body as it moved to the very tip of my toes.

The rough surface against my back suddenly changed to the soft comforter on Tate's bed, sending my heart rate spiraling as I came back down to reality. This wasn't a good idea; in fact, it was a fucking stupid idea. I couldn't do it.

"Tate." I groaned as his fingers went back to working me at a delectable tempo.

I needed to stop. I needed him to stop. Someone could get hurt.

"Tate… stop."

His body instantly stilled above me, his eyes searching for answers I couldn't give him. My head quickly snapped to the left, not wanting him to see the fear that shone behind my eyes.

"Baby, look at me," he whispered, grasping my chin between his thumb and finger, turning my head back to his. "Tell me what's wrong."

"I.. I can't," I said, closing my eyes and willing my thoughts to disappear.

"I will never pressure you into something you're not ready for." He pressed a feather-light kiss to my lips. "But it doesn't mean I can't make you feel."

His lips, so soft, so tempting, I was a goner no matter the outcome.

"Let me make you feel, Low," he whispered before gently pressing his lips against the hollow of my neck.

I was done for. I couldn't control the reaction my body had to his words, to him. Instead of pushing him off me, my legs clasped around his middle. Pulling him closer to my bare core, my hips moved of their own accord, seeking the delicious friction I knew I wanted.

"I need to hear you say it, baby. I'm not doing this without your full attention."

His voice rang out to my ears, a mixture of a gravelly husk and sweet lust wrapped around something I thought had hardened and vanished years ago, something I never knew I still owned… My heart.

My heart's a fucking idiot.

"Make me feel," I whispered on a shaky breath.

My eyes finally opened as Tate lowered himself down the bed, his lips gliding along my still covered breasts, kissing each peak before unclasping my black lace bra at the front. It seemed underwear was never going to be a barrier.

I watched in lust-filled awe as Tate moved lower, skimming my navel with his tongue before placing a slow, wet kiss against both my hip bones. My control was tearing apart, shred by tiny shred as he cast his hooded gaze to mine. His gaze burned against my skin as his hand cupped my right breast while simultaneously biting the apex of my left thigh. Holy god. The sensation rewoke the orgasm that had long faded, springing right back into action.

My hands fisted the comforter as Tate blew one long, slow breath against my sex, causing me to quiver and moan while squeezing my right breast in his hand. I waited, panting and needy, for his next move, but it never came. Pushing myself up onto my elbows, I came face to face with a cocky Tate, a smirk upon his lips and my breast in his hand.

"What are you… oooh," I moaned as his tongue ran up my sex in one sharp, swift lick.

Oh. Dear. God.

My elbows gave out as he slowly lapped, sucked, and probed me. The groans of approval that fell from his lips only spurred on the orgasm that was quickly growing in intensity. My hips bucked, begging for the friction I so desperately craved.

If I thought my mouth had no filter before, it certainly didn't now. The moans, groans and curses that fell from my lips seemed to ricochet in the room, seemingly encouraging Tate further and further before my orgasm suddenly crashed right through me like a damn freight train.

Black spots danced in front of my eyes as I rode out my orgasm as Tate gently kissed my sex as I shook and quivered underneath his touch. Once my breathing finally became slightly more even, my gaze landed on Tate, who was smirking above me.

"What?" I laughed, seemingly embarrassed.

"Mouth of a sailor." He smiled, kissing me fiercely, allowing me to taste my own arousal on his tongue before pulling back. "But sweet as a peach."

My cheeks flamed crimson as I bit down on my bottom lip, trying to hold back the fear I could feel burning the back of my throat. Shit, trouble doesn't even cover what the situation is right now. More like one gigantic clusterfuck.

"You okay?" Tate asked, raising his brow, moving a stray piece of hair from my face to behind my ear.

No. No, I was far from it.

"Yeah, I'm good." The quiver in my voice was hard to mask.

He stared at me pointedly for what seemed like minutes, but was more like seconds. A moment of uncertainty flashed in his eyes, and for my own selfish reasons, I did the only thing I knew would keep him at peace: I kissed him.

Our lips met in a slow, sensual kiss. I had no intentions of it being slow, but the minute his lips met mine, I was in a world of clichés, the ones I read about in romance novels that made me question love. Butterflies danced around my stomach like they were on fire, burning deep inside while my heartbeat skyrocketed to new highs as his tongue stroked mine slowly.

"Wow," I said, pulling back from his lips.

Tate chuckled softly as he rested his forehead against mine, but every time his breath fanned against my lips I could feel the emotional teenager break out from deep inside. The girl who just wants to be held, loved, worshiped; she's breaking through the hard inner shell and further cracking the fractures of the mask desperate to keep her hidden.

"Wow is right," Tate said, placing a small kiss at the tip of my nose before jumping up from my body.

I watched in fascination as Tate unbuttoned his jeans and dropped them to his ankles, clad in only his boxers he flashed a cocky grin my way. I couldn't take my eyes from his body, sculpted in a way that had me almost drooling.

"See something you like?" He winked before turning his back to me and dropping the last shred of material from his body.

Speechless. Completely and utterly speechless.

I was quickly up on my elbows, drinking in every single muscle that contracted underneath my gaze. He had back muscles. Back. Muscles. Drool worthy, core clenching muscles I desperately wanted to run my tongue over.

Jesus, what was I saying? I shouldn't be thinking about his damn back muscles, I should be ensuring that this… whatever this is, doesn't turn into the mess I know it could.

Snickering, Tate threw a wink over his shoulder before strutting his very fine ass into the bathroom.

"If you change your mind, baby, there's more than enough room in this shower!" he shouted from the bathroom and I heard the steady stream of water crashing against the shower floor.

The pull to run into the bathroom and show him just how much I'd changed my mind was fierce, my heart completely taking over my head. But the moment I heard a low growl from the bathroom, my head finally took that exact moment to tell me this wasn't smart.

My head's a fucking asshat.

Taking my head's cue, I threw on my discarded clothes that had been strewn across the floor in a careless heap. I needed to get back to my room: there was something I needed to do and I didn't want anyone around to witness it.

Once I had finally gotten my clothes back in order on my body, I knocked on the door of the bathroom. "Tate, I'm headed back to my dorm. I have a paper to finish."

I didn't get a response, only the pounding of the water against the shower floor. Grabbing my cell, I punched out a short text to Tate for him to see once he finished in the shower.

Got a paper to finish. See you at The Takedown. X

Biting my bottom lip, I quietly made my way out of Tate's dorm and up the flight of stairs to my own. My hands were becoming restless as I walked with purpose to my bedside. Reaching underneath my bed, I pulled out one of very few possessions I owned that I could never let go of. Sitting down on the rough carpet, I held the object close to my chest.

Sitting in a large glass jar was every lie I had told in the last six years. One hundred and forty-nine small pieces of paper representing everything I hated about myself, each holding one drawn black heart. My very own jar of broken hearts.

Unscrewing the mason jar, I leaned over to my bedside cabinet drawer, fishing out a small scrap of paper and a black marker. With a heavy sigh, I drew a medium-sized heart on the white paper, placing a kiss on top of it as a silent apology before placing it in the jar and screwing the lid back on tight.

One hundred and fifty little lies sat in the jar staring at me, boring a hole right through my own heart. One hundred and fifty lies, one hundred and fifty hearts broken over the years.

One hundred and fifty reasons for me to carry on running.

Chapter Four

The large crowd roared. Money exchanged hands as the cringe-worthy thump of bones being crushed echoed around the dimly lit room. Girls I recognized from college screamed and guys drank beer from bottles, but all eyes were in the cage in front of them.

Blood suddenly sprayed through the cage, soaking a couple in the crowd who only cheered in response to the deep crimson that stained their clothes. My eyes darted around the room, taking everything in. It had been a six months since I was last in a room like this, full of people waiting for the main event, but this wasn't just any main event: this was the event of the year.

I rolled my eyes as I watched one of the men in the cage go down, a right hook to the jaw sending his large frame straight to the mat. The crowd cheered for a second time as the winner was announced. It seemed we were right on time as I watched a hooded figure walk out of the double doors from the back of the room, his face hidden from view as his hood cast a dark shadow over his eyes.

Welcome to The Takedown: where anything goes.

"If I get a single splash of blood on my face tonight, I'm going to seriously hurt Ace," Neva shouted into my ear from beside me.

I couldn't help but giggle at her comment. Neva wasn't the best person to deal with blood, but Logan was far worse. As a kid, Logan fell out of a large tree, breaking his arm and passing out the moment he spotted blood pouring from the wound. Poor kid, the bone broke right through his skin. Still, I couldn't help but laugh when Tate told me he would give himself paper cuts just to see Logan pass out in school.

"I'll be sure to push Logan in front of you if I see even a speck of blood flying towards your face."

"Oh god, please don't. I don't want to pick his heavy ass up off that grubby floor." She laughed, shaking her head she looked back to Logan as he made his way towards us with Tate.

"He's not that heavy." I chuckled as Logan scowled at me from Neva's shoulder.

"Do I want to know how you know that?" She smirked.

"Eh. Probably not." I shrugged.

Suddenly the room's back in full swing as the man, who was still unconscious, was peeled from the canvas mat, and in his place was a towering figure dressed in board shorts and a black silk robe. The already dim lights were turned off and the room fell completely silent, the only noise audible from our spot on the floor was the heavy breathing from the victor of the first fight. I smirked; the victor was about to go down… and it was going to hurt.

The large strategically placed speakers around the room quickly came to life, the loud boom making Neva jump beside me. I chuckled.

"Ladies and gentleman, welcome to The Takedownnnnn!!" the announcer yelled through the microphone and the crowd cheered in response. "We have a very special treat for your asses tonight… after a six month break from the cage, we finally have him back for The Takedown Tournament. Hold up your beers, scream that name and welcome back to the canvas and metal… Ace 'The Law' Matthewssss!!"

Still in his black silk robe, Ace acknowledged the crowd with a single head nod while his opponent visibly growled like a damn lion. Oh yeah, his ass was Ace's.

"Facing The Law tonight is Kade 'The Marshall' Riverrrr!!"

The crowd roared with similar intensity as Kade bounced around on the balls of his bare feet while punching the air in front of him, whereas Ace just stared at his opponent with a blank expression. If looks could kill, Kade would be in a morgue by now.

I assessed the room once more. To my left was a crowd at least a twelve deep of hyped up fans. To my right was a little less intimidating; I chose this particular spot so Neva didn't feel as though she was caged in. Only a six deep crowd surrounded us. Then I spotted Jonah Rodriguez standing on a make-shift table, his hands grasping cash as fans all but threw bills at him, shouting out their bets on who would win the fight.

"Yo, Rodriguez!" I shouted over my shoulder. His eyebrows pinched together as he searched the crowd for the person matching the voice. Clicking my fingers in the air in his direction, his brown eyes landed on mine, a smirk gracing his lips. "Two hundred says Kade is KO'd in thirty!"

He pondered on my words for a moment before shaking his head, chuckling at what seemed like a ridiculous bet on my part.

"Thirty minutes? You ain't got much faith in your boy up there, Parker," he sniggered, his eyes never leaving mine as he took more bets from frustrated fans.

"Maybe you didn't hear me clearly… thirty seconds, you clown!" I countered, making my way over to him and thrusting two one hundred dollar bills into his greedy hands. "Place the bet."

Rodriguez nodded sharply, turning back to the queue of people that had formed to place bets on tonight's fight.

Walking back to my spot next to my best friend and her boyfriend, I watched with eager eyes to see what Ace had up his sleeve for the fight. Before I could even contemplate what sort of moves he could pull out, Neva's voice rang into my ear.

"Did you really just put down two hundred dollars on Ace KO'ing Kade in thirty seconds?" Neva asked as I stood beside her. My eyes were suddenly glued to the cage as the referee went over the cage rules.

"Yeah, Low. I know Ace is good, but he's been out of the game for six months. Plus, Kade is undefeated in fifteen fights," Logan added.

I didn't reply. The crowd in the room suddenly became quieter as we waited for the bell to chime, the signal that would tell us all the fight was on.

The bell dinged.

A body slammed.

Blood broke the barrier of the cage.

I lost my bet.

"Holy shit," Logan whispered, his eyes as round as saucers.

"I don't… Jesus. Low, is that… even possible?" Neva said, turning to face me.

I shrugged, a small smile playing at my lips as I watched Rodriguez balk in absolute shock. I threw him a wink before turning back to the blood-filled cage.

"Uh huh," I smiled, watching as Kade was pulled by his ankles, his limp body dragged from the floor. Noticing Ace's robe still hung from his body, I let out a sadistic laugh while shaking my head.

Ace didn't knock Kade out in thirty seconds… he did it in ten.

The smile quickly disappeared as I felt arms encircle my waist from behind, completely catching me off guard. My heartbeat accelerated, it was beating with such speed I was sure the whole room could hear it over their cheers. The fear I usually kept locked deep down inside me burst through the banks as a fine layer of sweat coated my body, the intensity of my fear refusing to let up. I was frozen on the spot.

Fuck.

"You lost the bet," a voice whispered into my ear, pushing the fear back to the confines of its prison and replacing it with… desire.

Shit.

"It wasn't about winning or losing," I replied, my voice suddenly husky from the close proximity of a hard, muscular body against mine.

Tate James. My god, what he did to me, and that alone was god damn terrifying. His name fell from my lips with ease, his scent could quickly fill me with lust, and his touch alone could turn me into a giggling teenager. Sometimes, there were no words to describe what he did to me physically, but emotionally I knew exactly what it was, and I was all too aware just how fucking dangerous that could be.

"So, what was it about?" he whispered, his teeth grazing the shell of my ear.

"Everything," I replied, my eyes as strong as steel.

Tate looked at me like I had lost my damn mind, but in truth, this was about everything. Life is like a cage fight: a little terrifying, a little reckless, a little intimidating. But it's also an adrenaline rush, blissful highs as well as depressing lows. You win some, you lose some, and it's up to the fighter to decide if they stand and dust themselves off, or stay down and kiss the canvas.

Life doesn't come with an instruction manual; it's a dog eat dog world and only you can determine if you're willing to be the eater or become eaten. In my case, I was the eater, while the eaten that stood around me were completely oblivious. I had lied, cheated, and sometimes bribed my way to where I was, never flinching at the consequences of my actions. But now, I was dealing with an internal battle that could ultimately seal my fate.

I was slowly unraveling around Tate, the stiches breaking at the seams with every whisper, every touch, and every kiss. It's been three months of blissful hell—trying to keep myself together around him, trying to keep my true self hidden from him and those around me. I was a ticking time bomb, and I wouldn't be the only victim when I detonated.

Tate's soft lips against my neck quickly pulled me out of my own little pity party, bringing me back to the here and now. My eyes moved to the cage; the guy cleaning the blood from the mat told me there was going to be a break between fights tonight. As Tate's lips dropped feather-light kisses against my skin, I tried to spot Ace within the crowd. It was no use. Either Ace had snuck off into a quiet corner, or I just couldn't concentrate normally with Tate so close to me. I only hoped it wasn't the latter; my body's reaction to his proximity was being a real problem.

"Low, can you show me where the bathroom is?" Neva said, grabbing my hand. I clearly had no choice in the matter.

I was dragged through the large crowd, now on hyper drive after another hour of alcohol and adrenaline, and weaving in and out of the sweat-lined bodies wasn't easy as I was being dragged by a determined Neva. What the hell'd gotten into her?

"Will you please let up on my damn arm? You're going to pull it out of its socket!" I yelled over the still booming music.

"Shut up and just move your legs," she grumbled.

"Kinda difficult to do ya know, Nev."

After a couple of ass grabs, hand pulling, and beer spillages, we finally made it to the confines of the ladies bathroom. A couple of girls around our age stood in front of the large mirrors above the sink, pouting their lips and adding a ridiculous amount of gloss to their already overly shiny lips. Ripping my hand from Neva's tight grasp, I crossed my arms and looked at her pointedly.

"What the hell was so urgent that you needed to all but rip my arm off?"

Neva's eyes flickered to the line of girls to her right who were shuffling their ridiculously large boobs around in their tops, trying to create cleavages that clearly weren't there. I rolled my eyes and sighed dramatically.

"Excuse me," I said, stepping towards the girl closest to me. Her eyes roamed my skinny jeans and plain black vest top, clear disdain written all over her face. "Does anyone have a sanitary towel? My cooter is weeping something fierce and I don't want to ruin my Saturday panties."

Neva snorted while the girls cried out "gross" and "that's sick" before swiftly leaving the girls bathroom. I waved them off as I kindly held open the door.

"Thanks anyway!" I smiled, shutting the door behind them.

"That was way over the top and you know it." Neva laughed as she took a seat on the sink counter.

"But effective," I pointed out. "Now, what the hell was all that about?"

Neva looked down at her knotted fingers, biting her bottom lip before blurting out something that completely sideswiped me.

"I think Logan is cheating on me."

What. The. Hell?

"You've got to be kidding me?" I said, arching my brow. "Neva, Logan would never cheat on you! He loves you."

Was she serious? I mean, shit. They had been skirting around each other for so long, and after everything that had happened between them, now she thinks he's cheating on her?

"I know he does," she said, casting her eyes to her left. "But I can't help but think he is holding something back from me, and it's making me freak out. After everything, Low, everything we have been through to get to where we are, he holds something back from me?"

I knew what she was referring to, and it ripped me apart not being able to tell her, no matter how much I wanted to. It's not my story to tell; it's not my place to tell it either.

"Neva, honey, I love you, but you need to read my lips when I tell you this. If he is holding something back, then you're just as guilty for holding back your thoughts and feelings on this. Go and talk to him about it; if he is holding something back from you, then he will tell you." Stepping towards the counter, I wrapped my arms around her shoulders, hoping my words may have sunk in. "What's brought all this on anyway?"

It didn't escape my notice that I was completely contradicting myself.

"I just… I don't know. It's just a feeling, I guess." She shrugged, pulling back from my arms.

If I thought Neva was vulnerable before, it had nothing on how vulnerable she was now. Christ, would they just give her a god damn break?

"Talk to him. If you don't, then I will. You know as well as I do it won't be pretty if it comes to that," I said with a wink.

She finally cracked a smile as she pulled me in for a hug.

"What would I do without you, Low?" she said, holding me tighter.

"I hope we never have to find out," I said honestly. It might have been the most truthful statement to ever pass my lips in the last six years.

My phone vibrated in my back pocket as I pulled out of her embrace. Plunging my hand into my pocket, I pulled out my phone only to gulp back an involuntary scream.

"I'll meet you back out there," I muttered to Neva as I walked into one of the stalls, locking the door behind me.

"Okay. Everything alright?" she asked, confusion in her voice.

"Fine. Promise, just need to deal with this," I mumbled, still staring at the screen in my hands.

The minute I heard the door slam shut, I finally pulled in a shaky breath I hadn't even realized I had held onto it until my head throbbed after the rush of oxygen hit my system. Staring at me right in the face was the reason I held myself back, why I couldn't get too close, why I decided to keep myself hidden. Now, everything people once knew about me was about to be blown out the window, and the truth was about to be revealed.

It's started.

Chapter Five

"Mom?!" I shouted as I toed off my Chucks, making my way down the hallway towards the kitchen. "Mom, where the hell are you?"

My mind was in a blind panic as I searched the entire house for her, my head throbbing as a migraine started to take hold. This wasn't good. I could feel my heartbeat hitting new highs as I made my way up the staircase to the second floor, shouting for her with every step I took. I ran out of the venue which held The Takedown, leaving everyone behind. The text message my only warning that something was happening and I needed to start protecting those around me.

"In here, sweetie!" she yelled from the spare bedroom.

Breathing a sigh of relief, I ran to the bedroom, my heavy footsteps against the floorboards sounding louder than usual.

Throwing open the door, I found my mom on the floor folding clothes. Her brunette hair styled into a high ponytail, while her clothes were her usual color, black.

She quickly swung her body around the minute she heard my panting breaths; she knew something was wrong. Oh, but if she knew.

"It's started."

The words poured from my mouth with so much distaste I almost vomited. Almost. I watched as pure shock registered on my mother's face; she knew exactly what I was referring to. She placed her head in her hands and wept uncontrollably. Shit, if I'd have known that was going to be her reaction, I would have toned it down a little bit. But why sugarcoat the inevitable?

My gaze was suddenly transfixed on her bare feet; it wasn't often she was barefoot in the house, maybe she had just had a shower? My eyes landed on the large scar that covered most of the top of her foot. Even after all these years, it was still a reminder of who we were. We all had scars.

"Mom," I said, snapping out of my thoughts. "Pack a bag. You're going to Vegas."

That was all I said before I slammed the bedroom door shut behind me. There was no comfort in my words, no softness to them at all. The ball had started rolling, and it was time to take back some of the control I thought I had lost over the years.

Heading down the staircase, I made my way into the lounge in search for something to calm my nerves. The room was large but intimate. My mom had tried to make this house into a home, but she knew as well as I did this wasn't a home. It was never supposed to be one either.

My shaking hands went straight to the liquor cabinet that sat to the right of the black leather sofa, I needed a drink. Pulling out a bottle of malt whiskey, I unscrewed the top and took one large pull.

"Fuck me." I hissed, the whiskey burning the back of my throat, straight down to my stomach where it bubbled nicely. Whiskey wasn't my drink of choice—merely a means to try and forget—but today I wasn't really picky.

"That shit's going to be the death of you," my mother said as she stepped into the room, placing a large bag onto the armchair beside her. If you took one look at her, you would have no idea she had just been crying uncontrollably. No, right now she looked like the prim and proper woman I've come to know over the years.

"You know as well as I do that this shit ain't going to kill me first," I said, shaking the bottle before taking another long pull.

"True." She sighed. "What happens now?"

Eyeing the bag she had packed, I sagged down onto the sofa, the whiskey bottle dangling from my fingertips.

"You take a cab to the airport, I'll get you on the next flight out. Just remember, wherever you go—"

"Pay in cash," she said, finishing my sentence for me.

"Right," I said, my gaze fixed on the window to my left.

Spring was definitely here, the flowers in the front yard had sprung and were in full bloom. It was a damn slap in the face: welcome to the real world, Low. Where life carries on even if you're dealing with the world's biggest clusterfuck of all clusterfucks.

"It's really happening, isn't it?"

The faint tremor in my mother's voice didn't go unnoticed; in fact, it was the sole reason why my gaze locked back onto hers. She was terrified, and I felt like a huge fraud. Years of wondering, waiting, and hiding turned me into a robotic version of the girl I once was.

"Yes," I mumbled, taking another large gulp from the whiskey bottle. "Yes, it's really happening."

Fingering the zip on her bag, she muttered, "But, why now? It's been six years."

"Why?" I asked, becoming angrier as the minutes slowly ticked by. "Why is the sky blue? Why is the grass green? Why do people have sex and introduce a child into… THAT world?"

Closing my eyes, I took in a sharp breath, I wasn't equipped to deal with this shit right now. Her questions were becoming beyond frustrating.

"We could ask questions all day about why the hell this is happening, but you need to quickly understand, Mom. This *is* happening, it isn't going to go away. You knew this was going to happen eventually. So if you want to make it out of this alive, I suggest you get your ass into a cab and get to the airport."

With a tight nod, my mother grabbed her bag and slung it over her shoulder before walking right out the front door.

The minute the door slammed, I was on my feet. Taking three more large gulps of the poison in a bottle, I held back the gag before gripping the neck of the bottle tight and throwing it against the nearest hard surface. Fragments of glass splintered and shattered across the carpeted floor like a blanket of glittering confetti. I laughed sarcastically. Welcome to the real world: where girls drank malt whiskey, where liars and cheaters were rife, and where your life is held in the hands of a single text message.

Welcome to my hell.

I stared at the glass fragments on the floor, watching as they glistened with moisture from the remaining whiskey. I looked around the quiet house, the one my mother and I had never really turned into a home, knowing full well that we'd eventually have to leave.

There were no picture frames housing family photos, there were no handmade ornaments from her little girl. There was nothing, nothing to say we had been here for six years. There were no memories here, only the ones that haunted us in the darkness of the night.

With the thought weighing heavy on my mind, I dived into the cabinet of alcohol, coming across my old friend. Jack Daniel's.

"Hello, motherfucker. It's been a while," I taunted the bottle, watching as the amber liquid sloshed around the bottom of the bottle.

Ripping off the cap, I sucked in a mouth full of the foul tasting shit, hissing as I gulped back the vomit that was quickly rising up my throat. I took another large gulp, wiping my mouth with the back of my hand as I ventured up the staircase on shaky legs. The alcohol already had me buzzed, but I didn't want buzzed. I wanted completely fucking annihilated, inebriated, and comatose. It was the only way to get rid of the rising guilt.

After negotiating the staircase, I stumbled across the hallway, making my way to my childhood bedroom. I laughed at the thought, not so much a childhood when you're on the run from it. I slumped my body against the door, turning the handle with one hand, bringing Jack to my lips as I did. I stumbled into the room with a loud thud, Jack almost slipping through my fingers.

"Slippery little fucker tonight, aren't you, Jack?"

I winced. This was when Willow came out of her shell, alone and... pretty damn wasted. I didn't want to be her. I wanted so desperately to be Low Parker, not who I was. The text message I received had sparked this, the need inside me just to break lose, to remember why I turned into Low. I hated Willow; she was nothing more than a poisonous memory, a part of the past that was now creeping up and tainting everything within its path.

"What you say me and you have a little party huh, Jack?" I hissed, sucking more of the alcohol into my mouth, feeling the irresistible burn that slid down my throat. "It's just me and you, buddy."

Without thought or feeling, I moved to my old dresser, finding my dusty CD player. With a flick of a button, I was thrown back six years. *Faint* by Linkin Park blasted through the crackly speakers and I threw my arms above my head, basking in the amazing alcchol fuzz that blurred my vision. As the chorus kicked in, I threw myself up onto my old single bed, the wooden slats beneath it creaking as I jumped around to the bass. Jack spilled some of his contents onto my bed, proving that even in alcoholic form men couldn't control themselves when it came to women.

I panted as I threw my head from side to side, still jumping up and down on the rickety bed. The bed moaned and groaned beneath me as I paused to take a large gulp from Jack, sucking him into my mouth and allowing him to swirl around in my mouth before I swallowed hard.

"Come on, Jack. It's a fucking party!" I yelled, dancing around like a freaking lunatic.

I drank some more, trying to drown the thoughts and feelings that were trying to consume me. I just wanted to blank everything out and be Willow for a couple of minutes, just to try and understand her. But, like always, I had no freaking clue who she really was. I had no idea who Low Parker was either. I was a nameless face with multiple personalities.

The thought made me laugh out loud, a full belly laugh that had me falling to my knees. My body hit the uncomfortable mattress but I didn't care. I couldn't control the laughter that bubbled from my throat, but as the laughter came, it slowly died on my lips as sobs vomited from my mouth. Hard, gut-wrenching sobs as I threw Jack from the bed.

I cried for the girl who I refused to be, for the girl who I wanted to be, for the girl I never could be. I was Willow Knoxx, the girl who was one monumental fuck up.

I lifted my head as I tried to survey the room; it swam with roaring intensity as I quickly realized I had cried myself into an alcoholic coma. My throat was hoarse, my muscles ached and my head throbbed like a bitch.

I took a look at the mess I had caused. My CD player was dangling from the dresser by its cord. The years-old green curtains were at an odd angle and the old posters on my wall were either completely shredded or hanging on by a thread.

Then I froze.

Crack.

Without warning, the bed I was lying on face first completely shattered beneath my weight.

"Oooof!" I winced as the bed hit the hardwood flooring of my old bedroom.

I sighed hard into the comforter. It was time to go home.

Three hours and many large glasses of water later, I sat in my usual spot on my dorm room carpet, my head spinning as I unscrewed the glass jar. I drew three little hearts, kissing all three before placing them safely in the confines of the mason jar.

One hundred and fifty-three reasons for me to keep on fucking running.

Chapter Six

It's never easy trying to carry on as if nothing happened, as if sending my own mother off to Vegas without warning wasn't a big deal. It was a huge deal. Trying to stop my damn knees from shaking underneath my desk in Dr. Voxen's class was becoming more difficult with every word he spoke.

Ace, as usual, was late. I hadn't seen him since the fight, and his lack of presence was making me jittery. I have never been one to deal with nerves, but right now, I was really fucking nervous. The text message was a warning, the next would be a threat, after that… it wasn't worth thinking about.

My hangover was monstrous, lingering in the back of my mind as my nerves took over. It was there but it was more like a pain in my god damn ass when I really didn't need it. I couldn't believe how trashed I had gotten, how fucked up everything suddenly was.

"Today's focus is US mob bosses and the financial impact they have."

Dr. Voxen's monotone voice rang out into my ears, his words bursting through my ear drums like a damn knife. Shit. I needed to get my nerves and emotions under control, this was not me.

Taking a slow and steady breath, I picked up my pen, ready to start taking notes. I looked down at my hand that held the pen, shaking and unsteady. Christ. This… this wasn't good. It was as if my own body was warning me of the danger I was in.

"Do I really need to ask why you're late to my class again, Mr. Matthews? This seems to be becoming a habit."

Looking up from my shaking hand, my gaze landed on a smirking Ace. I chuckled quietly as he just shrugged his shoulders in defiance, making his way to his seat that sat empty next to my own.

"This class sucks ass," he muttered as he parked his ass in his seat.

Grabbing the pen from my shaking hands, he flashed me a wink as he placed it between his teeth and twirled it around with his tongue.

"Some of us are majoring in this class, Ace. Shut the fuck up," I grumbled, my mood clear in my words.

"Just sayin'." He laughed softly as he noticed today's discussion. "Original, really original," he grumbled.

"Mr. Matthews, if you insist on disturbing my class, then please, by all means, come and teach it for me," Dr. Voxen said, rolling his eyes as he made his way up to Ace, stopping in front of him and flourishing his hand down towards his desk.

"Oh, Dr. Voxen, I thought you'd never ask." Ace smirked, bouncing out of his seat as if he had just been given a hit of pure sugar.

Oh shit.

Dr. Voxen took Ace's seat next to mine and I sat up straighter in my seat. What was it with a teacher's close proximity that made us quiver a little? I was worried he could smell the fraud seeping from my skin.

I rolled my eyes as I noticed Ace picking up a dry erase pen from Dr. Voxen's desk. He was enjoying this far too much for my liking.

Turning on his heel, Ace wrote the word *omerta* on the white board, underlining it a couple of times for effect before turning back to the rest of the class. I recognized the word, but didn't have much of an idea of what it meant exactly, all I knew was it was Sicilian.

"Omerta," he paused, placing the lid back onto the pen, "roughly translated means men of honor. It's a code, but also a way of life. It's known to be the Cosa Nostra's strict code of silence, meaning everything you learn in this class is based on rumors, stipulations, and the media's way of turning the Mob into a paper-selling enterprise."

I shook my head as I took notes, watching the professor from the corner of my eye as I did so. His fingers cupped his chin with one hand, while the other rested in his lap.

"It is basically to ensure the members swore total devotion to the head of the mafia family they're affiliated with. Meaning, if you were to become a rat, a contract would be placed upon your head," he said, cocking his brow.

"Some of the so-called facts you know today are based on the undercover work of Joe Pistone AKA Donnie Brasco, but most of the intelligence gathered from his twenty-year undercover work as a mafia member is classified. For instance, Michael Franzese, the former Colombo captain, was reported to have made millions of dollars through tax and business scams, and was believed to have made more money for the mob since Al Capone. Case in point, ladies and gentlemen: reported, estimated, classified. There is no factual information detailing just how much of an impact the Mob had on the financial US, merely guess work. Unless you speak to a real mafia member who is willing to break the code of silence, which is highly unlikely, you aren't going to have a paper that has any factual basis what-so-ever."

Ace finished with an over-exaggerated bow, the class cheering in response. I rolled my eyes once more as he flashed me his brilliant white smile before shouting, "Peace out!" and leaving the room without a backward glance.

Smart ass.

"Well, that was certainly interesting." Dr. Voxen smirked before getting out of the seat and making his way down to his desk. "Considering Mr. Matthews took the discussion in a whole new direction, your assignment is to argue this point. Do we really know how much of an impact the mafia has had on the financial US? I expect this on my desk within two weeks, you can partner up for this assignment to help collate research," he said, packing a stack of papers into his briefcase. "Well? Get some research done!" he said with a wave of his hand.

The room erupted with students chattering and chairs scraping against the floor as they filed out, all eager to get out of the stuffy classroom, the spring air making the pokey room suffocating.

Packing away my notepad into my backpack, I made my way out of the classroom. My head wasn't in the game, everywhere I turned my eyes trained on other students faces and their expressions, trying to comb out who could possibly become a danger to me.

"I've got your pen."

"Holy fucking hell!" I jumped, rearing my elbow before plunging it behind me, pulling a resounding "ooof" from the person behind me.

"Shit! That's a meaner elbow than some of the fighters I'm up against next weekend," Ace groaned from behind me.

I sagged against the nearest wall in relief, my heart thundering in my chest as I realized I wasn't under threat. This was getting ridiculous, I couldn't carry on like this. I needed to rectify this shit, and quick if I didn't want a god damn heart attack.

Turning around, I laughed as I watched Ace rub his stomach in mock pain. Flashing me a smirk, he thrust the pen he had stolen from me in class into my hands.

"Thought you might need this." He laughed. "If I'd have known you were going to fucking elbow me, I would've kept the damn thing."

"Thanks," I muttered, twirling the pen between my thumb and index finger.

"Hey," he said, taking a step towards me. "What's wrong?"

"Why would anything be wrong?" I asked, my chest rising and falling in quick succession.

"I know you better than you know yourself, Low, no matter how much you think otherwise," he whispered, placing his hand on my shoulder and squeezing gently.

A current of unease coursed through my veins while a mixture of relief and fear was churning my gut. Six years. Six years I had been hiding, holding everything back, and now I had no idea what my future held, or whether I would make it out the other side.

"Everything okay, babe?" Tate's arms quickly wrapped around my waist. Ace's arm fell from my shoulder as he gave a sharp nod.

"Remember what I said, Low," he said before making his way down the corridor, disappearing from sight.

"What was that about?" Tate growled into my ear, squeezing my waist tighter.

"Oh, just talking about Dr. Voxen's class," I mumbled, my gaze dropping to my feet.

"You sure?" Tate asked, turning me around in his arms, our faces inches apart.

"P… positive," I stuttered, trying to get my tongue to wrap around the words I needed to get out.

I couldn't help but shrink a little in his arms; his pointed stare made me quiver but also made me quake in need. My physical and emotional reaction to Tate was becoming unbearable, the pull towards him was strong, yet my heightened emotions were suppressing the pull at every turn.

"Good." He groaned as he place a gentle kiss on my neck, inhaling my scent as he did so. "I have practice tonight, do you want me to come over after I've showered?"

What the hell do I do? For the first time in a long time, I was so damn confused I couldn't think straight. Tate was no longer my best friend's brother, he was someone who could melt me, mold me, and bend me into the person I could become, the person I've been dying to be for so long. And that right there was the most dangerous thing of all.

"Not tonight, I've got a major headache coming on and I have to get a paper written for class. Tomorrow though?"

It was a cheap move, but it had to be done.

"Okay." He whispered, "You sure everything's alright?"

"Promise." I smiled.

The smile didn't reach my eyes, no matter how much I tried; lying to Tate was ripping me into tiny little shreds. I was so screwed.

I placed my head in my hands as I sat at my desk in my dorm room, the pounding of a slow throb in my ears becoming unbearable. I had been working for a good two hours, trying to get this paper written. It was no use, my mind was elsewhere. Namely with Tate.

Flicking my notepad closed, I got up from my seat and made my way into the bathroom, ready to take a shower, hoping to wash away some of the sin I could feel against my skin. Just as I reached out to turn the knob, I heard the dorm room door slamming.

My heart jumped to my throat, and my hands suck uncontrollably. Who the hell was that? Tiptoeing behind the door, I waited.

"Low, you in here?"

I sighed as I sidestepped the door and walked back out of the room. Sitting on the floor was what looked to be a very upset Neva. Her eyes were rimmed a deep shade of red, while she hugged her legs in a childlike manner.

"Hey, what's going on?" I said as I crouched down beside her.

"We had a fight." She cried, fresh tears springing to her eyes.

"So you spoke to him?"

"Yeah, it didn't go very well." She sniffed, wiping her nose. "He said that he would never hold anything back from me, that he loved me. But, I still feel like he isn't telling me the whole truth."

I bit my lip at her words; she was right, he wasn't telling her everything, and it made me angry. I suddenly forgot my own insecurities and feelings, suppressing them to try and get a level head, hoping I could help my best friend.

"I'm sorry, sweetie," I comforted, pushing a stray piece of hair behind her ear. I had no idea what else to say. I couldn't tell her what I knew.

"I just don't u—"

The room door suddenly flung open, and in walked a very pissed off Logan, his shirt absolutely nowhere in sight, only his jeans covering his bare body. Even his feet were bare. This couldn't be good.

"Neva, get your ass back to the apartment, or I'll drag you there myself," he growled, stepping into the dorm and kicking the door shut behind him.

Stepping back, I watched as Neva crossed her arms in front of her chest, clearly not interested in cooperating with him.

Turning to me, Logan eyed me suspiciously and grunted, "What have you said?"

"Don't look at me like that, Logan White, I haven't said shit, much like you."

I couldn't help it, it just slipped out. The moment the last words fell from my lips my hand instantly covered my mouth. Oh shit.

"What do you mean 'much like you'?" Neva said, standing up from her position on the floor. "What the hell aren't you telling me?!"

Her eyes flickered between Logan and me, her eyes prosecuting every inch of us.

"This is sooo not my place," I said, throwing my hands up in surrender.

Logan growled from beside me before stalking over to Neva, her hands dropped by her sides as he stepped against the front of her body.

"I love you," he whispered, placing a tender kiss against her lips.

Suddenly Neva was screaming, her body flung over Logan's shoulder as she pounded her fists against his back, her legs flailing in the air.

"Logan White! I hate your very fine ass right now!!" she yelled as he laughed, carrying her out of the door and down the corridor.

"Well that was interesting." I sighed, throwing myself onto my bed, flinging my arms above my head.

Closing my eyes, my mind rolled back to the text message, to my mom who was now on a plane to Vegas. How had everything gone so wrong so quickly? I wasn't naïve, I knew this day was going to come eventually. I just didn't think it would be when I was so close to unravelling. Minutes ticked by as I thought about what I was going to do, how was I going to fix the situation. But my body decided enough was enough, and I quickly fell into a deep, hellish sleep.

I gulped hard, slowly pointing the barrel of the 9mm at the woman who knelt in front of me. I had to do as I was told, I had to do this. The barrel pushing hard against the back of my own head reminded me why I was here, what I needed to do. The tears fell silently as my finger moved to the trigger, resting gently, waiting for my signal.

"Remind her why she's on her knees, little Willow," the voice that made my skin crawl whispered into the shell of my ear.

"You're in this position because you broke the family code. You lied, cheated, and snuck around, all for your own personal gain. Personal gain isn't tolerated, the only gain you should be searching for is the gain for this family. You created a… a bastard within the family. He can never be heir."

The words poured from my mouth but broke my very core. I stared into the somber eyes of the woman kneeling before me, silently begging her to fight, to kick back, to do something that would get her out of this situation. I didn't want to hurt her, I didn't want to do this. The gun that was pointed to my head moved back; it was no longer crushing against my skull.

"Good. Now make her beg for her life," he said in a slow, calm voice.

My body shivered from the cool tone of his disgusting voice, making my skin crawl. I had to make her beg; if I didn't, it would hold consequences, consequences that would cause unimaginable pain.

"Beg. Tell me why I should keep you alive," I whispered, the tears falling with every word that fell from my lips.

This was wrong, so wrong, I knew that, yet I was still here.

"You shouldn't," the woman said simply, not once flinching. "I would rather be dead than spend another day in this life, the life I was forced into. So, please. Shoot me."

I watched as the woman closed her eyes, turning her head and looking away from me. She couldn't look at me. Hell, I couldn't look at myself most days. She didn't want this life, and I was right there with her. I wanted to get out too.

"Do it," the male voice said from behind me. "Make her pay."

He wanted me to shoot her? I may have been trained to use a gun, but I knew my body wouldn't physically allow to me to do it. He was trying to win a losing battle. I wouldn't do it.

"No," I whispered.

The woman's eyes quickly shot open, her head snapping to mine. She knew exactly what I had done. I had defied him, I had told him 'no.' No one *tells him 'no.'*

"You stupid bitch!" he growled.

I suddenly dropped to my knees as pain sliced through the back of my skull, blurring my vision and sending the worst kind of throbbing ache through my body. I knew the sharpness of that pain, I knew it well. I had been hit on the back of the head with the butt of the Glock.

Blood trickled down the back of my neck as my fingertips grazed the deep gash. More stitches. I looked up into the eyes of the woman who only moments before had asked me to kill her, her face a picture of pain as she watched the tears fall.

"I'm sorry," I begged.

Then I felt it. The butt of the gun struck once more.

My eyelids snapped open so quickly I thought they were never there to begin with. My heart pounded as the blood rushed straight to the scar on the back of my head. My hand fumbled as I probed the thick blonde tresses, seeking one of the reminders of my past.

It was right there right then I finally decided enough was enough. I had been hiding for long enough, I had been denying a part of me for nearly six years. I was in too deep. I had people I cared about now, my heart was no longer my own; it was shared between the relationships I had made. I couldn't ignore the warning, I had to finally face the music – even if it killed me.

That night I placed five little hearts into the glass jar. Four for the lies I had given and one for good luck. I kissed each one and shed a small tear for the very last.

One hundred and fifty-eight reasons for me to start… fighting back?

Chapter Seven

Me: How long?

Unknown number: Soon.

Me: Keep me informed. Protocol is essential.

Unknown number: Understood.

I hadn't slept. My brain had been working at frightening speeds since I'd texted the unknown number back. I looked down at my wristwatch; I was already twenty minutes late for a class I wasn't sure I'd walk into again. Everything had escalated so rapidly it made my head spin and my heart hurt. Nothing was ever going to be the same.

My finger stroked the rim of my coffee cup, collecting the condensation as it soaked into my skin. I'd been sitting in coffee shop two towns away for the last hour, trying to hold back the nerves that were trying to escape and consume me. I pushed down the fear with a large gulp of black coffee, hoping the nerves would blend deep in my gut with my cheap, nasty coffee.

"Can I get you another?"

I balked back, almost toppling over my lukewarm coffee as I reared back in my chair. My jittery nerves quickly calmed when I noticed the smiling face of the waitress.

"Um, yeah. Please." I smiled tightly.

The waitress nodded and wrote down my order, making her way

behind the counter to make my coffee. As disgusting as the drink was, I needed to do something with my hands.

I had strategically placed myself in the far corner of the coffee shop, the table slightly hidden by a large pillar just behind the empty seat in front of me. I needed to be shielded from prying eyes, and this was the best place I could get on such short notice.

"There you go, my love," the waitress said as she placed my steaming cup in front of me.

My hands instantly cupped the off-white mug, the burning sensation warming my unusually cold hands but did nothing to heat the stillness of my bones.

"Thank you." I smiled, watching as the waitress moved around the room, filling more coffee cups as she went.

My eyes were suddenly drawn to the door on the opposite side of the shop. A figure dressed in black stood just inside the threshold, eyeing the surroundings. The figure's head was tilted down, masking their face with a cap and hood as they made their way towards my table.

I brought my cup to my lips, my hands shaking slightly in the process. Taking a large gulp, I winced as the burning liquid hit my tongue and throat, scorching its way down to my empty stomach. It tasted like mud, but I couldn't deny loving the burn against my tongue.

"You drag me all the way out here and you don't even get me a coffee?" The figure grunted at me, taking the empty chair in front of me. "Where are your manners, Willow?"

He made no move to pull down his hood or remove his cap. Instead he slouched in his chair, crossing his arms across his broad chest.

"Skip the bullshit, Jace," I said, sliding my cup across the table. He caught it without as much as a glance in its direction. "We need to cut to the chase."

"So cut to the chase," he said, taking a long pull from the cup, not once wincing at its foul taste.

"It's started."

I could feel the blood draining from my face as his heated stare met mine, his eyes hooded from the shade of his cap, but I could still see the deep, dark brown irises hiding underneath the shadow. I noticed the smallest frown line appear just beneath his plump bottom lip: he knew exactly what I was talking about.

"When did this happen?" he grunted, taking another large gulp of coffee.

"Last night," I muttered.

"Last night?" he said, sliding the coffee cup back to me, completely drained of its contents. "This happened last night and you're only telling me now?"

"I'm telling you now, aren't I?" I fumed, the nerves inside my gut morphing into anger the more his eyes penetrated mine.

He rolled his eyes, breaking the tension that sat between us. "Next time, you fucking tell me as soon as you know. Are we clear?" he said, cocking his brow at me. I didn't respond. "Are we clear, Willow? I'm not fucking around here, this isn't a game. You have some serious decisions to start making, and soon."

As much as it pained me to say it, he was right. Hard decisions needed to be made, big girl panties had to be pulled up, and balls needed to be formed. This wasn't just a game kids played, it wasn't the movies. This was real life, and we were right in the thick of reality.

"Fine. Understood. Jesus," I said, running my finger over the rim of the cold and empty mug. "What do we do now?"

"We just go with it. There isn't anything we can do to stop the inevitable, we've just got to damn well hope that we come out of the other side of this fuck up."

"I don't know if I can do it," I muttered, closing my eyes. It wasn't really a matter of not knowing. I was pretty sure I couldn't do it, no matter what the god damn outcome was.

The thing is with secrets, lies, and deceit, they tend to catch up with you. Past. Past has to be the most insignificant word in the damn dictionary. It's defined as 'gone by in time and no longer existing.' Since when has the past ever just been the past? Decisions, mistakes, demons: they creep up on you, walk all over you and spill open, exposing your present and future to the murky depths of your history. Yeah, past... not really that insignificant after all.

"You don't have a choice, Willow," Jace muttered, pulling me out of my thoughts.

"I know but it doesn't mean I have to fucking like it," I seethed.

I was done with this conversation. I didn't want to think about it. I knew I had to go back to normal, to make others believe I didn't have a history, that I was Low Parker. It was becoming exhausting, and I'd had enough.

"I'm not saying you have to like it, just… just deal with it, Willow, for all our sakes."

Dammit, I hated when he did this. I rolled my eyes like a petulant child.

"Fine," I grumbled, crossing my arms over my chest.

"You're cute when you go all pouty on me, Willow." He smirked, leaning across the table.

His left hand suddenly cupped my cheek, running the pad of his thumb over the skin that had quickly broken out in goosebumps. Crap.

"Hands off, Jace. This isn't a free-for-all. If you want to keep your dick attached to your body, I suggest you remove your hand right now."

I didn't know what had come over me. Maybe it was the shitty coffee combined with my delicate nerves, but whatever it was, I couldn't let it stand in my way of carrying out what I needed to do.

Jace's deep and throaty chuckle pulled me out of my thoughts, his large, warm hand leaving my cold flesh, folding back into the warm cove of his chest. He stared me down, the slither of sunlight through the windows illuminating one side of his face. I could finally see the deep brown depths of his eyes, like a never ending sea of dark chocolate.

"You know, your threats never really did anything to make me back off, Willow. Instead, they only made me want to come at you harder, faster… stronger," he said, placing his elbows upon the table, leaning forward. "You don't scare me."

The smirk on his face irritated me to the point of committing violence. I really wanted to punch him in his deliciously thick throat, but at the same time kiss that smirk right off his face. What the fuck was wrong with me?

"You and I both know," I matched his smirk, "that you'd be intolerably stupid if you didn't fear me."

I watched as his smirk turned into a full mega-watt smile, chuckling under his breath.

"I wouldn't count on it, babe." He winked, his smile morphing into a deep growl that did nothing for my conflicting thoughts.

"Jace, I have no idea what I'm doing right now," I confessed. I instantly regretted my moment of weakness when he dropped the hood from his head, staring me down with his brown eyes.

"Who the fuck does?" he said, pointing his finger in my direction. "Do you think I have any damn idea how to get out of this unholy mess? If I did, Willow, you'd be the first person I'd rescue from this shit."

I let out a small chuckle, the image of Jace on a white horse coming to my rescue taking over my messed up thoughts.

"My knight in shining armor, huh?"

"Damn fucking straight." He smiled playfully. "And don't you ever forget it, princess."

"How are things going your side?" I asked, noting to punch him in the throat if he called me princess ever again.

"There's movement, not much, but they know something big is about to happen."

Jesus.

"It's going to be pretty ugly, isn't it?" I asked, but in reality I knew the answer. I wasn't naïve: hopeful, but never naïve.

Jace was one of only two people I trusted. One of two who I had no doubt would kill to protect what we built. He saved me once, he'd do it again.

"It's going to be one hell of a battle, babe." He sighed. "Just remember what brought you to this point in the first place, that should be enough to help you pull through it."

"I wish it was that easy."

"Life's as easy as you allow it to be."

Jace's parting words vibrated through my mind throughout the rest of the evening.

Life's as easy as you allow it to be.

I didn't believe it for one second, but just watching Jace's relaxed posture as he said those nine little words to me filled me with more hope than I'd had in six years. Always hopeful, never naïve.

"You're quiet tonight," Neva said as she took a seat next to me on Logan's sofa.

I had walked from the coffee shop after my meeting with Jace and ended up at Logan's front door; it wasn't a conscious thing. I suppose it was my mind's way of telling me that something big was about to go down and I needed to spend time with the people who I surrounded myself with.

"Just tired. Dr. Voxen is pushing papers on us nonstop right now." I sighed. Another lie. Another heart.

"Tell me about it. My music class is becoming suffocating. It still gives me the creeps walking into that classroom," She replied.

I understood that. Neva had met Angel Walker in that very classroom: the man who gave her reason to heal only to break her back down again. I'm surprised this woman was still standing after everything she had been through. She was tough, no matter how weak she may think she is.

"Baby, dinner's almost ready," Logan shouted from the kitchen.

The scent of tomato and basil quickly surrounded my nostrils as I inhaled hard. It smelt delicious, whatever he was making.

"You know, he has to be the most domesticated man I've ever met." I laughed, turning to Neva.

"I know. But he was the man of the house after his dad left. He had to learn how to cook, clean, and do what he thought his father should have done for his mother. It's in his bones. Let him have his little moment." She giggled.

"If I find him in a pink apron, I'm totally bailing." I smiled.

"My lips are sealed," she said, grabbing my hand and dragging me into the kitchen.

One minute I was being dragged into a room, the next I was almost on the floor laughing. Logan wasn't in a pink apron—he was in a naked male apron. The front of the apron sported a model with abs so tight it looked unnatural, and funny as hell.

"What the hell are you wearing?" I said between howls of laughter.

Logan flashed his signature smirk over his shoulder, winking as he placed the wooden spoon into his mouth and groaning. I heard a small gasp escape Neva's lips. I rolled my eyes.

"If you start fornicating on the dining table, I swear I will cut you both." I groaned.

"Want some?" Logan laughed, holding out the wooden spoon to me like a child.

I raised my brow. "Have you had your mouth around that spoon?"

He looked at the spoon before looking back at me. "Yeah. Why?" he asked, taking a step towards me with the offending spoon.

"I'm not putting that thing in my mouth if it's just been in yours. I have no idea where it's been."

A small snort burst from Neva's lips as she took a seat at the small dining table. Logan winked at her before shrugging.

"My point exactly," I pointed out as Logan dished out the food.

Taking a seat at the table, I almost moaned out loud from the aroma laid before me on a plate. Logan had made spaghetti in a tomato and basil sauce. My mouth watered.

"You can cook," I said between bites. "Who knew?"

Logan winked. "I have a very particular set of skills," he started.

I laughed as Neva dropped her fork against her plate, groaning as she placed her head in her hands.

"Skills I have acquired over a very long career. Skills that make me a nightmare for people like you," I continued.

"If you let my spaghetti go now, that'll be the end of it." Logan smirked as he took a bite from his plate.

"Enough. What the hell is it with you two and Liam Neeson?" Neva said, shaking her head.

"I will not look for you, I will not pursue you," Logan carried on, chuckling at Neva as she groaned again.

"But if you don't, I will look for you, I will find you, and I will kill you."

Turning, I watched as Tate walked into Logan's apartment, flashing me a wink as he finished off the quote.

"You're all conspiring against me! I hate that movie," Neva said, standing, grabbing her plate she walked to the kitchen counter and placed it by the sink. Shaking her head, she made her way over to the sofa and sat down with a heavy sigh as she turned on the flat screen tv, turning up the sound as if to drown us out.

As Tate took a seat at the table, Logan and I burst out laughing, Tate smirking as his sister sighed dramatically.

"You know you love it, baby girl," Tate yelled over the tv to his sister. She waved her hand over her head in response. He chuckled deep as he plated himself some of Logan's spaghetti, his left hand wandering to my right thigh under the table.

The small touch made me shiver and damn if he didn't notice. Looking up through my lashes, I watched as Tate's eyes turned hooded and dark, laced with desire as his hand wandered farther up my thigh.

Just as Tate's hand came to rest on the very top of my thigh, Logan's door flew open, in walking the twins and Ace.

"Dude, you laid him the fuck out!" Colt cheered, punching the air in front of him. "You must have got some serious pussss… Hey!" Colt stopped mid-sentence as he became vastly aware of his surroundings and company.

"Is that Logan's mom's tomato and spaghetti I can smell?" Ace asked as he moved towards the dining table, Zane and Colt peering behind him.

"Am I the only one who didn't know Logan could cook?" I asked, taking another bite of the deliciousness from the plate.

"You always doubt me." Logan winked as he left the table, indicating to the guys to grab a plate as he took a seat on the sofa by Neva, wrapping his arm around her.

Ace, Colt and Zane all took a seat at the table, diving into their meals as if they had been starved for days. I sighed contently watching as the people around me, all of who had a special place in my heart… including the twins.

I watched as the guys joked around, discussing Ace's last fight and talking about the twins' latest conquests. Each and every one of them holding genuine smiles for those around them, each one seemingly happy. There was just one person within that room who didn't hold a genuine smile: me. I had been using a mask for so long I no longer remembered what a real smile felt or looked like. I knew it wasn't real, but how do you teach yourself to smile when deep inside you're crumbling?

After filling our stomachs, everyone I held dear to me relaxed on the sofa. We watched our favorite movie *Taken* with Liam Neeson, everyone repeating the quote, including Neva. I sighed once more as I laid my weary head on Tate's shoulder, his masculine scent surrounding me as he held me close.

That night, I placed two black hearts into the jar.

One hundred and sixty little lies. One hundred and sixty explanations of why fighting might not be good enough in the end.

Chapter Eight

Moisturizer.

Concealer.

Foundation.

My very own recipe for the perfect mask.

My scars were hidden, the brightness of my blue eyes taking everyone's eyes from the area where they were sure they saw something hidden beneath the makeup. I could see it in their eyes as their gazes would drop just a fraction, staring for a little too long, trying to see something they had no idea was there.

I sighed at the thought, throwing my mascara back into my makeup bag before adding a coat of gloss to my lips. I looked into the mirror, checking to ensure I was fully covered, that no scar was visible. I couldn't see any. Well, that wasn't strictly true. I could always see them, even with my expert hand of hiding it. You can't hide what's already tainted.

I ran my fingers through my blonde hair, trying to stop it from frizzing against the rising spring humidity. Once I was sure I could pass as Low Parker, I left my dorm room and exited the building. I didn't have any classes today; it was my only day of freedom against the persona I had created. Today I just wanted to spend some time alone, to think over things.

My heels clanked against the cobbled ground of campus as I walked towards the coffee shop. Coffee really was my addiction, my down fall. Amongst other things. I basked in the light breeze that gathered around my bare calves, swishing my floral dress in its wake as I rounded the corner to the coffee shop. As I got closer, I spotted Jared behind the counter, his usual chipper self as I noticed him singing along to yet another hit song.

Shaking my head, I entered the coffee shop. The music was on louder than usual but I didn't mind. It was usually a sign that the manager had gone on a break and this was Jared's way of saying 'I don't care.' We all knew Jared had a crush on his manager: his very male, very straight manager. He made sure to remind him every day too.

"Jared." I sighed, stepping to the counter. "I'm in need of a hit. Fast."

Jared's warm, lazy grin flashed across his face as he leaned both his elbows on the counter, holding his face in his hands.

"Is that so?" he chimed, smiling at me like the damn Cheshire cat. "What am I going to get in return for your hit?"

I rolled my eyes. "My god damn money?"

"Hmm, I don't quite think that'll cut it today, Low." He smirked, his eyes deviating to the left as he noticed his manager stepping back in from his break. "You get me a date with Preston over there, and I'll give you a double shot skinny frappe with a mile of cream every day for the rest of the year. On me."

"You wouldn't!" I gasped.

"Oh, I would. I might even throw in some of those mini marshmallows you love and… I might just sit my fine ass down with you while you devour it," he added.

I couldn't resist his challenge. Never wanting to back down from a challenge, I bit my lip as I nodded to Jared.

"Better warm up the machine, baby. I'm going to need that double shot skinny frappe in an extra-large mug." I winked.

Jared laughed as I made my way over to Preston who was wiping down a couple of tables in the far back of the shop.

I assessed him from afar. He was cute. His hair was a dark shade of brown, his eyes a warm blue. He was athletic, not too built, but enough to know beneath those clothes there's no doubt some impressive muscles.

"Hey, Preston." I smiled, stepping towards him. "Got a minute?"

Preston's eyes locked with mine and he smiled warmly.

"Sure, Low. What can I do for you?"

"Well," I said, winking over my shoulder at Jared who was leaning towards us, clearly trying to eaves drop on our conversation. Turning back to Preston, I immediately dropped the act. "Look, I know you're as straight as they come, but your friend over there has a raging lady-boner for you and he just challenged me to get him a date with you and he would reward me with coffee."

"Ooookay?" Preston replied, clearly shocked by my non-sugarcoating of the truth.

"I have a real addiction to coffee, Preston. So I'm going to make you an offer. I'm going to slip you five hundred bucks."

Preston's eyes nearly bugged out of his head at the mention of the money. I wasn't stupid, I knew Preston was struggling; his mom was sick and he could really use the money.

"If you accept that five hundred bucks it means you're going to take Jared out to dinner. I know you're straight as an arrow, Preston. But for Jared, for just a couple of hours, be as straight as a fucking circle."

"I… uh. I. Hmm."

"Don't talk." I laughed gently. "Just nod your head if you agree to the terms."

Without hesitation, I watched as Preston's head nodded slowly. Thrusting my hand into my pocket, I slid my cell number into his apron pocket that sat around his waist. "Call me. I'll set up the bank transfer."

With a tight nod, Preston quietly went back to wiping tables. A smile played on my lips as I turned and walked to Jared who was standing there looking about as nervous as a child on his first day of school.

"Coffee." I smiled sweetly.

"What the hell?" he whispered. "Do you know how long I've been lovingly violating him with my eyes? How did you do that?"

"I have skills, Jared." I laughed, thrusting out my hands and doing a gimme gesture. "Coffee."

With a smiling eye roll, Jared went to work on my coffee, sliding it across the counter into my hands in a takeout cup.

"Thank you, baby." I winked, "I've got some things to take care of. You remember I like my coffee at 9am sharp, right?"

"Get out before I shove this cream somewhere where cream should never venture," he threatened, pointing the can of cream at me.

I squealed, running for my life out the door and out onto the sidewalk.

I slowly made my way down the streets of Spring Water, stopping by small clothing stores on the way. I sighed heavy into the small hole on my coffee lid, clothes shopping seemed like such an ordinary thing to do. Pretty much normal. I wasn't normal. Even being out on the streets was a risk.

The thought made my bubbly Low persona wilt back in fear. I needed to get back to campus and get some studying done.

With a little more rush in my step, I walked back to campus. Throwing away my empty coffee cup as I threw myself onto my bed with a thud, I let my mind wander as I closed my eyes; for a second, I smiled. Just the action of being remotely normal with friends was something of a rarity, and this always happened after the happiness bloomed. Reality would high-five me in the face and chant "Don't be such a fucking moron."

With thoughts consuming my every breath, I slowly fell asleep. My mask still pretty much in place but doing nothing to stop the dreams that broke through the walls I had built around me.

"Answer the fucking question."

The dark and husky voice penetrated the walls of the Manor, ringing out like a horror movie.

I sat at the top of the first level staircase on my front, my chest squashed against the hardwood flooring. It was uncomfortable, but I didn't care. I don't know what pulled me to my spot, I hated this life, but something inside me told me to investigate.

"You better answer him or this pretty little blade will be sticking out of your kidney."

The voices were muffled from the echo of the large manor, so I couldn't tell who was talking. That only spiked my curiosity more. Then I heard it, the blood-curdling moan of pain that would forever be etched into the back of my mind. It was a cry that

I recognized, a cry that would stay with me until my last dying breath.

Suddenly, I heard crashing, as if someone was smashing plates against the floor, but I feared it was probably against the very person who was crying out. I was frozen to the spot, not wanting to leave but knowing my gut said otherwise. I pushed back the bile hitting the back of my throat and burning with ridiculous intensity.

"Little Willow."

As that voice that made my skin crawl danced on the skin of my bare shoulder from behind me, I instantly shrunk back.

"Y-yes," I stuttered, still frozen in place on the floor.

"I didn't know you liked to watch."

With that, my body was quickly flung into the air, landing onto a very masculine shoulder. With my ass in the air and my head near a jean-covered ass, I suppressed the scream that started creeping up my throat. I wouldn't give him the satisfaction.

I stayed silent as the man carried me down the staircase and into the very room where I had heard the screaming just moments before. I couldn't see anything, only the thick carpet beneath me.

"What the fuck's this?" the deep and vile voice asked.

"She was listening in. Thought I'd bring her down to see what all the commotion was about," the man carrying me said.

"Drop her."

I landed with a hard thud against the carpet, hitting it head first. I heard my lips burst before I felt it; blood trickled down my chin and onto my white t-shirt as I scrambled to my knees.

I gulped back the involuntary gasp that wanted to escape as I took in everything around me. We were in a room I wasn't supposed to be in for another couple of years. A table stood right in the center of the room, twelve chairs surrounding it with one single large chair at the very head. But that wasn't what tried pulling the involuntary gasp from my lips. No, it was the sight of Amelia on her knees, a knife sticking out of her stomach as she cried in utter pain.

Amelia. My god, Amelia. She had been disowned by her mafia family, and now she was in a room with the rival family of the mafia family she had been kicked out of. What the hell was going on?

"Amelia," I whispered, trying to get her to look at me. It was no use though. She knew her place right now, and it wasn't a place where she could even imagine looking at me.

"Silence!" a voice boomed from my right. "Amelia, such a pretty name for such a piece of trash."

I winced at his words. He was goading her and I had no doubt it was working. Her bottom lip trembled uncontrollably as she tried not to move, the knife not deep enough to cause internal bleeding, but enough so the knife would bounce every time she breathed.

"I'm sorry," I cried softly, still frozen in place on the floor as I stared at her blood-stained face.

I watched as she finally looked me in the eye. Acceptance of my apology evident as she nodded slightly.

And I screamed.

Amelia's face turned from submissive to completely defiant in one swift movement as she pushed the knife further into her body. Blood pooled around her: the crimson a color I would forever hate.

She didn't cry, she didn't wince. No.

She smiled. Smiled knowing no one could ever hurt her again.

The scream from my throat kept on coming as I was dragged backwards from the room by a stranger's hands. My eyes stayed trained on her as I was pulled from the room, watching as she slumped against the floor, bleeding out right in front of my eyes.

My body jerked me awake. I opened my eyes, staring around the room, trying to get my bearings. I was safe. Well, to a point. But I was safe and alone. How I liked it. I wiped at my sweat-lined brow as I inhaled a large gulp of air, letting it swell within my lungs before releasing it. Sitting up, I reached for my cell. I had a couple of missed calls from Tate. Sliding my finger across the screen of my phone, I noticed a couple of text messages from Tate.

Tate: Meet me? X

Tate: Where are you? X

Tate: You're worrying me. Where are you?

Tate: Answer your damn phone, Low!

Tate: I'm coming to find you.

The minute I read the last text message, a loud banging started on my door. I rolled my eyes: if he knew who I was he wouldn't need to worry so much.

"I'm coming!" I said, standing and walking to the door.

I opened the door, smiling as I saw a very unhappy Tate on the other side. He was panting as if he'd been running again, but I knew it was too late in the day for one of his runs.

"You okay?" I asked, chuckling slightly as his eyebrows pinched together.

"Am I okay? Low, you haven't answered a single one of my calls for the last six hours. So, no. No, I'm not fucking okay."

Six hours? Shit, had I been out that long? I watched him as concern gripped at his features, his eyebrows pinching further together as his gaze drifted from my eyes and landed on my lip.

"I'm sorry," I said.

Within an instant, Tate had me wrapped in his arms, his face diving into my neck.

"What's all this?" I asked, wrapping my arms around his waist.

He pulled back, looking at me like I had lost my god damn mind.

"I hate not knowing where you are. Answer your damn phone."

Okaaaay. This was a new side of Tate I hadn't seen, he was almost… desperate.

"Okay. I'll answer my phone, I'm sorry."

"Good," he muttered, turning and shutting the door behind him.

Grabbing my hand, he led me to the bed, pushing me back so I was sitting on the edge.

"What are you doing?" I asked as he knelt down in front of me.

Taking my right foot in his hands, he slid off one shoe then went to work on the other. It was slow and meticulous as he came to my bare feet. His large, warm hands cupped my right foot and slowly started rubbing it down.

"Wow." I groaned, falling back on the bed.

If he wasn't careful, I would fall right back to sleep with the slow way he was working the soles of my feet. I had no idea what had gotten into him, but I wasn't stupid enough to stop him. If this is what he needed, for whatever reason, who was I to deny him.

He worked my right foot for twenty minutes, moving onto my left foot, giving it the same care and attention he had with the other.

"Tate, what's going on?" I asked the minute he dropped my foot and stood.

"Just let me do this, okay?" he said, turning and walking into my bathroom.

I sat utterly bewildered, my head snapping towards the bathroom door as the sound of running water caught my attention. Was he… was he running me a bath?

Standing from the bed, I walked into the bathroom, only to stop at the door frozen to the spot. Tate's shirt was discarded on the floor as he crouched beside the bath, his arms in the water as he swirled it around with his hands.

I was transfixed on the way his back muscles contracted with every movement he made. If he moved his arm to the right, the left side of his back muscles strained against the movement. My mouth watered uncontrollably. Dammit.

"Strip, Low," Tate growled from his spot, never turning around to face me.

He wanted me to strip? Right here? In front of him? Fear quickly gripped every fiber of my body at the thought of him seeing the ugly beneath. I couldn't do it. I wasn't ready, he wasn't ready.

"I… I," I stuttered. Jesus, get a grip woman. "I can't."

Tate's head whipped around, staring at me long and hard until he stood, stalking his way towards me with a new intensity in his eyes. An intensity I hadn't seen before.

"Need a hand?" he asked, slowly sidestepping around me until he stopped at my back, resting his head on my shoulder.

I gulped. Hard.

"I'm not going to touch you, Low. I'm not going to give in to the raging hard on in my damn pants. I'm just going to wash you. Okay?" he whispered against my neck, pressing a soft kiss right on the spot that pretty much ignited my panties.

My hands shook as he slowly removed the left strap of my dress, letting it fall from my shoulder. I almost convulsed on the spot the second his lips came to the spot where my strap was previously sitting. Jesus.

I closed my eyes. I was breaking my rules. I shouldn't be doing this. But, right then, I was too far gone to try and stop it. This was what I was afraid of, falling in too deep. My god, was I in deep. I was in so fucking deep I could no longer see the damn sunlight anymore. I was in complete darkness, not knowing which way was up or down, not knowing if I was walking or floating. I suppose that's what love is. Love. Fuck.

Seconds rolled by as I tried to get my nerves controlled, all while Tate was slipping the second strap off my shoulder, placing another soft kiss there. I let out an involuntary moan. My head said "Run" but my body and heart said "If you move, we'll cut you."

"Jesus, you smell so good." Tate groaned from behind me as he inhaled against my neck.

I felt his hands wandering, coming down to my breasts as he pushed the material down my body. My dress pooled at my feet and I was suddenly bare, only wearing a black lace bra with matching panties.

I gulped.

I gulped again.

It was as if I couldn't swallow, my tongue thick in my mouth. I closed my eyes tight. The minute he walked around my body he would see it, he would see why sex was just not on the cards for us, that it would be dangerous if we tried.

His hands moved down to my waist, skating down from the top of my rib cage until they came to a complete stop.

Fuck.

He had found it.

His finger traced the deep jagged scar that sat just below my last rib, his breaths coming in hard pants against the skin of my shoulder. He lingered and I gasped. He didn't deviate from the scar and it had my hands shaking far worse than they had in a long time.

My eyes suddenly flashed open as I felt Tate's tongue against the sweat-lined skin of my shoulder, and that's when I saw them. My eyes locked on the mirror in front of me, taking in everything that was happening.

I almost cried out in agony as I realized what was exposed. Me. I was fucking exposed. Staring me right in the face were the scars I had been covering for years. The fragmented scars that sat just below my lips were out in full force for all to see. What the fuck? Then it clicked: my little flashback, my nightmare. I had been sweating, my makeup able to run freely from my face.

I wilted, my body almost buckling beneath my weight. Tate's arms quickly caught me, holding on to me as he placed a soft kiss just below my ear.

"It's okay," he whispered, his words telling me he had seen them, that this was the reason for the shift in him.

I whimpered. He'd seen my scars.

With quick movements, he stripped my bra from my body, my panties following swiftly behind. He lifted me into his arms, cradling me like a small child as he sat me down on the edge of the bathtub. He reached over, turning off the water before stripping off his own jeans and boxers.

The mood had shifted. No longer was I feeling an animalistic need to be close to him, to want him to take me. Now I was vulnerable, and something told me Tate knew it.

He lifted me from the edge, carrying me as he climbed us into the heat of the water. He opened his legs, placing me between them as he leaned us back into the soothing heat. We sat in silence for what felt like forever, my eyes completely closed as I leaned against the hard ridges of Tate's abdomen. Then, suddenly, the silence was broken.

"You don't have to tell me, baby," he whispered. "Only what you want me to know. If anything."

I responded to him with silence. I didn't want to tell him, I couldn't tell him. How could you tell the man you were falling for that knowing about those scars, about the ugly side of me, could potentially kill him?

"I can't, Tate. Not yet," I whispered after a beat.

"Then let me bathe you," he said into my ear, a shiver rolling through me.

I gasped as I felt the soft sponge against my skin. It only occurred to me right then that no one had done this for me, ever. I was built to be self-sufficient, built to be strong and unemotional. Having someone bathe me wasn't just intimate: it was loving. He was loving. I was loving.

With gentle caresses, Tate washed my body from head to toe. I noticed his breath catch as he washed the valley between my breasts, the evidence of what it was doing to him pressed against the curve of my back. He never acted on it: not once did he move up the pace, not once did he move to a place where I wouldn't take him.

His hands moved to my shoulders, drifting to my armpits.

"What are you doing?" I whispered.

"Turn around and face me, baby."

With a gentle lift, I was positioned back into the heat of the water, facing Tate.

His eyes roamed, taking me in as he held the sponge in his hand, suspended in the air.

"Breathe, Tate."

"Right, yeah. Breathing," he said, sucking in a hard breath and closing his eyes as if in pain.

When he opened his eyes, his attention went back to the sponge, dropping it into the water. Pulling it out from the warmth he rung it out before moving to my face. I stopped breathing. He started wiping my cheeks, then my eyes, finishing at my lips. He was wiping away my makeup. He was removing my mask.

There was nowhere to hide.

Nowhere to run.

Exposed didn't even cover what I was feeling in that moment. I closed my eyes as I felt his boring into my skin, seeking out every little scar that lay upon my face: fragmented ones below my lip, the one that stood out against my eyebrow.

Scars from lessons.

Scars from rules broken.

Scars from the way of life.

"Come here," he whispered, holding out his right hand.

Without hesitation, I dropped my hand within his. He pulled me towards him, my cheek resting against the smooth skin of his chest. I sighed deep, holding on as he cupped the water and let it trickle down my back. He washed my hair using my apple-scented shampoo, running his fingers through my wet locks before rinsing and moving on to the apple conditioner. He didn't miss a beat: between bathing me, he… loved me. Was this love? Was holding onto the man who had seen you for your scars and lovingly cleansed them with soap love? If it was then I had fallen, head first, with no chance of coming back up for air.

The water started to turn cold and I shivered as it sat against my skin.

"Come on, baby. Let's get you out." He placed a soft kiss against my wet hair before standing with me in his arms.

He grabbed two towels from the cabinet beside the sink, wrapping one around my shoulders then wrapping the other around his. Walking us into my dorm room, he bundled me up on to the bed with him. Pulling back the covers, he lay me down beside him, the silence of the room our only witness.

"Sleep," he whispered, slowly drying my hair with the towel.

He worked the towel into my hair, drying every strand. Within minutes, my eyes were fluttering closed, darkness surrounding me as Tate lulled me into a deep sleep. Thoughts, memories and flashbacks filtered through my mind, trying to make me remember, to let Willow out of her cage. But something suppressed them, something pushed them back.

"I love you," Tate whispered.

Chapter Nine

"Mornin', beautiful," Tate's gravelly morning voice rang in my ears.

I opened my eyes, blinking back the sleepy glaze. Where the hell was I? Then it clicked, it all fell into place, pretty much like throwing an ice bucket over my body. I was in my bed, but I wasn't alone. Then I felt it. Tate's body wrapped around my own. His very warm, very naked body. I wiggled slightly, gasping as I realized he wasn't the only one who was naked. He groaned out as I registered the hardness of his morning erection sitting thick and heavy against my hip bone.

"Er. Mornin'."

I cast my gaze around the room, eyeing two white towels on the floor. Oh, Jesus. Everything came back to me like a freight train derailing in front of me. The nightmare. Tate turning up at my door. The makeup that had left my face. The bath. Tate holding me while he wiped away the remnants of my mask. The whisper as I fell asleep.

And out of all that, the only thing I could think of was...

He had seen me without my mask. He had seen my scars.

I groaned out, rolling over onto my other side, away from Tate's sleepy eyes.

I pushed my face deeper into the softness of my pillow, as if it would help hide my true self. Fuck, I'm such an idiot.

"Baby?"

I could feel the fresh morning breeze as I realized the sheet had fallen away from my body, resting on my waist and exposing my chest. Exposed and fucking vulnerable, not something that was in my mind's capacity. I needed to get out of here.

"Hmm," I said into my pillow.

I quickly understood my mistake when I felt Tate's hardness against my ass, resting there like it was made to. No. I couldn't do this. I needed to get out.

"You okay?" he asked, placing a small kiss on my shoulder.

I trembled from the contact. I wanted his touch, I wanted it more than anything, but I wouldn't take it. I wouldn't let him go there. I wasn't made to be loved, to be touched, to be held. I was made to... well, I didn't know what I was made to do, but it certainly wasn't what Tate clearly wanted. Me. All of me, in every way possible.

"Yeah." I yawned, trying to mask the lie. "What time is it?"

The bed dipped, indicating Tate had rolled over. His morning erection moved from my skin and I breathed a sigh of relief; the longer it was there the more likely it was I would throw myself at him, not thinking about what the consequences would be.

"Nine-thirty," he said after a beat.

"Crap," I muttered.

"What's wrong?" he asked, moving back into a spooning position, his leg draping over mine, locking me in.

"I said I would meet your sister for coffee. She wanted to do the girl thing today," I lied. My god, I completely lied. Even worse I lied about the one person who was pretty much Tate's everything.

"I've got to go for a run anyway," he said, his arm snaking around my bare chest. "Although, this seems more enticing."

I gulped. The feeling of utter bliss overcame me and I wanted so desperately to bask in the silky smooth feeling of Tate's body. But I couldn't. It wasn't smart, it wasn't cleaver and I had no doubt that it would ruin us both in the end.

"Tate." I groaned, pushing my ass against him.

Okay. That wasn't smart. Jesus. I was trying to push him away, trying to distance myself from him so I could get the hell out of there. The only thing it did was send a shockwave of lust right down to my core.

Fuck.

"Be careful, Low," he growled, pushing against the crook of my ass. The temptation to stay put was so freaking strong, the moan that quickly escaped my lips evidence of it.

Okay, time to get the hell up!

I literally jumped up from the bed, leaving behind a very relaxed looking Tate, wearing one hell of a smirk on his lips. Ugh. The sheet was pooled at his waist, tented and standing proud. Holy hot Jesus. He was like a work of art, a sculpted piece of utter perfection. I averted my eyes, no need to ogle the poor guy.

"I'm grabbing a shower then I'm going to head out and meet your sister," I said, opening my closet and throwing myself inside it. If I didn't look at him it would be easier, right?

"'Kay, I'll call Logan, see if he's got his whiney ass up and ready for a run," he grunted.

I grabbed a tank top and some jeans. Turning, I closed the closet door, nearly dropping my clothes in the process. Tate was no longer lying in my bed; he was standing. Naked. Deliciously naked.

My eyes instantly located that sexy V, my tongue itching to explore it. Dammit.

"My eyes are up here, baby." He smirked, grabbing at his jeans and roughly pulling them on. No boxers. Oh dear lord.

My head snapped up, locking with those green eyes of his that did amazing things to my panties. I coughed, trying to hide my embarrassment. Sucking in a lung full of air, I stepped towards him, placing a short but chaste kiss on his lips.

He groaned. I immediately pulled back, biting my lip.

"Are we going to talk about what happened last night?" he asked after a moment.

Hell no. He already knew too much. I need to keep him safe.

I shook my head, my gaze fixed on the floor between us.

"Soon, Low. Soon," he whispered, placing a soft kiss on my hair before throwing on a shirt and leaving the room.

I exhaled. I hadn't even noticed the lack of oxygen to my brain until I felt dizzy.

"What are you doing?" I grumbled out loud to myself. "You know the rules. Stop thinking with your vagina."

With that, I threw a text to Neva before leaping into the shower, trying my hardest not to think back to how much I wanted Tate.

Me: Coffee and the girl thing in an hour?

Neva: Yes!! Logan is driving me crazy.

Me: Uh oh, what's he doing now?

Neva: Breathing?

Me: Ha! See you at Black Bean in an hour?

Neva: Sure, if I don't get arrested for murder beforehand.

An hour later I was sitting at the table in the coffee shop, my amazing coffee that Jared had grumbled at making in my hands. I sat in the window, a first for me. I would usually pick the farthest, darkest corner, and I knew Neva would have something to say about it.

"Mornin', babe!"

Speak of the devil.

"I hate that you're a morning person," I grumbled as she took a seat beside me.

"Who jumped up your ass this morning?" She smiled, signaling Jared for her coffee order.

I almost spat my coffee all over my best friend's face. Coughing, I tried to hide my sheer embarrassment beneath it.

"Wrong hole." I threw my face in my hands and groaned. "I walked right into that one."

"Yes. Yes, you did." Neva laughed, smiling to Jared as he placed her coffee on the table.

"Okay, enough about holes and asses. What's going on with you and Logan?"

"You mean why haven't I punched you in the throat yet?" she quipped, raising her brow and staring at me pointedly.

He's finally told her. Thank Christ.

"You know it wasn't my place. Besides, it doesn't look like you've committed murder so I'm presuming everything's okay?"

"He has a fat lip. I smacked him in his stupid mouth for being so damn careless." She smiled.

"That's my girl." I winked. "So, what do you want to do today? I've got class at four so we need to get our asses moving if we want to do anything."

"Shopping?"

"You hate shopping," I said, my brows pinching together.

"Yeah but you don't. You get new clothes all the time," she fired back.

"Yeah, it's called the internet. I hate physically shopping, too many PMS-ing women around for my taste," I lied.

It wasn't that I hated physically shopping for clothes, it was that it was risky. I couldn't do risky.

"We could grab a bite to eat at Bones? Dex and Trix will join us." She smiled, taking a sip of her coffee.

"Sure. I could murder a cheeseburger right now," I said, rubbing my stomach.

One thirty minute cab ride later, we were sitting at the bar. The place was empty, since it was a couple of hours before opening.

"Get your damn grubby hands off my tits, Dex! Jesus!" Trix yelled, rolling her eyes as she swatted away Dex's hand.

I chuckled quietly to myself as I took a large bite of my burger. Yummy.

"You had no complaints last night, hooker." Tex winked, leaning his elbows against the bar, eyeing my fries.

"Don't even think about it," I stated flatly. Damn idiot thought he could steal my fries.

"Leave her alone, Dex. It's too early to deal with your ass today," Neva grumbled beside me.

"Cowgirl, I'm hurt." Dex smiled, covering his heart with his hands.

"No, you're not. You love the attention, now scoot. I need to go into the back room," Trix said, holding an armful of small mixer bottles.

"It going to cost you." Dex smiled playfully.

I rolled my eyes. Dex caught me.

"For that," He leaned in, "I'm stealing one of these."

My reflexes reacted before I could even blink, catching Dex's hand mid-air, the offending fry falling from his fingers as he gazed at me in absolute shock.

My mind suddenly filtered back to a time where having rapid reflexes was absolutely necessary. A time that made me breathless every damn time I thought about it. It was my past. I had become somewhat of an expert at lying, keeping things hidden, but lately, since that single text message, everything was falling through my fingertips.

"Fuck me." Dex gasped.

His whispered gasp was enough for me to snap out of my thoughts. I instantly released his wrist as if it would burn my skin.

"Girl must love her fries," Trix said, shrugging, pushing past a still speechless Dex.

Yeah, I loved my fries but my reflexes were notorious. Moral of the story? Touch my fries and I will break your damn hand.

"Okkkkay. So, moving on," Neva said with a nervous chuckle. "You guys going to make it to The Takedown? Ace is fighting Big Willy tonight."

"Did someone say big willy? Count me in!" Trix fist pumped as she walked back behind the bar.

"What? You don't get enough of mine?" Dex balked, the fry situation a passing thought.

"Christ, when was the last time either of you got some? This sexual tension is making me nauseous," I quipped, throwing another fry into my mouth. "Do you need us to leave? So you can, you know? Fuck."

I smiled sweetly at Dex. He responded with a wink while Trix gave Dex the evil eye. Uh oh, trouble in paradise? They both claimed to have the perfect relationship. They would hook up when they wanted some, then they would go their separate ways. Seems that was no longer the case.

From what Neva told me, Trix had been crashing at Dex's house. She had been kicked out of her family home, something about her father not approving of all the ink she adorned on her body. Her father would probably have a damn stroke if he saw her array of piercings.

"Low, text me time. I'll meet you over there. It's my night off anyway." She smiled, turning to Dex and scowling at him before heading into the back room again.

"Jesus, Dex. What the hell have you done?" I asked, Neva and I exchanging glances before she nodded her head in agreement at Dex.

He sighed hard, his usual cocky self completely disappearing.

"I did what most men do when they come into contact with Trix." He shrugged.

"What's that?" I asked, curious.

"I fell in love with her."

"Jesus," Neva and I said in unison. This was Dex and Trix, the couple that were completely wrong for each other but at the same time completely right. They were chalk and cheese, but peanut butter and jelly. Complete walking contradictions.

"Have you told her?" Neva asked.

"It may have slipped out," he said, scratching the back of his neck. "She's fucking fragile. Handle with care should be tattooed on her damn body. She's got a bad past. It wasn't pretty; she came to the bar one night looking for a job and I instantly gave her one after having her make the most complicated cocktails known to man. One night we got trashed and fucked on this very bar."

I inwardly cringed, removing my hands from the bar.

"Her name isn't Trix, she gave herself that name because it suited her lifestyle at the time." He winced as if realizing what he had just said. Pointing at us, he continued. "You know nothing about *any* of this. Okay?"

Neva and I nodded.

"She called herself Trixie, or Trix for short because at the time she was turning tricks. She was whoring herself out just to make enough money to leave her past behind. Her life had been shitty and the men… Jesus, the men she fucked would tell her they loved her and then drop her instantly. The minute I told her I loved her, while we were having sex, she fucking bolted."

Well, shit. I didn't expect that with my midday cheeseburger.

"I'm going to check on her," Neva said, leaving her seat and wandering into the back.

"What do I do, Low?" Dex asked, pain clearly evident in his eyes.

I pondered on his question for a moment. "Time. You give her time."

I inwardly rolled my eyes at my own words. I was the worst person he could possibly ask for advice. Guilt gripped me as a slow, winding pain hit my chest. I rubbed at the valley between my breasts. That hurt. I needed some air.

"Can you tell Neva I had to get to class?"

I stood from my chair, nodding at Dex and leaving the bar. I opted to walk; walking seemed to help me organize the mess within my own head. I just wished there was something to help me organize my damn past.

The sun was still blazing as I made my way back to campus, thinking back on my own words as I did. *You give her time.* Time: it was something I didn't have. My time was limited, I knew that, but then I wondered: if I had the time I so desperately craved, would I have opened up to Tate sooner? What if my past was erased? What if I knew nothing of the life I had lead, would I still be the same person dealing with the battle between choices and consequences? Because when you make a choice, you also choose to deal with the consequences, but was it better to cross the line and suffer those consequences than to just stare at it and wonder what if?

There I go hoping again. Always hoping, never naïve.

It took me only thirty minutes to get back to campus, just in time for my class with Dr. Voxen. I slowly made my way to class, my eyes downcast as I dodged on-coming students as they bustled through the corridor. I was on edge today, my nerves peaked and my senses completely aware of everyone and everything going on around me.

I made it into class without a single eye gazing into mine; taking my seat, I waited as the room filled up with excited students, clearly eager to get this class over and done with so they could start the weekend. I took in my surroundings, noticing some familiar faces who are regulars at Bones or at Ace's fights. My gaze flickered to the doorway, people were cheering. Speak of the devil.

Ace sauntered into the room while girls hung on his every word and movement; it was like they were eyeing their prey, ready to pounce the minute he chose one of them to mate. Damn idiots.

"Why the long face, beautiful?" he said, throwing himself down into the chair beside me after shrugging off the mauling women.

"Are you trying to say I have a long face?" I countered, raising my brow.

"Out of that sentence, the only thing you got was that? Did you miss the part where I was being unusually gentleman-like and called you beautiful?" He smirked.

I rolled my eyes.

"You're in a chipper mood today. Who did you screw?"

"Seriously, this chick had thighs that could crush concrete and—"

"I really don't want to know." I cringed, cutting him off.

"Who crawled up your butt? Or better yet, who hasn't? Blow off some steam and get laid, Low. You sound like you could use a real hard—"

"Okay, settle down!" Dr. Voxen bellowed, cutting Ace off just in time. "In today's class we're going to discuss the papers you handed in. Your arguments were good, although some were lacking in creativity. But there was one that stood out. Low Parker?"

The pen I was holding dropped from my fingertips at the mention of my name, hitting my desk and rolling onto the floor in one fluid movement. Oh, shit. Remind me why the hell I picked this damn major?

"Um." I coughed, trying to conceal my utter horror. "Yes, sir?"

"Your paper was outstanding. You had clear and precise reasoning and your research was well-documented. I'm going to use it for today's discussion."

I gulped, nodding my head in a robotic fashion.

"You okay there?" Ace whispered, his hand grasping at my thigh.

I felt him squeeze. My eyes traced his long fingers that rested against my jeans before snapping to his face. He winced slightly, moving his hand away.

"I'm fine."

I stayed silent for the rest of the class, my eyes downcast just like before, my head pounding with a sheer intensity I didn't know existed. Dr. Voxen went from one paragraph to another, explaining why my findings on the mafia were very well-educated around rumors and guess work, not only from the international media but from the general public.

The minute we were dismissed, I jumped from my seat, bumping into Ace as I all but ran from the class. What the hell was wrong with me today? It was if my body could sense something but my head was like a clueless sitting duck.

Yeah.

Quack.

As I made it out of the classroom, I noticed the corridor was pretty much empty. Taking my chances I slipped into the empty classroom opposite and slammed the door shut behind me. My head flew into my hands as I slid my back against the door, dropping onto the floor.

"Okay, er, body," I said out loud to myself.

Your body isn't going to respond to you, you idiot! Still, I didn't see why it would hurt.

"What the hell is going on? What do you know that I don't? You're making my brain hurt."

No response. Huh.

I was quickly pulled from my minor lapse in sanity the minute I heard banging against the door I was leaning on. Great. Five minutes. Would it hurt for five minutes to freaking think on my own?

"Low, open this damn door. I know you're in there. I can still smell your fucking perfume. It smells like unicorns and rainbows, by the way, what is it? Some kind of pre-teen shit. It stinks." Ace laughed through the door.

Har har. Everyone's a fucking comedian these days.

"Go away, Ace. I'm busy!" I shouted, my head still in my hands.

"Fuck no. Open the damn door." He grunted.

"Ace, I'm serious, leave me alone!"

"Dude, open the fucking door. Dr. Voxen is looking at me like I'm a nut job for talking to a fucking door. Open it now."

"No " I shouted back.

He growled something I couldn't understand, and for a minute I was sure he said something along the lines of 'Little Willow.' Fuck. My body instantly froze. My blood boiled, seemingly melting away the frozen feeling I had and bringing me right back down to earth. Motherfucker.

Jumping from the floor, I flung open the door and grabbed Ace by the shirt, pulling him inside the room. Slamming the door, I whipped my head around to his.

"What did you just call me?" I growled, my eyes hard, my stance even harder.

"Nothing." He sighed. "Are you okay?"

"I'm fine. I just wanted some time to think, that's all." I smiled, slouching my shoulders. "Anyway, what time is the fight tonight? Trix is going to meet us there."

"Trix? Yum." He smirked, winking at me like the cheeky fuck he was.

"You know, you're almost always surrounded by vagina, yet you're the biggest one out of them all."

"Sweeeet!" He laughed, over-exaggerating as usual. "Fight's at nine, doors close at eight. And please for the love of all things holy, do not bet on me again."

"How did you know I put a bet on you?"

"Rodriguez."

Dammit.

"He talks a little too much for my liking," I grumbled.

"I need to get over to the gym for a pre-workout. You good?" he asked, placing his hands on my shoulders. I nodded. "Good. And remember what I said: get laid. You're like a cranky old woman, I'm sure Tate will be all too willing to clear the cobwebs, Old Mother Hubbard."

"Ace." I grunted, shrugging his hands from my shoulders.

"Uh huh. Got it, overstepped the mark. Laters!" He smiled, making a dash for the door.

I sighed hard as I stared at the closed door; finally some quiet so I could think. Fear was keeping me on a tight leash, restricting me from dealing with the situation at hand. It did nothing but piss me off more. Swallowing down the large lump that had formed in my throat, I opened the door and walked out into the corridor, keeping my eyes downcast as

I made my way discreetly out of the building.

I made it to my dorm room without a problem, releasing a sigh of relief as I shut the door behind me. Pulling out my cell, I fired a text to Trix, telling her the time of Ace's fight. Once I'd done that, I sent another to Tate.

Me: Fight night? X

He replied instantly.

Tate: I'm thinking you, me, pizza and a movie? X

Me: I'm thinking you're a genius. I'll let Neva and Trix know.

Tate: ...and hot, sexy, gorgeous. Don't forget those.

Me: How could I forget?

Tate: Are you trying to tell me you have the hots for me? ;) Now that's hot.

Me: Do you need me to stroke your ego? Is that what this is?

Tate: I can think of other things that need stroking.

Me: I walked into that didn't I?

Tate: No idea what you're talking about ;)

I laughed at his cheeky mood. We texted for a good twenty minutes before I decided to jump into the shower. I needed to try and wash away today's fear and guilt from my skin. I walked into the bathroom and turned on the shower, stripping off my clothes I waited for the water to heat up as I stared at my reflection in the mirror. Low Parker stared back at me: brilliant blonde hair, icy blue eyes, makeup that was made up to perfection. It was time to drown her, for now.

Shaking my head, I walked into the shower, immediately stepping under the hot spray. Water cocooned me, wrapping me within its warmth as I washed my hair. The next step wasn't as simple as the first. Now it was time to remove the mask. Tentatively, I reached for the wash cloth and started slowly washing away every layer I had built up on my skin to hide what was beneath. Someone I didn't want to be.

After peeling away most of my skin, I turned off the shower and wrapped a towel around my body, adding another to my hair in a twist. Out of instinct, I walked to the mirror once again, staring at the woman in the reflection. Mission accomplished: Low Parker had disappeared and in her place was Willow Knoxx. The scars that were recently revealed to Tate taunted me. Never have I been ashamed of my scars, but with Tate it made me want to bolt and hide.

Those scars made me who I was, but more importantly, made me strive to be someone else. I wasn't bound by my scars, I was bound by my past, which was much worse. My scars were a physical reminder of what I had faced, but my past filled the emotional hole in my heart. The child in me wanted love, the love of one man in particular but that thought was quickly pushed away.

"Time to hide, Willow," I said as I reached for my makeup bag.

I was playing hide and seek with my own identity.

Chapter Ten

"Baby, did you hear what I just said?"

Tate's voice penetrated my thoughts, thoughts that were on something that was consuming every second of my slow creeping days. It wasn't so much what I knew would happen, it was the journey towards it. In the end, everything was going to come out, and I was certain I would be just as alone as I had been six years ago.

"Hmm? Sorry, what?" I asked, my gaze finally finding the eyes that haunted me daily.

"Do you want pepperoni on your pizza?" he repeated as he spoke into the phone for our takeout order.

It had been two days since my meeting with Jace, a meeting that was very dangerous. If anyone ever saw us together… I didn't even want to think about what the outcome would have been.

"Sure," I answered.

Tate nodded, but his eyes latched onto mine as he stood from his bed, his phone still attached to his ear as he made his way over to me. His gaze never wavered as he stopped at the foot of the bed I was sat on. I watched as he bent his right knee and placed it beside me, ending the call as he did so.

"What's on your mind, baby? I can feel the cogs turning in your head," he asked as he placed the weight of his body onto the bed in front of me, watching me intently as he sat on his knees.

"I have a couple of essays I really need to get done, they count towards half my grade," I babbled, running off lie after lie, becoming tangled within my own web of deception.

"Are you sure?" he asked, tilting his head to the right.

No. I'm lying! I'm lying. Please stop me from lying, please stop me from adding to my little glass jar! I begged him in my head over and over again, but it was no use. I couldn't put him in a position that could potentially put him at risk. My heart wanted one thing, but my head pursued another. I had an internal battle that would soon break out into an outright war, and I was powerless to stop it.

"I'm sure." I smiled.

"Good." He smirked. "Because I only want one thing on your mind right now, and that's me."

I laughed at his cheesy remark. The sound that left my throat sounded foreign, it was a genuine sound that I hadn't experienced for a while. When you're trying to push your emotions down into a deep dark box, it's hard to keep them hidden. The box is always there, a little reminder of the person you once were. It's also a temptation, you know what's inside the box, and once in a while you have to open it. It's human nature… curiosity.

Curiosity killed the cat.

Stupid cat.

"You, huh?" I smirked, mentally slamming the lid shut on the box of emotional blackmail. "I think I have enough room in my mind for you, Tate."

"Enough room?" He growled, his brow arching at my comment. "Baby, I don't think you get it yet. I want to consume your every thought, every movement, every desire."

His hands suddenly cupped my face as he leaned in close, his breath caressing my lips like soft silk. My pulse skyrocketed at his closeness, as it did every time he was near, sending me dizzy with lust. I could feel the vulnerability snaking its way through my body, latching onto my crimson blood as it slowly seeped through my skin. I could physically smell my vulnerability as it permeated the air around us. I could smell it, taste it, see it.

"Okay," I squeaked, the fear of my secrets dripping from my soft voice.

"Listen, and listen good, Low. I *will* consume every part of you. I *will* consume every thought, every movement, every desire. You won't be able to breathe without thinking of me, feeling me, wanting only me. Am I clear?"

Oh dear god.

I could feel the lump in my throat forming, choking me with every second that passed, seconds that felt like torturous hours.

"Yes," I replied on a shaky breath.

Words had yet again failed me. I was sprouting one word answers because Tate did something to me that no man had ever accomplished. He made me feel.

His lips suddenly crashed against my own, the power he held over me pushing boundaries I didn't know were there. His teeth scraped against my bottom lip, pulling and tugging as if pleading for entry. My head screamed, begged, and bartered, yelling at me to stop, to push back and leave. But his lips and teeth held me captive, my heart jumping at the chance to finally overpower my head, all too willing to be his victim.

My palms smacked against his solid chest; the intention clear in my mind that I was supposed to push him away, but the push never came.

I pulled.

My hands suddenly held onto his shirt for dear life as I finally allowed his tongue into my mouth. A growl escaped his lips as he searched, probed and stroked my tongue with his. This wasn't like any other kiss we'd shared. This was World War III exploding inside my own body, fighting over which voice was going to win in the end… and in the end, my heart took my mind by surprise and dominated it without a single protest.

"Jesus, Low." He groaned as his hands grabbed at my ass, squeezing tight as he lifted me onto his lap.

We were nose to nose, the evidence of his lust for me completely evident beneath me. I was no longer in control of my own body, my hands wandering underneath his shirt, my nails scraping against his solid abs.

I said I wouldn't do this, I wouldn't put him at risk, but right now I was so far beyond the point of listening to the tiny voice in my head. I was like a bull in a china shop, crashing through the walls I had built to protect the people I loved. Love, is that what I felt? I knew love, the kind of love friends have for another, but love between a man and a woman? I've never had to try and decipher that emotion, and now was tumbling between the fine line of love and lust.

A slow rising moan ripped from my lips as Tate ran his palms up my tank top, the rough texture of his hands leaving a path of fire in their wake. His fingers made short work on the clasp of my bra, his hands moving against my flesh before reaching under the cup of my bra. I hissed in the pleasure that thrust its way through to the bottom of my spine as Tate's tongue and teeth claimed my mouth, the pure overload of bliss feeding my desire to finally let go, to finally let him in.

"God, Tate." I groaned as he took my puckered nipple between his finger and thumb, rolling with just the right amount of pressure to blur the lines between pleasure and pain.

Euphoria poured through my veins as he removed my tank top from my body, one of two barriers between his mouth and the flesh of my breasts. He made short work of removing my bra, but just when I thought he was going to plunge in, he took me completely by surprise.

My entire body quaked as he ran his nose between my breasts, caressing me with a slow, sensual touch that engulfed my body in flames. I could already feel the knot deep inside me tightening like an elastic band, ready to snap at any given moment.

"God damn, you smell so fucking good, baby." Tate groaned as his nose made his way up to my neck, settling behind my ear, inhaling my scent before nipping my skin with his teeth.

He sighed contently as he gently kissed the spot he had marked with his teeth, and all movement stopped. His hands dropped to his sides, leaving my breasts exposed as his hardness stood proud between my legs.

"What's wrong?" I whispered, not understanding why the hell he stopped.

He sighed as he hid his face in my neck, still not putting his hands on my body.

"If I don't stop now, I don't think I ever will."

Something in my chest swelled, and I was suddenly feeling needy like a damn teenager. My mind had completely switched off: no longer were there thoughts about how dangerous it was to be close to Tate, no longer was I questioning everything. Right then, I needed him in a way I had never needed another man.

"What if I don't want you to stop?" I panted as he inhaled deep into my neck.

He froze against my skin, a growl escaping his lips that was so deep I thought my panties might actually combust from the delicious sound.

"Do you have any idea what you're asking of me, baby?" he said, dropping kisses across my jaw. "If you give yourself to me, there's no going back. You'll be mine and no one will stand in my way from taking you whenever and however I can have you."

His words tightened the knot deep down in my stomach, sending licking flames to every crevice of my body. I had finally switched off my mind and yet I was still nervous. I had lied to him, told him I was innocent, that I was a virgin. And if we go down that path he'd soon find out I had deceived him. I had to tell him.

"Tate, I…"

"I know, baby. I knew a long time ago."

Huh? He knew what? Suddenly my heart was hammering against my chest at frightening speeds. He knew I wasn't a virgin?

"How?"

"You wouldn't kiss me like you do if you were a virgin, Low. Plus, my sister isn't very good at keeping secrets. Her own? Yes. Yours? No." He smirked. "I was just waiting for the time you'd finally let me in and tell me.'

I was speechless: what the hell do you say to the man who was hard beneath you? The man who knew that you had lied about being a virgin?

"Are you ready to finally let me in, baby?" he asked, his thumb slowly running along my bottom lip.

He had no idea what he was asking. Was I ready to let him in to screw me seven ways to Sunday? Yes, because right now I needed him to make me forget everything I knew, everything I knew was going to happen. But was I ready to show him the side of me only one person in this state knows? No, and I don't think I'd ever be ready.

"Yes."

"Fucking finally." He groaned as he sealed our fate with an earth shattering kiss.

His hands roamed my body as if tracing every inch and committing it to memory before finally settling on the waistband of my tight skinny jeans. His right hand moved to the center of my chest, flattening against the crevice between my breasts, pushing me down flat onto my back.

"I can't do this slow, I won't do this slow," he said as he pulled his shirt over his head, dropping it on the floor beside the bed.

My eyes were no longer on his; instead they stared at the tanned, defined abs that called out my name. Suddenly, I'm hungry. Hungry for Tate.

"Baby, you have to stop looking at me like you're going to eat me up. I'm already hard as steel and you looking at me like I'm your next meal is only making me harder."

I bit down on my bottom lip to hide the smirk that was begging to release, but it quickly disappeared the moment Tate dropped his jeans.

He wasn't wearing underwear.

He was hard.

My mouth watered uncontrollably.

"See something you like?" He chuckled, pulling me out of my drool fest.

Right in that moment, watching as Tate crawled back onto the bed, I mentally threw down the vulnerability, the fear, the lies and deceit. Just for now, I was the girl I had always dreamed of being, the girl who could take control and never have to think about the consequences.

"Yes," I said, cupping Tate's face in my hands as I pulled his weight on top of me. "Yes, I do."

Without thinking, I pulled his lips to mine. Moans erupted from my lips as Tate's tongue plunged into my mouth, dominating as his lips wrapped around my tongue and sucked hard. He was showing me who was in charge; little did he know the girl who I was desperate to be wouldn't take anything lying down.

"Holy fuck." He growled as I wrapped my legs around his naked waist and flipped him onto his back, his hardness pressed against my stomach.

Unbuttoning my jeans, I slid them down my legs, pulling my black lace panties along with them. Throwing the unwanted barrier on the floor beside the bed, I was completely exposed to the man who could unravel me like no other.

"Jesus, Low." Tate panted as his slid his fingers between my legs, the sensation tilting me off axis as he moved in to a slow, torturous rhythm. "You're soaking wet."

"Ah." I moaned as he slid a single finger inside me, his thumb rubbing slow circles against my clit.

The knot deep in my stomach was becoming too much to bear, the urge to slide him inside me was unlike anything I'd ever felt. I needed him like I had never needed anyone before, wanting the pleasure to outweigh the burden placed upon my shoulders.

"Baby, I need to be buried inside of you, I need to feel you," he growled, the deep husk at the back of his throat only fueling my need for him.

"Condom," I whispered huskily.

"Shit," he cursed, reaching over to his bedside cabinet drawer and all but ripping it from its wooden confines. Handing me the condom, I set to work.

Lifting my hips, I steadied myself above him as he held his cock in his right hand while his left gripped my hip. Tearing the wrapper with my teeth, I quickly sheathed him. His tip rubbed against me as he slowly maneuvered me, but I didn't want this slow. I needed this to be fast, unthinking, and enough to send me to the blissful place that I prayed took away all of my conscious thoughts.

"Jesus, fucking shit!" Tate groaned as I suddenly powered down hard, impaling myself on him.

Pleasure and pain erupted and mixed together deep inside me, the sting from the fullness grounded me but the pleasure overtook the pain and threw me into mindless bliss.

"Jesus, Low. You're going to be the death of me," he growled as I started to move, slowly adjusting to his size and the full feeling that consumed me.

Every movement I made, Tate matched thrust for thrust. My hands moved down to his pecs, using his body as leverage as my movements became more frantic. I was quickly losing my rhythm as the pleasure spiked through me, I was so close to orgasm I could taste its freedom.

I was no longer in control. I was in a power hungry frenzy, trying to chase the orgasm that just wouldn't come. I needed the orgasm. I needed my escape from the thoughts that ran through my mind at ridiculous speeds.

Guilt gripped me. I was using Tate as a means to escape, an escape from the past. I wasn't proud of it, in fact it sickened me to my stomach.

Tate sat up, placing my arms around his neck as he hit new places inside of me with every hard thrust. I watched as he bit his bottom lip with his teeth, the long vein in his neck threatening to burst with pressure. He was holding back, waiting for me to topple over that edge with him. But, as much as I was trying to run to the edge, there was something holding me back. Guilt. So much guilt.

Tate's hands went down to my hips, holding on for dear life as he flipped me onto my back. I was panting like a damn dog: so close yet so fucking far.

"You're going to come with me, Low. Hold on, because I'm not going to be gentle," he growled into my ear.

A single moan escaped the confines of my mouth before the breath from my lungs was stolen right from my chest. Tate pounded hard inside me, so hard the bed groaned with every movement he made. Pleasure spiked to new highs, my toes curled with every thrust, and my mouth was spilling cuss words that would put any sailor to shame.

Tate's right hand wrapped around both of my wrists, pinning them above my head as he hit a new angle that had me seeing stars. Without warning, ecstasy ripped right through me with Tate following swiftly behind. My legs shook uncontrollably as I moaned hard, the intoxication of finally being in a place where I couldn't think about anything other than pleasure making me lightheaded.

For the first time since the text message hit my cell phone, I could hope, dream, and feel like the normal girl I wanted to be. But the ecstasy didn't last. It never did. Three minutes of pure peace. I had sacrificed myself and Tate for just three minutes of blissful thoughtlessness.

My head crashed against Tate's hard chest as I panted for a breath I didn't know would come. I was gasping for air as the realness settled in, and everything I had locked away only moments before threatened to burst through the seams.

Tate lazily stroked my hair as we both tried to come down, but there was only one question on my mind as fear and guilt quickly consumed me.

What have I done?

Chapter Eleven

Same place. Same disgusting coffee. Different waitress.

I was back at the coffee shop, waiting for the one person who could help me deal with this fucking mess. It had been less than twenty-four hours since I handed over everything to Tate, albeit unknowingly, but handed over just the same.

Tate and I had finally gotten a couple hours sleep after three more rounds of him showing me exactly who was in control, but little more than two hours after falling asleep, I received the text message I had been dreading.

I re-opened the text as my right hand clasped around the coffee cup, reading the two words that made my skin crawl and stomach knot.

Unknown Number: He's coming.

He was coming for me. Oh, fuck me in hell! He was coming… and I had no idea what to do.

I left Tate's dorm room in the early hours, leaving a note behind that merely said 'Gone to class.' It was pathetic really, another string of lies bound in an impenetrable web. I couldn't even bring myself to say the words out loud. I couldn't even say who I was without feeling the urge to vomit.

That morning, before leaving for my meeting with Jace, I placed two little black hearts in the jar.

One hundred and sixty-two little lies.

"Us meeting here is like an itch," Jace said as he sat in the chair opposite me. "I've got to fucking scratch it otherwise it'll never go away."

I rolled my eyes as I shook my head, trying to rid my mind of my jar of lies. Fucking typical, he was trying to do a funny.

"I'm not listening to your shitty jokes today, Jace. We have confirmation," I stated flatly, the seriousness in my voice ringing through the air around us.

I watched as Jace lowered the same black hoodie he had worn at our last meeting, his brown eyes staring back at me as he reached for my nearly cold coffee.

He took a large gulp of the cheap coffee, holding my gaze as he emptied the contents of the mug.

"You need to go to him," he said as he wiped his mouth with the back of his hand.

His statement had me nearly backing out of my seat in utter surprise.

Was he fucking deluded?

"Jace, if this is one of your jokes, you better cut the crap. I'm going nowhere near him of my own accord. If he wants me, he can damn well come and get me."

"You think he wouldn't do that?" he asked, a ghost of a smirk gracing his lips. "Willow, he will come for you, why not save him the trouble and seek him out? You have an informant, they can tell you where he is."

For a moment I contemplated punching him in the dick for his ridiculous idea. Why the hell would I go to the man who had me quaking in fear after all these years? He was deluded if he thought for one moment I was going to seek him out.

"Six years on and you still have the worst people skills known to man," I stated flatly, not an ounce of humor in my voice. "Get a fucking clue, Jace. I'm not going anywhere near him if I don't have to."

Jace sighed hard, it was overdramatic and for a minute, I could feel a small chuckle worming its way up my throat, but I quickly pushed it back down.

"Do you ever truly think about who you are, Willow? About what it would be like had we not left?"

I sighed. Of course I thought about who I was, who I could have been before we left, but that was six years ago; I'm no longer the same person.

"It would have been hell, and you damn well know it," I said, pointing at him.

"Forget that." He paused, seemingly searching my face for something… anything. "You would've been respected, you would've been the girl I grew up with who didn't take shit from no one. Since we left you turned into this shell of yourself, and to be honest, it's fucking depressing. I know the person you could be, and no matter how much I deny it, I *know* I should fear you but it doesn't mean I will."

"It's fucking depressing? You think?! Fuck me, Jace. I'm still waking up six years later with flashbacks. How do you not have them? You saw all the shit I saw, and yet here you are, telling me that because I'm not the girl I once was, that it's fuckin depressing."

"That's not what I meant and you know it! Don't twist my words, Willow. All I'm saying is you were someone to be reckoned with… go and show him exactly why people respected you back then."

I let his words sink in for a moment. He was right, I was once respected for who I was. But was I willing to go to the one person who made me feel so fucking small? If I went to him, was I going to seal my fate and that of everyone around me?

"It could be a trap," I muttered, glancing down at my lap.

"If it is, I'll be right there to pull you out of it," he stated.

His comment was enough to move my gaze back to his, locking onto the eyes that had been holding my attention for more than a decade.

"You can't," I whispered. "It's dangerous and adding you to the mix would be downright stupid."

"When have I ever deviated from danger… or stupidity, for that matter?"

I paused. Why the hell were we even having this conversation? Did he honestly think I would go to him, never mind adding Jace into this fucked up mess?

"I won't do it."

"If you don't do it, Willow, he'll just think you're weak. He will have the upper hand, and he'll know just how much *you* fear him," Jace said, standing from his chair, the loud scraping noise against the floor making me flinch. "You need to step out of the mind of Low, and remember who you really are, Willow."

"I don't know who I am anymore," I muttered, the weakness in my voice apparent even to myself.

Jace stepped around the table, kneeling beside my chair and grabbed at my chin with his thumb and finger. He turned my face to his, our gazes locking and a smile gracing his lips.

"You're the girl I grew up with. You're the girl I admired for years. You're the woman who I knew you would turn into." He paused, his mouth turning into a flat line upon his face. "You're also Willow Knoxx, and no one from your past is ever going to let you forget that."

I pondered for a moment, trying to work out Jace's angle; there was always an angle when it came to Jace. Always.

"You're also a pain in my ass, you always have been." He chuckled as he straightened from his position beside me.

Something at the back of my mind told me he wasn't telling me something, that he was holding something back. In my experience, that was fucking dangerous.

"What aren't you telling me?"

"You have to go to him." He sighed. "Or I will."

With that, he left the coffee shop, leaving me with a god damn ultimatum and a headache from hell.

I could feel my skin on my forearms becoming itchy, the need to scratch becoming unbearable as I sat stunned in my chair. I knew all too well what would happen to Jace if he was true to his word. Jace was always true to his word, no matter the consequences.

I slowly rubbed my temples with my fingers, trying to elevate the headache that just wouldn't let up. My head pounded hard as I considered my options… but they all stopped at the same conclusion and that was what frightened me the most.

"Motherfucking shit," I hissed as I pounded my fist against the table.

Heads turned and stared as I tried to get my shit together, but every time I thought I had arrived at a new outcome, reality set in and I realized this was so much more than I could handle on my own.

"Fucking asshat," I grumbled as I pulled on my leather jacket.

Throwing down a twenty, I made my way out of the coffee shop, stopping on the sidewalk briefly to send a text message.

Fuck protocol.

Chapter Twelve

The Last Judgment was referred to as the Day of Reckoning, a time when the effects of one's past mistakes or misdeeds catch up with one. That thought repeatedly jumped to the forefront of my mind every second step I took towards my desired destination. Although, my destination wasn't truly desired, it was more of a necessity. I promised myself years ago the only communication between myself and my informant would be via text message. This was my Day of Reckoning.

My legs burned with every long stride I took down the sidewalk. I had been walking for three hours straight but I wasn't about to burn out any time soon. My cell had been blowing up with phone calls from Tate, clearly wondering where the hell I had gone to, considering my class with Dr. Voxen finished an hour ago.

I was doing this to protect him.

"Fine job you've been doing," I mumbled out loud to myself.

My chest was tight with the adrenaline that pumped through my veins, pushing to heights I hadn't been to in over six years. But now I felt it. I felt the need to push through the fog that had attached itself to my retinas over an hour ago. I was two towns away from the coffee shop, five from campus. I needed to be as far away as possible so I could clear my head.

I slowed my assault on my body, falling into a leisurely walk. The sun beat down on my exposed skin on my chest, warming me from the outside. Couples walked hand in hand down the sidewalk through the small town I had found myself in. What I would give just to do that with Tate, to be normal. Small children laughed as they ran past me, chasing each other and enjoying the spring sun.

The chiming of my cell quickly pulled me out of my desire to be normal. Jace's name flashed across my screen as I rolled my eyes in defiance. I really didn't want to deal with him again today. Sliding my finger across the screen, I rejected the call without a glance.

Just as I went to place my cell back into my pocket, it chimed again. Groaning, I noticed Jace was calling me again. Persistent ass. Rejecting the call, I turned my cell on to silent mode, hoping he would eventually get the hint.

The minute the weight of my cell hit the inside pocket of my leather jacket, my world suddenly turned askew.

My heart accelerated as a large hand muffled my scream begging to be released, the smell of stale cigarettes on the hand choking me. I kicked out my legs and arms, hoping to make contact with someone, but my attempts where useless.

"Stop struggling, little Willow. I will cut you," the gravelly voice sneered into my ear.

I recognized the voice. It was a voice that would appear in my nightmares from time to time. It was a voice I wasn't ready to face, a voice from my past I was hoping to be rid of.

Tears threatened my eyes as his name rolled over in my mind, the connection between us hard to hide.

Dominic Knoxx.

His name made my stomach clench with fear, the last name we shared turning my tongue thick and immobile in my mouth. We're family, half siblings to be exact, and I hadn't seen him in close to eight years. I feared him then, and I would be fucking insane if I didn't fear him now.

I stopped struggling against his hold on me, my legs becoming heavy and limp as he dragged me down a side alley. I tried to take in the area, trying to spot something that would give me some sort of clue as to where he was taking me. But I saw nothing other than piles of trash and stray cats. I couldn't even spot something I could use as a weapon. I whimpered in defeat.

"Shush, little Willow. I don't plan on hurting you… yet." He laughed huskily into my ear as we came to a stop just outside a small building.

My body was quickly maneuvered, my front now facing the ugly building, my hands wrapped behind my back with my brother's hands encasing them. If I screamed, I would be killed, and I had no doubt no one would hear me if I did. If I tried to fight back, I would be killed, and I wasn't stupid enough to even try it. Instead, I kept my mouth shut and my body relaxed.

I was quickly marched into the building, the steel door slamming hard behind us as we made our way over a large space. It looked like a small warehouse building, crates were scattered about the floor space, some opened, some sealed. My eyes glanced over one of the crates, hoping it wasn't what I was imagining. The minute my eyes settled on the contents I almost balked in shock. Almost. Inside the crates sat row upon row of weapons, ranging from your usual hand guns to AK-47s. What the fuck?

A figure before me broke my contact with the weapons. I instantly recognized him from the large spider tattoo that sat proudly on the side of his shaved head. It was my god damn informant, my only connection to my past. The person who had been sending me text messages for the last six years. Spyder Monroe. The most notorious liar. My lies didn't have shit on him. They named him Spyder because he was known to have his fingers in lots of pies and he was one of the best internal spies there was. Now he was wearing his name with pride… tattooed onto his head. Jesus.

"Spyder." I grunted as a smirk played at his lips. "You son-of-a-bitch!"

The smirk quickly faded and my eyes nearly bulged out of my head as I watched the Glock in his right hand rear back. The blow came hard. I saw stars and black spots as the pain splintered through my right cheek bone, no doubt fractured from the butt of the gun.

"Motherfucker," I hissed, the tang of copper swirling around my mouth.

"Learn your fucking place" were the only four words Spyder

growled at me before turning around and walking towards another steel door.

Dominic pushed me hard, my knees buckling as I was thrown forward, the hard concrete against my palms and knees breaking my fall.

"Get up!" Dominic grunted, gripping me by my jacket and hauling me through the steel door.

I decided right there I would keep my mouth shut. I knew they took pleasure from my pain, I wasn't going to give it to them. Just like all those years ago.

I stumbled into the dark room, only the silhouettes of roughly nine other people were visible. I squinted hard, trying to make out who the hell I was dealing with. Anything was possible, I was dealing with my brother and who I'd thought was my informant.

"She know where she is?" a voice grunted from somewhere in the room.

I still couldn't make out which direction I was supposed to be looking, everything was so dark I could barely see my hands in front of my own face.

"She wouldn't be stupid enough to tell anyone if she did." Dominic laughed sadistically.

I silently rolled my eyes to myself, wondering if they knew who the hell I was. Did they think I was just some girl off the street that my brother had picked up? Surely Spyder and my brother would have told them?

"Good."

Suddenly the room was illuminated in light. My hands quickly flew up to my eyes, shielding them from the painful brightness that consumed the room.

"Holy fuck," a strangled whisper broke the room as I tried to see through the light.

"What the fuck have you done, Dominic?" another voice said.

My vision finally cleared and I moved my hand, finally able to see ten large men standing in a semi-circle in the small room. My eyes darted around my surroundings; the only furniture visible was a small dark desk coupled with a clearly worn out office chair. There were no windows and only the single door we had just entered through.

I tried to work out the eyes of the faces that stared back at me, wondering if I recognized any of them. I saw two sets of bright blue eyes that were fixed on mine and I recognized them instantly: the Gomez twins. They booth stood at around six feet tall, their frames matched in muscle and build. The last time I had seen them we had been in the Manor, it wasn't pleasant and I knew exactly the kind of damage they could do.

"She is the key to getting this locked down," my brother said, breaking the silence.

"You brought your fucking half-sister to help us with this? Are you fucking deluded? She could blow the whistle on this whole operation, you dumb fuck!" a man I didn't recognize yelled.

"You have no fucking idea who she is do you, Nicolai?" My brother laughed.

Nicolai. The name registered in my mind but I couldn't put together the pieces of the puzzle that were confusing the shit out of me.

"No. And by the look on your sister's face, neither does she." Nicolai leered as he took a step towards me. "Who the fuck are you, little girl?"

Little girl? Little girl? Rage boiled deep in my gut as the fractures in the walls I had built cracked and burst open with an all-mighty roar. I was done playing games. Without warning my mask shattered into millions of pieces before my eyes.

Out came Willow Knoxx.

Ex-mafia.

"I suggest you watch your fucking mouth, Nicolai. You have no idea who I am," I said, leaning into him. "And that, is very fucking stupid."

"Do you know who I am?" Nicolai roared at my outburst, clearly surprised.

I briefly closed my eyes as I tried to work out who the hell I was dealing with. His name was familiar, and without warning my mind tumbled back to six years before. Nicolai du Lude.

"Nicolai, of course I know who you are. Being the daughter and heir to one of the biggest mob bosses within the US kinda puts me in a particular position, you know?" I smiled sweetly.

Just saying it out loud broke my heart. I hadn't admitted to myself, never mind anyone else, who I was in such a long time. My mother had tried to get me to talk about it, to open up about our time with my father, but I wasn't going to let him taint our new life. Now I was standing before my past: tainted, exposed, released. Low Parker had disappeared so easily it scared me and made me want to vomit at the same time.

"Who are you?" he whispered as he played with a strand of my blonde hair.

Thrusting out my hand, I laughed as he looked at me like I had just lost my damn mind. "Willow Knoxx, nice to finally meet you, Nicolai." I winked. "Jaxson Knoxx is my father," I added, just for clarification, even though his name made my stomach turn.

The room erupted in gasps and chorus of 'holy shit' as Nicolai just stared at my hand in front of him. "You know, where I'm from, if a mob boss's daughter offers her hand, you damn well take it," I growled.

"Jesus, Dominic. What the fuck are you doing?" Nicolai said, rolling his eyes.

My hand was still between us, hanging there like it didn't matter. I wasn't happy.

"Hey. Hello?" I said, using the same hand to wave in front of Nicolai's face. "Are we going to stand here all day and pussy foot around the fact I have a vagina? I kinda have somewhere to be."

My hand was suddenly gripped tightly in Nicolai's, squeezing hard as he leaned into my personal space.

"Don't push it," he growled.

"If you want to walk out of here with your dick still attached to that worthless body of yours, I suggest you remember who the fuck I am and let go of me. Now."

"She's feisty. I like it." Nicolai smirked over my shoulder, his hand releasing mine slowly.

"That ain't even the half of it. Now, can we move past this shit and talk about the plan?" my brother said, gripping my left shoulder, pulling me back a step.

My brows furrowed. I was interested to see what the fuck they had to say. What plan had they got up their sleeves, and what the hell it had to do with me and my brother.

"You know what I want, Nicolai. I need to be at the head of that table, blood will spill but I want *his* blood smeared across that fucking throne."

Holy shit. The realization of what they're talking about suddenly hit me full force. Dominic was my half-brother. Our mother had an affair a few years into her marriage and thus produced my father's pride and joy. A first-born son. He was destined to take over the family business, to become my father's second in command when he became of age at twenty-one.

Three years later, my mother bore another child. Me. This time I was definitely my father's, everything about me was him. From my crystal blue eyes to my platinum blonde hair. I was a Knoxx, there was no doubt about it.

Some years later, a gentleman by the name of Luca pulled up to the Manor in a Rolls Royce, claiming Dominic to be his son. By that time, my father had put my brother into training, showing him the ropes of the business he was destined to take over. Three weeks later a DNA test confirmed Dominic to be illegitimate, and it was too late for his real father. Jaxson Knoxx shot him dead in his flashy Rolls Royce, his driver stepping on the gas to take back the message the Knoxx family weren't to be fucked with.

The minute my father read the DNA results, he became quiet, closed off, unreadable. He was a sadistic man before, but after that, he was pure evil. My half-brother was thrown out of the house, his name never to be used to gain power. If he did, he would be shot on the spot.

My father soon turned his attention to me, the pure blood, his only heir. The training Dominic was given over the years was crammed into me in a few short months. My protests would go unanswered as my father thrusted a Glock into my hands, and by the tender age of sixteen, I could shoot a moving target without blinking.

My mother mourned the loss of her son, of her first born. There was nothing she could do; if she went to him, my father would shoot her for being unfaithful, again. My mother wasn't without punishment, the nights were long and painful as I listened to her cry herself to sleep. The image of the scar on her foot jumped to the front of my mind. My father had waited years, waiting for me to turn sixteen to give my mother her 'just deserts.'

One night, three days after my sixteenth birthday, I was pulled from a restless slumber. My father gripped me by my nightdress as he ushered me across the long hallway to my mother's room. They had been sleeping separately ever since my father had learned of her betrayal; his nights were usually spent with paid women while my mother cried herself to sleep in the next bedroom.

My mother slept soundly within her bed as my father tiptoed us further into the room, stopping at the foot of her bed before thrusting that same Glock he had been training me with into my hands. I looked at my father to try and find some understanding in his eyes, but there was nothing there. There never was, just darkness clouding the purest of blue eyes.

"I don't understand," I whispered to my father as he made his way around to my mother's bedside.

"You will learn, little Willow. That breaking the code, being unfaithful, and tarnishing the family name comes with consequences." He smiled before gripping my mother by the hair.

Her screams still haunt me to this day as he forced her down on her knees before him, her sobs breaking through the stillness of the night. My father waved me over and I slowly stepped towards his side, wondering what the hell he wanted me to see.

"Point the gun at her," my father stated as he held with a tight grasp in my mother's brunette hair.

I stuttered for what felt like minutes until my father grabbed at the gun, pulling me forward with it. The Glock that sat heavy in my hands was pointed to the woman who had created me, who had soothed me after I would come home spent from a day of training for something I didn't want.

"Remind her why she's on her knees, Little Willow," he whispered into my ear.

I gulped down hard as I tried to clear the large lump in my throat. I had to do this; if I didn't, he wouldn't just shoot me, he would also shoot her.

"You're in this position because you broke the family code. You lied, cheated, and snuck around, all for your own personal gain. Personal gain isn't tolerated, the only gain you should be searching for is the gain for this family. You created a… a bastard within the family. He can never be heir."

I closed my eyes as I tried to push the painful memory back into the little box in my mind. I didn't want to think about that night, I didn't want to deal with the poison of my past.

"I need collateral, Dominic. What am I going to get in return for pulling your father from the head of the table? This could cause a war I don't think you're ready for," Nicolai said, his gaze landing on me. "And you're not even next in line. She is."

Nicolai de Lude was smart. Surprising, considering his father was a vile leech that would take any job that would come his way, including sex trafficking. The de Lude's were hitmen, the ones you went to when something or someone needed to be dealt with. I was under no illusion Nicolai would kill my father; he was just like his, vile.

"She doesn't want to be at the table, she never has. She can get out if I make them vote, and you'll all be at my table," Dominic said, his voice sure.

"How are you going to get rid of the originals who sit at that table, Dominic? Do you want me to take those out too? You're putting a lot of blood on my hands without so much as a guarantee."

I felt as though I couldn't breathe, like a lead weight was sitting on my chest. My brother was planning to kill off my father and the original members of the mob family, just so he could take a seat at the head of the table. Didn't he realize this could cause an outright war? That killing members of your own Family means you've committed something far worse than breaking the code of silence, you've committed mutiny. Payable with blood.

"Dominic, have you lost your god damn mind?" I grunted out, the weight on my chest becoming heavier.

He laughed as he turned to me, his dark brown eyes staring back at me. "I lost what was left of my mind when your snake of a father kicked me out of the fucking house and had me fend for myself. He deserves this, and you're going to help us."

"I'm not putting blood on my hands for you, Dominic. I won't do it for anyone."

"You will do as you're damn well told, Little Willow. Nicolai is going to get rid of your father, make it look like a mob hit and you're going to take the seat at the top of that table. Then you will get Nicolai to sit at the table alongside you, you will vote him in. Nicolai will start killing from the inside, making sure the only two originals left are no longer able to sit their old asses at that god damn table. You'll sway the vote, Little Willow. You'll then vote me in, and I'll take over the chair you clearly don't want."

"Are you fucking deluded?" I screamed, my voice echoing around the room. "If any of the other families find out about this, you'll be killed, Dominic. You're not playing around with school kids here, you're talking about killing off one of the most sadistic men in the mob world and could involve mob families from across the country."

"I know what I'm doing. You want out of that seat? Then I'm going to take it and ensure those ridiculous business deals your father has made gives us more revenue and we can branch out."

"By those ridiculous business deals, I presume you're referring to the Irish weapons deal that has been in place for nearly a decade?"

"I can get bigger and better weapons for the Irish, I can supply every two weeks rather than every four. Not to mention that I can supply larger weapons."

"I won't do a damn thing to help you do this," I said, squaring my eyes at my brother and Nicolai.

Nicolai laughed sarcastically, his Adam's apple bobbing with every breath he took. He looked towards Spyder, my now ex-informant, who took a step towards me.

"Little Willow, you don't think your father was the only one watching you all these years?" Spyder smirked. "I know exactly what you have now: college, friends… a boyfriend? Just think how quickly we could take those away."

A gasp escaped my lips at his threat; he had been watching me for six years. We had come to an agreement I would never take the chair at the top of the table the day I got out, and over the years he had sent me updates via text message on my father's movements. Now, he was coming for me, and Spyder had gone back on our agreement.

"You wouldn't," I said, almost instantly.

"Actually, Spyder probably wouldn't. Even though he is on this side of the fence, he still wouldn't betray you like that. But I have no fucking problem doing it," Nicolai chimed in.

My head spun as I tried to come up with a way of stopping this, of trying to grasp everything I was hearing. But I came up with the same conclusion over and over again. If I wanted to protect those I loved, I had to sit at the damn table.

"From the blank stare on your face, I'll take that as a 'Yes, Nicolai, I'll do it.'" He smiled.

I felt the heat quickly drain from my face as I stared at the men in the room, not one of them giving anything away. What choice did I have? If I didn't do what they wanted, they would destroy anyone who stood in their way. I wasn't about to let anyone get close to the people I loved.

I sighed before nodding sharply.

Welcome to World War III.

"You'll go back to your pathetic life until you're called upon." Nicolai smirked, pointing to the steel door behind me. "If you run, I will find you."

Dominic stared at Nicolai, nodding, which I presumed was aimed towards me. I had been dismissed. No goodbye, no fuck-you-very-much. Nothing. Just the threat on the lives around me if I didn't do as I was told.

"Oh, and Ms. Knoxx?" Nicolai chuckled, flicking his gaze to mine. "I will kill you."

Gulping hard, I slowly backed out of the door, ensuring I never once turned my back on the room of large men. I had no idea if they would shoot me on the way out, but I wouldn't take the risk. My hand fumbled behind my back as I tried to open the heavy steel door. Closing my eyes briefly, I heard the large creak of the door and as soon as the gap was big enough… I ran.

I ran so hard my legs burned with so much intensity I thought I might pass out. The three hour walk I had already pushed my body through before being grabbed by my half-brother and his minions splintered through my bones.

I needed distance from my experience with my own past. Running fast, I made it six blocks before nearly passing out from lack of oxygen. With my hands on my thighs, I bent over as I tried to catch my breath, the air around me feeling thick as I gulped in air like it was water.

It took several minutes for my body to register I was no longer running, the burn from my muscles almost having me cry out in pain as I stood upright. I assessed my surroundings, I was in a small town with quaint little stores. One of the stores was painted a yellow color, the light from the mid-day spring sun reflecting against the brightly colored building. Spotting a coffee shop, I made my way towards it. Stepping inside, I quietly took a table in the back, my hands shaking as I rubbed the aching muscles of my thighs.

"What can I get you?" a waitress said from beside me.

"Coffee. Black," I muttered, never glancing in her direction.

She must have taken the hint as she moved from my table, coming back a couple of minutes later with a steaming cup of coffee.

"Excuse me," I said, my gaze locking with the waitress. "What town is t…this?"

Shit. I was a stuttering mess.

"This is Charlottesville, my love." She smiled warmly.

I returned her smile and turned back to my coffee.

I pulled my phone out of my leather jacket, punching in one of two numbers I knew by heart.

"This is becoming a habit, Willow," Jace's gravelly voice rang into my ear.

"I… I…" I stuttered, my nerves finally catching up with me as I tried to spit out what I wanted to say, but nothing came out.

"Tell me where you are, babe."

I could hear rustling in the background, followed by large banging footsteps.

"I... I don't know," I whimpered, my hand moving to the center of my chest as I tried to stop the fast-rising panic taking over my body.

"Describe what you see, babe. Tell me what you can see from where you are," he said softly, the roar of an engine creeping through the phone.

"Small stores. Small town. Bright yellow store on the left." I paused, pulling myself together. "Charlottesville."

"I'm coming for you."

That was all he said before the line went dead and I was left alone, surrounded by people.

Chapter Thirteen

Check the time. Sip my coffee. Check the time. Sip my coffee.

I seemed to have turned two normal, everyday things into a ritual as I waited for Jace to come for me, the routine making me feel safe, calm. Or calmer. My left index finger ran along the lip of my cup as I noticed the steam that was once floating freely had completely disappeared; my coffee was cold and I hadn't even noticed.

"Babe!" Jace's voice rang out as I spotted him crouched beside my seat on the floor, his hand on my forearm. "Tell me what happened."

"Dominic," I whispered, the sound of my own brother's name was like a nail running down a chalkboard in my head.

"Motherfucker." Jace grunted. "What did he want?"

"I... Jesus, Jace. I..." I sighed, forcing myself to get the words out. "I have to take the chair."

"You ain't got to do shit, Willow!" he growled.

Standing, he took the seat opposite me, just like every meeting we've had. It was a sign of respect. I didn't want respect. I wanted to bolt and run.

"No, Jace. I *have* to take the chair." I paused, looking down into the murky depths of my half-empty coffee cup. "If I don't, they'll hurt them."

I closed my eyes as the words spilled out of my mouth, trying to erase the picture of my half-brother's venomous face from my mind.

"How the hell did he find you?" Jace asked, his eyes searching every inch of my face for some sort of clue but, as always, my face was blank, never giving anything away.

"My informant." I cringed, memories of Spyder's smirk as he took sheer delight in my pain flashed right before my eyes. "Spyder Monroe."

Jace's hand moved to my right cheekbone, rubbing gently with the pad of his thumb. "That the fucker who did this to your jaw?" he asked.

My gaze quickly locked with his. In truth, I had forgotten about the pain from when the butt of Spyder's Glock thundered against my jaw. But the subtle pressure of Jace's thumb against the throb of my skin stung like a bitch, reminding me just how real all that back there really was.

I nodded sharply as my head deviated to the left. I closed my eyes. I could feel the hesitation in Jace's hand as it left my skin. I didn't have to look at him to know he was pissed, raging, and just waiting for the right time to release.

"I have to take the chair, Jace," I whispered, my eyes still closed.

I waited for Jace's protest, but nothing came. Seconds passed before I opened my eyes again, and when I did, my heart broke.

"I know," Jace whispered on a gravelly breath. "And I've got to take mine."

His admission stung. We had left that life, tried to start a fresh once we finally thought we were free. But there's no such thing as a retired mob member, and there's certainly no such thing as an heir denying something they were born into. The mob wasn't just a way of life, it was a family. Blood in, blood out – except, there's never really an out. The mob looked after their own. If you're too old, too sick, you're looked after, placed into a part of the Manor and only called upon if necessary.

"What happens from here?" I asked.

"They'll summon me the second you step foot back in that manor. The minute you take the chair, I have to take my own. That's the way it is. Fresh blood on one family throne means fresh blood for another.

"You need to listen to me, Willow. If my family or yours knew about... about our new life, we'd both be punished. Do you understand?"

I nodded my head, tears forming behind my eyes as I took in everything he was telling me.

"I helped you get out, we helped each other. We broke loyalty, we broke the code."

"I know. I just wish this would just go away, I don't think I'm strong enough to deal with this," I admitted.

"Yes, you are," he said, reaching for my hands that now sat on the table in front of me. "You're Willow Knoxx, daughter to one of the most notorious mob bosses in the US. You need to wait for Dominic's call, and no matter how much you want to run, you better stay put and stand the ground you deserve to walk over."

"What about my father? He's still going to be looking for me, I have no doubt he's already found me by now."

"It's dog eat dog, babe. It's whoever gets to you first."

That night, I placed twenty tiny black hearts into my mason jar.

I had no idea how many lies I had accumulated, but I knew twenty paper hearts would never be enough to help me over the next couple of days.

One hundred and eighty-two tiny little lies, enough to tell me…

I was a fucking liar.

Chapter Fourteen

A day. A night. A lifetime.

Waiting, wondering, hoping.

Holding on to something worth fighting for.

Chapter Fifteen

"I'm sorry," I whispered.

Watching, taking in every inch of Tate he slept soundly beside me.

Hiding in plain sight.

Chapter Sixteen

Withdrawn, hopeless, a complete fraud.

One week and not a single shred of news. Nothing, no one.

Tate knew something was wrong. I was breaking into millions of pieces and he knew it. Every night was the same as he clung to me in my bed, as if he was trying to hold me together while he slept.

Tate holding me. Me holding Tate while my other hand was secured around the Glock beneath my pillow.

Living through my worst nightmare.

Tate and those that I loved right in the firing line of my past.

Chapter Seventeen

"Motherfucker!" I shouted, snapping my nail as I threw my clothes into my old and tattered suitcase.

I hadn't been prepared—I was always prepared for every eventuality—but this time I was completely caught off-guard. The phone call from Dominic came late in the night. I'd never been a heavy sleeper, years of being woken in the night by every tiny noise prevented me from sleeping more than a couple of hours. But last night I was sleeping heavy for the first time in a long time; it was the worst mistake I could have possibly made.

As soon as I saw the number on my phone light up the screen, I knew. My world all but fucking flipped on its head, crumbling beneath me. I had fucked up, big time. People were going to get hurt, people I cared about, people I loved. All because I had gotten comfortable, careless. I wasn't brought up to settle in one spot for more than a couple of years, but here I was: six years later, settled in the same spot. Christ, I'm such a fucking idiot.

My gaze flickered to the dorm room door, I knew Tate was going to walk through it any second. God, Tate. What had I done? I had given him no warning, just ran from Logan's apartment without a word, leaving everyone behind without a thought. Pulling myself from my damn pity party, I furiously started throwing the rest of my essentials into my case. Clothes: only jeans and loose fitting t-shirts. Shoes: mostly Chucks or black boots. I'm moved in robotic mode: get my shit and then get the hell out of there.

Stepping around my bed, I picked up the only family photo in my possession. It was a picture of my mom and me ten years ago, not long before we ran. We had been running for so long, never settling, only passing through. The longer I stayed in one place, the easier it became to be found. I couldn't be found, I wouldn't be found. But, this time, it looked like I had been found and it could cost me my life, and the people around me.

I could hear heavy footsteps making their way down the corridor of my floor, the sound throwing me off for a moment. I was sure it was going to be Tate, but the sound coming from the footsteps weren't Tate's, but I recognized them instantly. Ace.

Fuck.

I quickly threw the photo frame into the case on my bed before reaching underneath the bed for my mason jar. My little jar of hearts. Kissing the glass briefly, I placed it into the case, shutting the lid and zipping it up. Just as I pulled it from the bed, I heard the distinctive click from my door. I closed my eyes and waited.

"You have got nine minutes until he walks through this damn door. Explain. Now," Ace growled as he slammed my door shut, walking towards me.

Ace had a quality that wasn't to everyone's taste: opinionated, vain, cocky and honest… mostly. But what people didn't see was his protective side; it's instinct and most of the time necessary. Ace was misunderstood, deemed to be this big, scary guy who was hard on the outside and soft on the inside. Ace wasn't soft, anywhere. Neither of us were, that's how we had been brought up.

No, dragged up.

I opened my eyes, but I didn't make eye contact with him. I didn't need to say anything, my silence alone would give away what was going on, that or the small suitcase in my right hand.

"Oh shit," he whispered.

Oh shit. Yeah, that sort of sums everything up. It's time, it has been for a while now, but I wasn't ready to accept it. But the phone call confirmed everything. It's time to run, and I couldn't look back.

We stayed silent for minutes, the realization of what was about to happen building tension in the room so thick, you could slice right through it.

"Little Willow, look at me," Ace whispered, stepping closer into the room.

"Don't call me that!" I boomed, the rage associated with that name boiled to the surface, and I could feel my restraint breaking.

"Raise your voice to me again, *Low*, and I will take you over my god damn knee. Now, look at me!" Ace growled, stepping even closer than he was before.

My eyes quickly snapped to his. I wish they hadn't. Every time I looked in those eyes, I remembered the day when he came for us, the day we ran. When people looked into his eyes, all they saw was the dark brown irises staring back at them. What I saw was years of pain, obedience, blood and even death. Now, in that moment, all I saw was awareness. Awareness of me? The situation? Or that we stood in a room together alone, actually acknowledging who we were for the first time in over six years?

"Take another step, and I will blow that growl right off of your god damn face," I sneered, my fingertips brushing against the Glock sitting in the waistband of my jeans. Always prepared.

Ace raised his right brow at me and smirked. Arrogant piece of shit. "Try it," he grunted, taking the last step between us.

He was so close I could feel his breath against the skin of my forehead as he towered over my small frame, but I wasn't intimidated. I was anything but, but his closeness took me back to when we just kids, dragged up into a fucked up adult world.

"Do you still remember where I hide my Glock?" I asked in a calm, collected voice, cocking my brow at him. My trusty Glock, it had been with me ever since he pulled me out of the disgusting, vile place I was hiding in. When you come from our background, you learn to have a weapon on your body, no exceptions. My Glock was pushing against the skin of my waist, the familiar pressure a welcome feeling, but at the same time terrifying.

Ace chuckled as he quickly stuck his right hand in the waistband of my jeans, pulling out my trusty Glock by the grip and scratching the barrel against the stubble on his chin. "I always remember," he said seriously.

Stupid man. "Now, do you remember the weight difference between a loaded and unloaded Glock?" I laughed as I watched his brows furrow, weighing my Glock in his hand. I took advantage of his confusion as he started to pull out the magazine, bending down I pulled out a second Glock from my ankle strap and pointed it straight between Ace's eyes.

"What the fuck?!" Ace blinked, and I couldn't help but smirk. But he quickly regained his composure. "Get that fucking barrel away from my face. Quickly. We have shit to discuss!" he barked.

My confidence wavered, and I placed the Glock back into my ankle holster. It seemed over the years we had changed: Ace had forgotten what the weight of a loaded gun feels like and I had lost my hard outer shell. This wasn't good.

Ever since my family reunion with Dominic I had been carrying my weapon, always hidden from sight but most definitely there. The people around me needed protecting from the demons of my past. That included Ace too.

"Your momma still in Vegas?" he pushed; he clearly wasn't going to drop the subject.

I hadn't spoken to my mom since the night I told her she had to leave. The day Ace had come for me, he had made sure we took my mom with me. But we knew we couldn't all stay together, it was too dangerous. I missed her like hell, but we had to do it to protect each other. I made sure she only used cash, shipping her off to Vegas with an alias, one that should get her by for at least a year. So I hoped.

"Last time I checked, but I need a pre-paid, I need to get the message to her," I whispered, the words sliding off my tongue like second nature. This was me, all of me. The fucked up girl with the fucked up family.

"I'll deal with it," Ace grunted, abruptly ending my self pity.

He was doing it again, trying to protect the people he shouldn't. What he was doing had consequences, and his actions could cost him his life. I wasn't prepared to let him carry on doing it; he had been doing it for far too long.

"No, Ace. I will deal with it. I need you to stay here and help with damage control," I said. I needed to deal with this, not him.

"Damage control? Are you fucking serious, Low? This won't be damage control, this will be fucking chaos. You need to deal with it before you leave. Talk to him, but don't think for a second you can take him with you. You can't give him that. You can't give him the option to go with you; he can't see what we see." He stared pointedly at me, like a god damn child and it boiled my blood.

"Don't you dare talk to me like a petulant child, Ace. You do remember who the hell we are dealing with here? You remember my father and my brother, right? I know I can't take him with me, I know that. But what the fuck am I going to tell him when he asks me why I have to leave without him? I can't just tell him who I am, Ace. You know I can't do that!"

This was becoming messy. I didn't do messy, I couldn't do messy. My heart practically lunged from chest cavity with lightning speed, lodging itself within my throat as I heard the audible gasp from behind Ace. My knees buckled, and I had to find strength from deep within to keep standing on my own two feet. Ace slowly stepped to the side, crossing his arms in front of his chest and keeping his eyes directed to the floor. It was a stance I was all too familiar with.

Standing in the doorway of my dorm room was Tate, his skin pale and his eyes showcasing the utter fear and dread I had been accustomed to seeing for years. I held back the lump that formed in my throat, trying to settle where my heart was already lodged, fighting for front row seats to the biggest clusterfuck of the century. I could only wait, hoping Tate hadn't heard what I had all but screamed at Ace. But I knew otherwise. His face morphed from fear to complete rage within a matter of seconds.

"What the fuck is going on?" Tate boomed, taking another step into the room and slamming the door shut with the back of his heel.

The loud bang vibrated through every bone in my body as the door slammed into place. I hesitated. I was mentally about to slip the mask back on, the one I had perfected over the years of hiding. But I knew I couldn't hide behind it anymore. Tate knew more than he should.

"Tate…" I started, but I was quickly cut off with a wave of his hand.

Did he really just cut me off like that? Then it hit me. I needed to push him away; I couldn't get him tangled up in this mess, it could prove fatal. My heart shredded inside my throat, the realization of what I was about to do consumed me. Fuck.

Before I could utter a single word, Ace opened the hole in his face.

"I wouldn't cut her off like that if I were you, Tate. Take my advice: you can't dominate a woman who can skillfully break every single bone in your body… and count with every snap."

My stomach dropped. Oh shit. When I cleaned this mess up, I was going to shoot Ace in the dick. Twice.

I groaned as Tate turned back to me, confusion written all over his face. Then I saw the pain. Pure, unhidden pain danced in his eyes. Oh god. I could feel my body reacting to his pain; it was drawing me in, pushing me to take hold of him and never let him go. I ached. Ached to touch him, to hold him, to love him. I knew that if I did, it could potentially kill him.

"What the hell are you talking about, Ace?" Tate spat, taking a step towards him.

Ace's stance turned hard. I couldn't help but gasp as the memory of just what Ace could do to another person flashed in front of my eyes. Utter torture.

"Don't, Ace. You do and I will blow your dick off," I growled.

Tate's eyes flashed with venom, and the realization of what I had just said sunk in. Tate probably thought I was sleeping with Ace. Tate had no idea that I had a Glock in my ankle strap. Hell, he didn't know anything about Willow Knoxx.

"You son of a bitch!" Tate shouted, his voice filling the tension filled room.

Tate's face had morphed into something I hadn't seen for a very long time: absolute hatred. Before I could think, I jumped in front of Ace. Throwing my arms out either side of me, protecting Tate. He didn't realize just what Ace could do if pushed, and Ace was holding on by the thinnest of threads.

"Little Willow. Move. I might have to snap him in half," Ace growled into my ear.

I kept my stance; if I moved, Tate was going to leave this room in a body bag. I wasn't having any more lives on my conscious, especially the man who owned me mind, body, and soul.

"No," I grunted.

"Little Willow? Only your mother calls you *Willow*," Tate spat in distaste, as if he had just sucked on a sour lemon.

The tension rose higher with every passing second that I didn't respond. What the hell do I tell him? I couldn't tell him everything; if I did, it would be the worst decision of my life. But I had to tell him something. Should I let him believe I was sleeping with Ace, just to protect him? It would hurt him, but if he knew the truth, it could potentially ruin him. I made the split second decision, and I only hoped I didn't regret it.

"No, Tate. My mother isn't the only one who calls me Willow. People I have been hiding from also call me that," I whispered, the words tasting vile in my mouth.

"Who are you?" he said breathlessly.

Here goes.

"My name is Willow Knoxx, daughter and heir to the Knoxx family business. I'm a trained killer. I can shoot a moving target quicker than you could blink, I can put a grown ass man on his fucking knees with just my index finger, and I could do things with a pocket knife that would turn your stomach."

Silence.

Dead silence.

Tate's eyes widened, and as I turned to Ace, I couldn't help but notice the thick vein that throbbed against the skin of his neck. The room was tense, so tense I almost couldn't stand it.

"The fuck…" Tate whispered, shaking his head. "I… I… don't understand. What the fuck is going on? Some explain this to me. Slowly."

Chapter Eighteen

"Willow, be careful what you let slip here," Ace grunted, raising his brow.

"Ace, shut that fucking hole!" I growled, rubbing the tight muscles in the back of my neck.

"You know what could happen if you say too much, don't turn this into the mess that I had to deal with." Ace sighed. The pain of what he had endured during our teenage years flashed across his hard face.

"I'm still fucking here, you know! Someone explain!" Tate yelled, breaking through the memories.

I was torn. Telling Tate too much wasn't an option, but telling him nothing wouldn't solve anything.

"Think, Tate. Willow. Knoxx. My last name should start ringing some bells soon enough," I said, the tremor in my voice hard to mask.

I didn't want to watch when he would recognize my name. I just wanted to leave and keep the people I loved safe. But, sure enough, Tate was quick off the bat.

"Knoxx? As in… No. It can't be," he whispered, his worried eyes staring right into mine.

There it was. He knew.

"Willow," Ace warned, but I didn't take any notice. I didn't want to.

"Jaxson Knoxx? Jaxson Knoxx the, the… Fuck!" Tate growled.

Tate suddenly turned, crashing both of his fists into the door with a loud bang. He finally got it. He understood who I was, and all I felt was pure shame. This was why I hid, this was why I didn't want him to be here when I left. I couldn't stay and fix this. I had to leave.

As if Ace could read my thoughts, he suddenly broke through the thick tension of the room. "It's time."

Tate suddenly whirled around, anger flaring in his eyes as he looked at Ace with distaste.

"It's time for what?" he growled, stepping towards me.

His gaze locked with mine before dropping down and landing on the suitcase that sat on my bed; he would understand soon enough.

"I'm coming with you," he grunted, grabbing my case and pulling it from the bed.

"What?"

"Are you fucking crazy?!" Ace and I shouted at the same time.

Tate didn't say a single word. He only walked towards the door with my case in his hand.

Before I could even think, I dived for my ankle strap and pulled out my secondary Glock, aiming it right at the man I loved. My hand tightened around the grip as Tate turned towards me. His eyes flashed with fear, and a gasp left my mouth as I realized what I was doing. It was kill or be killed: he needed to understand exactly what that meant.

"Low," he said breathlessly before shaking his head. "Baby, what are you doing?"

"I'm doing what has to be done, Tate." I sighed, but quickly regained my composure as I signaled for him to move from the door with the Glock. "You will do exactly what I say, and I don't want any arguments about this. I will shoot you, Tate."

"Fuck," Ace whispered, moving to my side and bending so his mouth lingered by the shell of my ear. "Give him enough so it won't hurt too much, but don't give him too much. You know the drill."

With that, Ace left the room. He would be waiting outside the door, making sure no one could disturb us. Too many people were involved already.

"Bab-"

"No, Tate. I'm going to talk, and you're going to listen." I waited, seconds went by before Tate nodded in defeat before taking a step to the right.

"Okay," he mumbled, confusion written all over his face.

"You know who my father is, but you only know a small percentage of what he can do. His name is splashed all over the media, but they can't ever get anything to stick. There's a reason for that, Tate. They can't get his ass in jail because he has judges and governors on his payroll. He's untouchable, Tate. If you get in his way… you will also become untouchable, unreachable, and completely unfindable."

"But I can help you," he begged, but it was no use: no one could help me now.

"Help me? Tate, I have been running for six years, running from him. I am the sole heir to the family business. He is coming for me, Tate. Too much blood has been spilled. I won't be responsible for any more," I whispered, the memories I had kept locked away in the far recesses of my mind slowly started to filter though.

"Any more?" he asked, the hesitation evident in his voice.

"I am the daughter of a mafia boss, Tate. Don't ignore Ace's warning. Blood has been shed, and some has come from my very own hands."

I watched as the cogs turned, waiting for Tate's reaction. Sure enough, the cogs slowly clicked into place, and rotated slowly.

"Who is he?"

"Who is who?" I asked nonchalantly. I knew this was coming, but I didn't know if he could handle the truth.

"Don't fuck around with me… shit, I don't even know what to call you! Do I call you Willow or Low?"

I winced. He was hurting, badly. I couldn't comfort him; if I did, it would only make things harder, much harder than they already were.

"My name doesn't really hold any importance, Tate. But you wanted to know who Ace is?" I asked, trying to divert his anger.

He nodded.

"Ace Mathews is an alias. His real name is Jace Rowe."

Tate's eyes bugged out at the mention of Ace's last name. He was quicker than I thought he would be.

"What the fuck?!"

His hands flew into his hair, and pulled tight. Yeah, my sentiments exactly. It was public knowledge who Ace's family was too, they were just like mine. Completely fucked up.

"His father is–"

"Julius Rowe." Tate muttered, swiftly cutting me off. "What. The. Fuck."

Julius Rowe was the lead member of a rival mafia family: to be more exact, the rival of my mafia family. Yeah, completely fucked up. There's been hate between the two families for nearly two decades, each one trying to get to the top and stay there.

The mafia are like a family: mostly made up of blood relations, but from time to time the top bosses bring in some outsiders. They were all loyal and were trusted. You didn't get anywhere in the mafia unless you're trusted, as soon as that trust had gone, so did you.

The Knoxx and Rowe families had been on tender hooks ever since the Rowe family's fuck up over ten years ago when their men took out the wrong person in the Knoxx family. They took out someone who was female, blonde, and in her early teens. They took out the wrong girl. That bullet was meant for me.

"Everything is a lie... everything," Tate mumbled, throwing his hands over his face and slowly sliding his back down the wall beside the door.

My stomach suddenly dropped. Gone was Willow Knoxx; in her place was Low Parker. The mask was back on. My grip loosened around my Glock as my heart pounded, the sound deafening to my ears. What was I doing? I had pointed a fucking gun at Tate, the one man who didn't take my shit. Now I'm threatening to shoot him? Oh god.

"Baby-" I started, but my mouth quickly shut, and I quivered.

Tate's eyes were laced with so much fire, and I was quickly feeling the burn. It scorched me from the inside, the intensity catching me completely off guard. The slow burn crept from my toes to the very tips of my fingers, encasing me completely in flames. I gasped as the Glock dropped from my hands, landing with a thud on the ground.

Gone was the trained killer, gone was the cocky attitude. In their place was the woman who was completely head over heels in love with the man who was crumbling on the floor.

"Are we a lie, Low? Was everything we had a lie?" Tate asked as he slowly moved from the floor to stand before me.

Was it a lie? No. It had never been lie with Tate, with my feelings for him. I may have lied about who I was, but my heart told only the truth. Tate owned me, and my heart was breaking knowing I have to let him go.

"No, Tate. We aren't a lie," I whispered, staring into his eyes.

"Then why are we standing here like this? You lied about who you were, Low. I feel like I don't even know you," he muttered, pushing a stray strand of hair behind my ear.

My body quickly covered in goosebumps from his touch, my body recognizing him, only him. Ten minutes ago I could have walked out of that door and not looked back, knowing what I was doing may have broken my heart, but in turn saved the man who held it within his hands.

"You do know me, Tate, you have known me right from the beginning. You're the only person who really knows me."

His hands cupped my face as he leaned in close, so close that his breath caressed my lips.

"No. No, I don't. Ace… Jace, whatever his name is, knows you like no one else. How can I compete with that?" he whispered before ever so slowly grazing his lips across mine.

I whimpered from the sudden heat that ignited my bones, grabbing onto his shirt, trying to stay up right. Heat. It was everywhere. My lips, my skin, my bones… my heart.

"Jace isn't even in the running. It's only you, it's only ever been you," I whispered breathlessly.

He was so close, so close I was sure he could hear my heart pounding against the cage of my chest. My hands flexed around the cotton of his shirt, as if holding on for dear life, not wanting to let him go.

"Then why does it feel like you're about to walk out that door with him?" he whispered before placing a feather light kiss to the crook of my neck. "And never come back."

Everything tingled from the smallest of touch as pain sliced through my chest. He knew, we all knew. I was going to walk out of that door and run again, but it was the best thing for everyone. If my father was to catch up with us, there would be blood, and it could well be Tate's. I wasn't willing to risk him being hurt.

"I have to go, Tate. I love you. I always will, but it's because I love you that I have to leave you. You can't come with me, baby, I can't let you do that. I'm so sorry."

A sob broke free from my lips as the realization of what was about to happen took hold: I was about to leave the man I loved because of the man I despised. My father was notorious for being a ruthless man. If you didn't do as he ordered, you were punished, and the punishment would be painful. Now my father was just the tip of the iceberg. My brother had me up against a very heavy, very solid brick wall and I couldn't see anyway out from my vulnerable position.

Tate sighed in defeat against my neck, his breath like a soft caress against the sensitive flesh. I couldn't help but cling to him, holding on for as long as I could.

"I love you, Low," Tate whispered as he pulled back and looked deep into my eyes, pausing for a moment. "I need to come with you."

"Tate." I sighed. "If you make one move to follow me I will shoot you. Don't think I won't. I love you, but this is for your own safety."

"I-" he started but was quickly cut off by a banging against the door.

"It's time to go, Willow," Ace said as he opened the door slightly.

I nodded hard. My eyes landed on my case propped up against the wall beside the door. It was definitely time. Keeping my gaze on my case, I walked to it and picked it up. I couldn't look at Tate. If I did, I was sure I would crumble and stay. I couldn't stay.

As I sidestepped to the door, my foot hit something on the floor. Looking down I spotted my second Glock. I needed it now more than ever, but if I knew my brother and Spyder well, they would already know about Tate. He was now a part of the mess that had been created over a decade ago. He needed protection.

Picking up the Glock, I handed it over to Tate. His eyes were weary as he took it from my hands, looking down at the gun before looking back up to me. He started to say something before I cut him off, making sure he understood.

"Just in case," I whispered before running for the door, quickly leaving the room.

My heart shattered within the confines of my chest, splintering and breaking into tiny little pieces as Ace followed me down the stairs and out of the building.

"We should go on foot for the first couple of miles," Jace mumbled beside me.

I felt the warmth of a hand against the waistband of my jeans, then the weight of a Glock against my skin. Turning, I watched as Jace discreetly placed my trusty Glock back into my waistband. The weight was heavier. He had loaded it for me.

I gave him a small smile as he took the case from my hands. We walked from the campus in silence, not once looking back at the place we called home for so long.

"My heart hurts," I admitted out loud as we rounded the corner to a residential street.

"Good," Jace said, stopping mid-stride.

Turning, he placed both hands upon my shoulders and stared straight into my eyes.

"That's what separates you from that world. You have compassion, sympathy, and empathy. It is what makes you different from your father, from the mafia world. You were not meant to be a killer, Willow. You're placed here to love, and be loved. But we can't control our past, or the world that we come from. Every girl deserves a love that can make her heart forget that it was ever broken."

His words seared through my chest like a sharp blade, penetrating my skin with so much force it left me breathless. He was right, we can't control our past, but I was determined to control my future.

"Come on, the Escalade is just around the cor-"

"Oh fuck!"

Chapter Nineteen

Tires squealed and brakes screeched all around us. My heart leapt into my throat, restricting my breathing as I took in the scene in front of me. Two blacked out trucks and an unlicensed car stopped haphazardly in the middle of the road: it could only mean one thing.

I had been found.

Instinctively, I reached for my Glock, wrapping my hand around the grip I was ready to take on whoever got out of the vehicles. I suddenly stopped when Jace's voice penetrated my ears, telling me to keep my hands out of my waistband. He was right: if I pulled out a weapon, they would shoot me in the foot. A flesh wound, enough to cause searing pain but not enough to kill me. I dropped my hands to my side as a mob of men jumped out from the confines of the trucks.

"Stay smart," Jace grunted as a thick black sack was placed over his head.

Three men walked Jace towards one of the trucks. He didn't once struggle against the hold of the men. He knew he was collateral damage; he knew that they could kill him without a thought or care. Me? I was the prize, the one that they wanted. Jace was just along for the dangerous ride.

I watched as Jace was bundled into the back of the truck, and tears pricked my eyes at the loud slam of the door shutting. Then my whole world turned to darkness. My wrists were bound behind my back, by the painful bite of a cable tie, the clicking of it moving into place made my body shudder with fear. God only knew what was in store for me.

I didn't struggle. It was pointless. If I struggled it would only give the men more reason to wound me, and I didn't have the energy to deal with the pain I knew they could inflict. It suddenly felt like I was flying into the air, my ass hitting a solid surface only moments later.

"Coof!" I winced.

Pain rocketed through my spine, rattling my neck as I tried to lean against another flat surface. It was no use. I presumed I had been thrown into the middle of the truck, so if I leaned back I would fall onto my back, and then I would be even more vulnerable than I already was.

"Time to get you home to daddy, Little Willow."

Fuck. My father was behind this. Terror filled me. Dominic was expecting me. I was going to be killed.

The husky voice came from my left; he was close to the sack that covered my head. I could feel his fowl breath against the shell of my ear. I held in the retch sitting at the back of my throat. I knew that voice, it had haunted my dreams for years.

"Nice to see my father has demoted you to head bitch." I growled, turning my head to the left ever so slightly, ensuring he knew I was talking to him.

"Fuck," I hissed as a jab rocketed into my side.

The sharp throb burned through my ribcage, the force of the blow taking the air straight out of my lungs. That wasn't smart. I needed to reign in my stupidity and smart mouth, it wouldn't get me anywhere.

"Your cockiness doesn't work with me little Knoxx, cut the shit," he grunted beside me.

I stayed silent. There was no use lowering myself and becoming a human punching bag. The journey was slow and painful. I knew instinctively they were detouring, ensuring no one was on their tail before they got to their destination. I tried to make sense of where we were, counting the corners as we took sharp turns. It was no use. They had taken at least twenty corners, and we had driven at least ten miles between. But I knew the destination; it was an image I would never be able to rid my mind of.

The Manor.

I calculated we had been in the truck for around forty minutes, maybe more, before we finally came to a stop. The sound of the gates screeching against the hinges indicated we were right back at the place I ran from all those years ago. I had no idea how I was going to get out of this. I didn't have enough time to even plan an escape before the truck doors slammed open and I was being hauled out by the scruff of my jacket. The toes of my Chucks scraped against the rough surface of the ground while some douchebag dragged me along.

My ears pricked as I heard the slam of a second truck, the grunting of around six men told me they were hauling Jace along with me. Jace was twice the muscle mass of an average male, obviously making it difficult for him to be dragged along.

My skin noticed the temperature change before I did, the goosebumps that once covered my skin disappearing instantly. We were inside. I felt the different in surfaces as we were dragged through the Manor. Moving from hard ground, which I presumed was the hardwood flooring, to a soft textile beneath the toes of my Chucks, before swiftly changing back to hard.

My heart was still in my throat and my stomach in my ass as we came to a stop. I was pulled upright and I heard the distinct sound of heavy feet leave the room. I was alone. That meant Jace was somewhere else in the Manor, which wasn't good. I didn't try to move, nor did I try to free my hands of the cable tie; as painful as it was, it would be much worse if I did.

"Take off the sack," I heard an unknown voice grunt in front of me.

I had gotten too much into my own head, I hadn't even heard anyone come in the door, never mind approach me. I suddenly had to blink back against the harsh light as the sack was pulled from my head, but the light still penetrated when I closed my eyes.

Shaking my head, I managed to keep my eyes open and squinting against the light, I took in my surroundings. The room looked exactly the same as it had ten years ago. In front of me stood a grand fireplace, antique in style and burning brightly before me. The room was large, a mixture of deep reds coated the walls, while a mixture of dark and light gold accentuated the historical fixtures that ran along the tops of the walls. The same dark oak hardwood floor stared back at me as I looked down, the same flooring I had been accustomed to nearly a decade ago. Moving my gaze, I assessed the furniture. Lining the wall to my left was a large bookcase, housing classic literature of the last century, no doubt all first editions. To my right was a large dining table with twelve chairs: the meeting table. I was in the meeting room.

A cough came from my left and I hardened my gaze. The person on the receiving end of my glare smirked when we locked in an unblinking battle. It was Moz, the man who had spoken to me in the back of the truck. I took in his appearance from the shoulders up. He had gotten more portly, the muscle once carried on this thick shoulders had all but disappeared, turning to fat. His hair had receded so much it looked as if he had shaved right to his scalp. His eyes held mine as I investigated the rest of him; his eyes had become more grey and cloudy, then I noticed the wrinkles. He had aged. A lot. He was no longer someone of importance either; he had been demoted, by the looks of things.

The door clicked open, and Moz was the first to break eye contact. Walking through the door was a group of six men who looked to be hauling Jace into the room, the sack still secured over his head. He was placed beside me, the sack whipped from his head. Flicking my gaze over, I gasped. Jace's face was laced with red blotches, some already starting to turn a deep blue in color. My gaze dropped to his lips, they were covered in blood from a small gash at either side.

Suddenly the door was thrown wide open as more men piled into the room, only stopping to drop off two more limp bodies. Once they were placed beside us, they removed the black sacks from their heads. I gasped. Lying semi-conscious on the floor beside us was my half-brother Dominic, and his vile little minion, Nicolai.

"Did you stay smart?" Jace mumbled, wincing as he turned his head to me.

"Barely," I muttered back, a smirk taking over my lips.

Jace chuckled before quickly wincing; it seemed they had given him a good beating before bringing him into the room.

I could feel eyes on me, making my skin prickle with every passing second. Looking up, I noticed eight men staring right at me, never breaking contact with me. I couldn't help but release a growl at the disgusting men that stood before me.

"She got her mother's good looks," one grumbled to another.

"Yeah, but Mr. Knoxx's temper," another muttered before exiting the room, leaving only Moz and us in a stand off.

I rolled my eyes: I was nothing like my father. And sure enough, as if on cue, the door clicked open and in waked the man whom I called Dad.

I straightened, my younger self stiffening at the sight of him. Obedient as ever.

Jaxson Knoxx took six long strides and stood in front of me, casting a wary eye over my face. I noticed the deep set wrinkles before I noticed anything else; he had also aged, the years unkind to his appearance. It must've been all the whiskey he consumed. His bright blue eyes scrutinized me hard as he walked around me, checking each and every available surface of my skin. I shuddered, his eyes were always my pitfall, the only thing that could make me quiver in fear, but also disgust.

"You're skinnier than I thought you would be," he said in a clear and husky voice.

He finally stopped his investigation of me, making his way to the mantle above the fireplace and pulling out a Cuban. He chuckled as he clipped off one end and pulled the other to his lips. Moz walked over with a lighter and lit the end of his cigar. He couldn't light his own cigar now? I rolled my eyes, but swiftly ended my minor rebellion as my father glared at me.

"You also have a disgusting attitude, it's very unbecoming of you, Little Willow."

My name rolled off his tongue with distaste as he took a long pull on his Cuban. Smug piece of shit. My head quickly whipped to my right when I heard the deep chuckle from Jace. Oh god.

"Something amusing, Mr. Rowe?" my father sneered, taking a step towards him, "You're not in the best position here, young man, so I suggest you keep that foul mouth of yours shut."

Jace's body language didn't once waver as my father leaned in close to his face. My father growled, his lip curling in disgust.

"What the fuck do you want, Knoxx?" I asked, my voice cool and calm, a stark difference to the quivering of my insides.

Deep laughter filled the room at my outburst. My father wiped his eyes as he tried to control the laughter that erupted from his bulging stomach. Soon, Moz was in fits of laughter. It only made my blood boil and my head throb. My father was goading me in a way he knew would get to me.

"What do you think I want, oh stupid daughter of mine?" he said once the laughter had subsided. "I want you, at the head of that table."

He pointed to the meeting table on the other side of the room. It was were the Heads of Department sat and discussed operations, rivalry hits, and anything else that needed to be delegated. I was sole heir to that seat, the one that held the power of this mafia family. He was deluded if he thought for one minute I was going to park my ass in that chair.

"I would rather suck off Moz over there," I said, flicking my head into Moz's direction. He gave me a wicked smirk in return. "I would also rather stick pins in my eyes and have Jace pull my nails out with pliers. So, dear fuckhead father of mine, what you want isn't always what you get."

I heard Jace's quick intake of breath beside me. Yeah, what I just did probably wouldn't go down very well, but I wanted to make myself clear. I wasn't putting a single piece of my body on that seat, no matter what the cost.

Suddenly there was a gun shot. Instinctively, Jace and I ducked, searching for the shooter and offending weapon. The blaring echo of the gunshot quickly brought Dominic and Nicolai out of their forced slumber. I was shocked when I noticed the shot was from my father, even more so when I turned and looked at the wall behind me. Staring at me right in the face was a hole with the bullet still lodged inside it. Fucker nearly shot me!

"Sorry, Father, did I push a button?" I growled as I turned back to face him.

I quickly shut my mouth when he took the last couple of steps towards me, aiming his Glock right between my eyes. Blood drained from every corner of my pale and quivering body. I had gone too far, my brain to mouth filter seemed to have become non-existent. Perfect timing, filter!

The room had become tense and strained as the barrel sat right between my eyes. The shift had been quick, so quick I hadn't noticed Moz pulling out his weapon. My eyes quickly flicked over to where Moz stood on the back wall, taking in what he was carrying. My heart sank. An AK-47. Someone was going to get shot today, and this time I knew it was going to be me.

"On your knees, all of you," my father ground out.

I didn't hesitate. I had said enough. There was nothing else to say that would get me out of this mess. Jace, on the other hand, had other ideas. He wasn't moving.

"Something you wanted to say, boy?" my father pushed.

Jace smirked, shaking his head before dropping down onto his knees. Smart ass. He was trying to take the upper hand on my father; even in an unforgiving situation, Jace always had to have the upper hand.

"Didn't think so. Shame Amelia did."

My eyes widened in utter shock. What did he just say? My father removed the barrel from my head, another one of his minions taking over. He didn't like to do the dirty work. Turning to Jace, I watched as his chest heaved in what seemed like both pain and absolute fury. My father had just made his first mistake.

Amelia was Jace's first love: his only love. She was part of his mafia family, taken under the wing of his father when her parents disowned her for having violent streaks as a teenager, kicking her out onto the streets. One night she stumbled upon the Rowe mansion, discreetly jumping over the heavily guarded gates and took shelter under one of the large trees at the back of the building. As the story goes, she was caught, but she put up a good fight and somehow managed to pull a gun from one of the guard's holsters. She was the first one to pull a smile from Julius Rowe in five years. She wasn't given a free pass into the mafia, if that is what you're thinking; she was pushed to her limits, her loyalty tested, and her violence tamed. She proved herself at every turn, keeping everyone on their toes. Including Jace.

Fraternizing between mafia members within another family was a no go, but fraternizing between in-house non-blood mafia members would lead to exile. Jace made the mistake of not only fraternizing with Amelia, but he made the most vulnerable one too: he fell in love. Now, almost six years on, and Amelia hadn't been seen since the night I had been listening in on them torturing her when she pushed the knife in deeper.

"You have my attention, Knoxx, now what the fuck do you want?" Jace growled beside me, impatience pouring from him.

"I want my daughter at the top of that table, and I will stop at nothing to get her up there," my father grunted, clearly pissed at Jace's attitude towards him.

Jace chuckled, the rough texture of his laugh shocking me.

"You think putting her or me at gunpoint will put her on that seat? You're becoming delusional in your old age, Knoxx. She won't flinch if you pull a gun on her again. You taught her that, remember?" Jace laughed sarcastically.

Shit.

"You little f-"

My father was swiftly cut off as we heard raised voices and what sounded like a struggle on the other side of the door; something was happening and it didn't sound good. Suddenly, the room spun beyond all proportions and my heart hammered, hard. Being dragged into the room with his hands tied behind his back was Tate. He was slumped with his head down and his shoulders drawn in. He was unconscious.

"No," I whispered.

My father seemed to have caught the alarm in my voice as a venomous smile crept across his face. He knew, but I had just verbally confirmed it.

"So, this is what was keeping you in one spot for so long." My father chuckled as his gaze swept over an unconscious Tate.

"You're sick, Knoxx!" Jace growled.

"Sick? No. Mafia boss? Yes. Huge difference, son. You should know that by now," my father said seriously. "You know what I can do, what my family can do. Yet you still think it's acceptable to talk to me like the scummy piece of shit family you come from."

Jace suddenly grunted out in pain as a butt of a gun struck him across his cheekbone. It was so unexpected that, for a minute, I had no idea what was going on. Bile quickly threatened to break the confines of my stomach as the room spun once more. Fuck. Breathing in through my nose, I slowly started to feel semi-normal. That was until Tate groaned, making my heart race and my skin prickle.

I still had no idea who had hit Jace in the face with the gun, and I still had a barrel pointed at my head. A hand clasped around my arm and I was quickly being pulled to my feet. Tate and Jace were both pulled to their feet as Moz moved from his position on the back wall. I gulped hard as I noticed him rolling up their sleeves of his shirt as he stepped forward.

"I don't believe I have made myself clear," my father started, inhaling hard on his Cuban before releasing a large cloud of smoke. "You WILL sit at that table, Little Willow. You will fill your obligations as part of this family."

Was he for real? Hell no!

There was a reason why I ran, a reason why I didn't want to have any part with this family. It was because of the mafia my sister was killed, why I was still a god damn target, why Jace still protected me to this day.

My father wanted me at that table with him as a second. He was getting old and the family knew it was only a matter of time before he would need to be voted out. If he was voted out, he was at risk of being gunned down. I was his safety net, keeping his position at the table and getting rid of the target and his back and my own.

The mafia wasn't always based on drugs or human trafficking. The business that my family dealt in was firearms. The same for Jace's family. Two mafia families in the same state dealing in firearms… not a good mix. It all started with a cocky Irishman named Mickey Donahue. To most his name wouldn't mean shit, but in mob circles it meant money: lots of money. Donahue was the Irish mob leader. His reputation would make even the fearless of mob bosses quake within his presence.

Ten years ago, Mickey Donahue held a meeting with Julius Rowe, Jace's father. They discussed a business opportunity in which the Rowe family would supply unmarked firearms to the Irish mob, anything from Uzis, AK-47s, to standard Glock 19. They weren't fussy: all they required was a safe, secure shipment once a month at the drop-off point. It went on for two years, business was good, and both mafia families were content with their business deal. Until my father intervened.

My father swooped in and stole the business away from the Rowe family, offering the Irish a deal they couldn't pass up. Julius Rowe was furious, raging for days until he finally decided to place a hit on a member of my father's family. That family member was me, heir to the 'throne.'

The hit went wrong, dramatically. They shot an innocent girl they had mistaken for me. We were the same in every single way, from our blonde hair to our blue eyes, even our height and weight. The hit was ordered and later that night a doctor pronounced the girl dead. The mafia was poison, my family was poison, I was poison. So, I did the only thing that would protect everyone else while at the same time protecting the invisible target drawn on my own back.

The target was still there. I was still wanted dead by the Rowe family, by Jace's family, to get back at my father for fucking up a steady stream of income. But I would never go back to the life I once knew: the life where blood was spilled, hits were ordered, and people vanished.

"No," I said in the most defiant voice I could muster. "I am not filling any obligation you seem to think I have."

"No?" he said, raising his brow. "I'm sorry, I forgot to tell you what would happen if you don't."

I trembled from the sudden change in my father's voice; it had dropped several octaves and was beyond terrifying.

Suddenly, Dominic and Nicolai became aware of their surroundings, grunting as they finally came to. The moment their eyes locked on my father's, two shots rang out. My father shot my half-brother and Nicolai in the head. A small whimper escaped from my lips as blood poured from the gaping wounds in their heads, their bodies instantly becoming limp.

"Stupid fuckers didn't know I knew their plan. Spyder is a very fucking good employee." He grunted. The realization hit me: Spyder was playing off me and Dominic for my father. I had no doubt he was paid well for his deception.

My father dropped the gun to his side before turning back to me.

"This is what is going to happen. You're going to sit at the head of the table and become my second in command, until the time I feel you're ready to take on the whole of the business. You're going to do as you're told. Otherwise I will make sure the Rowe family knows of your little vacation home. If that doesn't please them enough, I will inform them that their rogue son is with you. I'm sure they would love to know he has been with you all this time."

My gut felt as though it was about to fall out of my ass. If my father informed the Rowe family of any of that information, I would become a walking target and Jace… would disappear. Just like Amelia. Just like Dominic and Nicolai would.

Chapter Twenty

"Don't do it, Willow," Jace whispered beside me.

My gaze drifted over to Tate, who was still semi-conscious on the floor beside Jace. I was torn: what the hell did I do? For a fleeting moment I wondered if all of it was worth it, whether my love for Tate was worth fighting for. Then I glanced at him.

I was ready for war.

"You'll have to kill me first."

The words I had been longing to say to the vile man standing before me lingered on the very edge of my tongue: why? Why now, why me? I slapped them back down, they would only be seen as a weakness to the hard exterior he had built around me all those years ago.

My father's gaze quickly locked with mine, a wide smile taking over his face before he broke out into another fit of laughter.

"Just like your mother, stubborn and dramatic." He chuckled. "You think I wouldn't kill my own blood? I wouldn't even hesitate, Little Willow."

I flinched. I closed my eyes, and for the first time, I prayed for someone to pull me out of this hell. The absolute disdain in his voice was what gutted me open, his emotions towards his own daughter completely untraceable. Did he always feel this way towards me? For one fleeting second, I cried on the inside for the poor little girl who could never be a daddy's girl.

Sucking back my own little pity party, I smirked, shutting out Low Parker, who begged for a relationship with her father. Instead, I brought out the worst of the worst: I brought out his daughter.

"You don't scare me," I hissed. "In fact, you repulse me. You think you can force my hand with a damn Glock? Come on, Daddy, you need to do better than that."

That earned me another strike from the butt of the Glock I was mocking. Yeah, that one fucking stung.

"Who do you think you are talking to me like you're something? You are nothing, Little Willow. This life is the only one you know. No matter how much you tried running from me, you still look like me, you still act like me, and you can shoot a moving target better than most of the men in this room. Remember who holds the fucking power here, daughter. You may have skills, but I have one thing that you'll never have."

I rolled my eyes. "Please enlighten me."

"Control." He smirked, chuckling as he noticed how my eyes widened slightly. "Ah, you still haven't figured it out yet, have you? You crave control, Little Willow. You've fought for control for six years. Don't think I haven't been watching."

My skin crawled instantly. Knowing he'd been watching me sent a shockwave over my flesh, like tiny bugs crawling across my skin simultaneously. I didn't respond, too shocked to give him an answer, a smart ass comment, or breath. I wasn't breathing.

"I can give you control. You've just got to submit until the control is earned."

He was talking about the table, about putting me at the top of it. He knew I didn't want that disgusting seat, but he also knew I still had a target on my back from his own deception all those years ago. Once my name was tainted, it became forever remembered as the girl who walked away. Taking the seat at the table would remove the target, but it would also spark the Rowe family to place Jace at the top of the table too. Change in one family meant change in all of them.

"I won't submit. I'll never submit, especially to you. I'd rather live without control than park my ass on a seat that disgusts me more than you do."

The room was eerily silent. Moz, who had stepped towards us, faltered, looking at his leader for some sort of direction or command. It was clear he thought I would forgo my new life and jump back into the vile life I had run from.

My head throbbed as my heart all but stopped beating as a groan sounded from beside Jace. No!

"Ah!" My father smiled, moving over to Tate. "Back with the living, are we? Good. We have some news for you."

"What the… where the hell am I? And where is Low?!" Tate grumbled as he slowly came back around.

"You mean my daughter, Willow? Oh, she is just over there," he said, pointing to me. "A gun's pointed at her head. I'm being exceptionally nice and giving her the little push she needs."

"A … what? She's—"

"Yes, smart ass, you've been fucking a mafia boss's daughter. One that is going to sit at *that* table over there," he said, pointing at the seat I feared and despised. "Congratulations. I normally would have blown your dick off for fucking her, but hey, I have plans for you." My father winked.

I couldn't look. I couldn't watch as the latest secret of mine crumbled Tate again. I had made myself vulnerable, giving my father a way to get to me. Tate.

Every action has a consequence.

"What the hell do you plan on doing? You going to shoot your daughter, really?" Tate snapped, the rumble in his voice confident. "I love her. You shoot her and I will torture you within an inch of your life."

Oh dear god. Did he really just say that? Not only had he threatened a freaking mob boss, my father, but he staked his claim on me. He might as well have written his own death warrant.

"Really? Maybe I'll just shoot you first, then her." My father laughed.

I could feel tears building. My relationship with my father had always been non-existent. I had no love for my father, but I couldn't help but feel a sense of pain as the words slipped out of his mouth with ease. Not a single hesitation.

"You'll be arrested and thrown into jail, Knoxx. You know that,"

Jace hissed.

"You think I'll be convicted? Ha! I have most of the judges on the bench in my pocket, I'll never see the inside of a jail." My father smiled.

"The cops are on their way, I called them before your men decided to use my rib cage as a trampoline," Tate said coolly.

He called the cops? Oh shit. It wouldn't do any good, we all knew that—he would be arrested and questioned but released a couple of hours later. Nothing stuck. Nothing ever stuck.

"You did what?!" my father hissed, the fury written all over his face. "Do you want to see the consequences of going up against me, boy?"

Consequences. Consequences. Consequences. I couldn't breathe, my chest tightened with every struggling breath I took. Suddenly, I didn't know if I would breathe again.

BANG.

Flashes of light danced in my eyes, distorting my vision as a heavy weight held me in place. I couldn't get my bearings, making me vulnerable yet again. My ears rang in a strangled whisper of pain, sending another slow throb to my head. Everything happened so fast I didn't know where the hell I was, or how I had gotten there.

I could see visions of red. I had no idea whether my eyes were even open, but either way, red was all I could see. Was the red from the deep rouge coloring the walls of my father's meeting room? Or something else entirely? The weight on top of me grew heavier, pinning me down with so much force I winced in pain.

My legs shook and quaked as I tried to move my hands, but they were pinned underneath the unidentified weight above me. Slowly, the ringing pain in my ears started to fade, and when it did, I decided I wanted my hearing to disappear again.

"Move and I will blow your brains right across this polished fucking floor."

Was that Jace? I couldn't tell. Where the hell is Tate? Oh god.

Finally, I managed to pry my right hand from under the weight but what greeted me when I looked at my fingertips sent unbelievable pain throughout my body. Red. All I could see was red. Was I bleeding? Had I been shot? Pushing hard, I managed to move the weight from me.

My eyes roamed my body, searching for a bullet wound, but all I could see was red. My top was soaked; it clung to my abdomen like a second skin, but I still couldn't find a bullet wound. Where the hell was all the blood coming from?

"Low."

Oh fuck no. I was on quickly on my knees, crawling over to the painful groan that would forever be imprinted in my mind.

There was blood everywhere. Everywhere I turned it was there, mocking me. The puddle grew by the second, wrapping around my jeans like a liquid blanket, scaring the ever loving shit out of me. My head throbbed as I finally registered everything that had happened.

"Noooooooooooo! Tate! Tate, stay with me, baby!" I cried.

I was suddenly frantic. I didn't care what was going on behind me, all I cared about was stopping the flow of blood that poured from Tate. My hands were everywhere, trying to find the source. My hands stopped on his abdomen as they brushed a large hole. No! He had been shot in the stomach: this could kill him.

Gripping his shirt collar, I pulled, hard, ripping the shirt straight down the middle, exposing the nightmare that had become my reality. My thoughts and movements had become robotic. One palm down, the other on top. Tense. Press. Hold. Blood poured between my fingers, covering my skin in its deep red hue.

"Low, I can't breathe."

Blood. It was everywhere: every part of my skin had been saturated in it, his body completely drowned in it. A mixture of fear and fury overcame me. I knew someone was going to die today, but for the life of me I didn't think it would be Tate. There was a good chance he may not survive this, and the pain of that cut so, so deep.

I went into a blind panic. Tears streamed down my face as I tried to stop the never ending flow of blood. I knew that if I didn't stop it he was going to bleed out underneath my fingers. Nothing I was doing was stopping the bleeding. Keeping one hand on the wound, I ripped my top from my body, balling it up and pressing it down hard on the area.

I didn't understand. What the hell had happened? The questions that had been swimming around in my mind fizzled out when I felt a hand on my shoulder.

"Leave me the fuck alone!" I screamed, throwing the person's hand off, a strangled sob breaking through my lips.

"Please, Tate. Please, please stay with me." I cried.

I watched as the color slowly drained from his face, as my body shook with sobs. I sobbed so hard I couldn't see, couldn't hear, couldn't process what was going on all around me. All I could hear was muffled shouting, but all I could concentrate on was Tate: the way his body cooled under my touch, how his eyes had turned from vibrant green to brown to a smoky grey, how lifeless he had become underneath me.

"I love you," he whispered.

"I love you too. God, I love you, baby. Please don't leave me, please."

I begged. I begged for someone to help me, for someone to save him. But the words never came; they stuck in my throat alongside my heart, which shattered into so many pieces.

"Look after her," Tate said breathlessly.

His hand, so weak and shaking from the pain he was clearly facing, slowly pressed against the flesh of my cheek.

"Look after her," he repeated, his voice just a gentle caress against my aching soul.

"Always," Jace whispered. "Always."

"Please!" I cried, desperately trying to keep him talking, to keep him with me for as long as possible.

"Strong." He coughed, blood splattering from his lips. "Strong. Stubborn."

A gut-wrenching sob broke the confines of my lips, echoing in the room around us. It was just us: Tate and me. I wondered, I wondered for a fleeting second, what our future would look like, would we get married? Would we have children? If our little miniatures would look like him; would our children be as fierce in protecting? Would they have the smile could build you up as quickly as you fell down? Would they have his eyes, ones that could tell a thousand secrets but hold a hundred fears? Would they be so much like him I couldn't take my eyes from them?

Suddenly, I was being ripped away, physically and emotionally. I was dying inside as the love of my life was dying in front of my eyes. Hands clutched around my waist and pulled me from the ground, taking me away from the heartbreaking scene that laid in a pool of blood on the floor.

"No. Please. I need to be with him! Let me go!" I screamed, punching and kicking as I tried to scramble back to Tate. It was no use. I wasn't strong enough.

I was cold, so cold that I flinched when I finally registered the warm hands that surrounded my abdomen. I didn't want those hands on me. I wanted his, I wanted him to hold me and never let go. I tried to scramble away once more, trying to get back to the man who had irreversibly changed my life with just a kiss.

"Low, calm down. Let them do their job."

The whisper was so low that it caught me off guard. It was Jace. What did he mean, let them do their job? Let who do their job? I didn't understand, nothing made sense.

"Look," Jace whispered in my ear as he held me tight against his chest.

For the first time since I can remember getting to the Manor, I truly opened my eyes. The scene around us had completely changed from being hell in a room to a nightmare come true. On the floor was Tate, lying in a pool of blood, surrounded by paramedics trying to save him. The room was quiet, the only sounds audible were the paramedics' hushed voices. My father was nowhere to be seen, nor were his disgusting minions. It was as if they hadn't been here in the first place.

"I don't understand," I whispered. "How did this happen?"

"He was going to shoot you, Low. But, before anyone could even blink, Tate jumped in front of you and took the bullet. Low, we are trained killers, masterminds of the criminal world. But Tate? Tate saw it coming before any of us did, and didn't once hesitate. His love for you took over, and his primal instincts told him what to do. He took the bullet that was meant for you."

Oh my god.

"Jace, he's dying," I whispered, the truth of my words sending pain straight through my chest.

I watched as pain morphed across Jace's usually hard face; it was there, for the smallest of seconds, it was there.

"He's stronger than you give him credit for, babe."

Suddenly, the silence of the room disappeared, in it's place were loud voices barking orders, machines beeping wildly, and the jolt of another machine.

"We need to move, now!"

My head spun, my heart broke, and my soul was destroyed as I watched Tate flatline on the floor.

Chapter Twenty-One

White walls. Grey floor. Green seats. That was what I had been staring at for the past hour, the hour of absolute hell. I paced the floor. Sitting down made me want to vomit from my overactive nerves. My stomach flipped and rolled with every tick of the clock that seemed to be overly loud, while my hands shook so hard I thought they would never settle again.

It was just me in a lonely corridor, waiting, wondering what the hell was happening. The love of my life was hanging on by a thread while I was crumbling into tiny little pieces, hoping within this dark hell there was a tiny glimmer of light, a glimmer of hope. For the first time, I hoped, and for the first time in a long time, I was being naïve.

I had been handed doctor's scrubs when I had arrived at the hospital, my clothes drenched in blood from the disaster at the Manor. I couldn't help but look down at my hands, hands that had already been soaked in blood, spilled many years ago. Now they were soaked in blood for another reason. The deep crimson had dried and cracked against the creases of my skin, the blood staining my fingernails. No matter how hard I scrubbed, the blood was there; it was always there reminding me just how fragile life can be, how vulnerable we truly are.

I bit down on my bottom lip, trying to stop the sob threatening to escape from the vision before me. I needed to get his blood off. I couldn't have any more blood on my hands, physically or emotionally. Before I could make a break for the bathroom, a large noise jolted me back a couple of steps. Running down the corridor was Logan, and before I could try and say a single word, I was pulled into a tight embrace.

I couldn't breathe, but I welcomed the winded feeling that overtook my chest. I held on with white knuckles to Logan's shirt. The man I once didn't trust was the man who would hold me up while I crumbled. The tears came thick and fast, sobs choking me without forgiveness. The walls I had built to protect me, to protect the people I loved, had come crashing down, smashing into ash and dust, leaving me exposed.

"Shhh. It's okay, he will be okay," Logan whispered gently, but I could hear the uneasiness in his voice.

He pulled my hands from his shirt and held them between our bodies, staring me straight in my tear-filled eyes.

"He will get through this, we will get through this." He sighed, pulling me back into the warm cove of his chest. "Jesus, Low, what happened?"

I cried. I cried harder than I ever thought possible. My pain and fear melded with the tears staining my face, drying against my skin and leaving a permanent reminder of what had happened. The saying "you don't know what you have until it's gone" rang through my head. I had lost the man who came into my life like a bulldozer, smashing his way through my walls, pulling away my mask and seeing me with fresh, nonjudgmental eyes. He truly saw me: the girl frightened for her life, unable to take the risk of getting to close, unable to settle for too long. He saw me. He loved me. He understood me.

"My god, Low!" Neva cried, taking me from Logan and holding me tight in her arms.

My god. What this could do to her… this could push back the progress she had made. What have I done? I looked into the eyes of the girl who had so many demons in her past, but so much fight in her eyes, eyes that were full of unshed tears, waiting to burst.

"I'm so sorry," I whispered. I cringed. Those three little words were useless to convey what I felt.

"It's not your fault, Low. None of this is your fault. My god, Low, I can't lose him," she pleaded, her arms becoming tighter with every word she spoke.

The minutes ticked by as Neva kept hold of me in a tight embrace, it was like a painful slow torture. Everyone had arrived—Neva, Logan, Zane, Colt, and Lorena—all holding pain-struck expressions on their faces. But there was one person missing, one person who had been right there when this mess had started. Jace. I had no idea where he'd gone. Everything that happened between the paramedics arriving and Tate being transferred to the trauma unit was a blur. But, right there, we were waiting. Wondering. Hoping. Until finally, hope walked right through the double doors.

"Mrs. James?" the doctor asked gently.

Lorena stood on shaky legs from the chair, gulping back the tears that threatened to come.

"Y… Yes," she stuttered.

"Your son lost a lot of blood. He went into shock upon the paramedic's arrival, going into cardiac arrest," he said softly.

I waited, waited for the blow I knew would come, waiting for him to say the words that would irreversibly change my life and all the people in it.

"We managed to stabilize him, but the bullet was lodged in his large intestine, so we had to perform emergency surgery to remove it. He is stable, but critical. We should know more in a few days' time when we can wake him from sedation."

My knees gave out, buckling under the weight that turned to lead within the minutes the doctor had been talking. I dropped, the solid ground slamming painfully against my knees. My hands shot out, my palms slapping against the grey floor with an angry thwack. Neva didn't have a chance to even break my fall; she was as stunned as everyone else. As my breathing became erratic, the sobs hit me full force.

He was alive.

"Shit," I breathed, panting as pain suddenly sliced right through me.

"Low?" Neva whispered, placing her hand tentatively on my shoulder.

I couldn't answer. The pain pulsing through my veins rendered me completely speechless.

"Low. Jesus, sweetie, look at me," Neva begged, cupping my cheeks with her warm hands. "He's okay, he got through it."

She didn't understand. No one else understood. The pain I had endured as I watched Tate flatline was fierce, but the pain that was running through my body right now was completely consuming. Something was wrong.

"Holy fuck!" I cried as another wave hit me again.

"Out of the way!"

From my position on the floor, I slowly looked up. Tears streamed down my face as I watched Jace glide down the corridor towards me. I was quickly in his arms as he carried me towards the doctor who, only moments before, gave us the news of Tate's condition.

"She needs a doctor," he grunted.

"What's going on?" Zane asked behind us.

"Bring her into the side room, I'll have a colleague lock at her," the doctor instructed Jace.

I nodded slowly, trying to hide behind Jace's enormous chest. Another wave of pain sliced through my chest once more.

"She's in shock," Colt whispered from somewhere in the room.

I felt Jace tense against my body, his arms tightening around me.

"You," he said, turning to Colt, "shut the fuck up and grab that fucking door. If I hear any more stupid shit come out of that mouth of yours today, I will not only kick the living shit out of you, I will also shoot you in the god damn ass. Yes, she's in shock. Now get the fuck over it so we can make sure she's okay rather than pointing out the damn obvious."

If I wasn't in so much pain I would have laughed at the large gulp Colt swallowed, but I was in pain. Heartbreaking pain that burned with every wave.

"Down the corridor, first door on the left. Tell them Dr. Carter sent you from ICU!" the doctor shouted down the corridor as Jace carried me through the double doors.

"You'll be okay, babe," he whispered.

Would I? My father had been arrested for shooting Tate, almost killing him. I was in shock, my half-brother had been shot dead along with his sidekick and I still hadn't gotten in touch with my mother, whom I shipped off to Vegas. Would everything really be fucking okay?

"I need to see him," I mumbled leaning my cheek against Jace's hard chest.

"He's still in recovery. Let's get you seen to first, then you can be with him. Okay?"

"Okay." I paused, I was too weak to argue with him. "Where were you?"

"I . . . I." He stopped, staring down at me. "It's best I don't tell you. You have enough to deal with."

"Oh, Jace, what have you done?" I whispered.

"Nothing that wasn't deserved."

Jace carried me the whole way to the small side room at the end of the corridor, pausing every time another wave of pain sliced through me. He stroked my hair, held me close, and whispered how everything would be okay. He was doing what Tate would do. He was protecting me, knowing that's all Tate would want. Me, protected.

I climbed into the unflattering gown once Jace carried me into the small room. He insisted on sitting outside, informing me he'd wait for me, cringing as he took in everything around us. He hated hospitals and the look of utter distaste on his face made me smile when all I really wanted to do was cry.

I tied the gown at the back, even though I knew my ass was completely on show for all to see. Sitting down on the large hospital bed, I pulled my knees to my chest as if trying to regain some sort of control, control that was ripped from me so long ago.

"Low Parker?" a cheery voice rang out as a petite young woman pulled back the curtain.

Jace had told me to use my running name, just in case anything were to happen, there would be no evidence of a Willow Knoxx attending that hospital.

"Yes." I nodded.

The nurse smiled before motioning for me to lie down as she pulled out her stethoscope.

"Dr. Carter has filled me in on today's events," she said, pressing the cold metal against my chest. "You've been through a lot today, your body is just trying to process it all."

I nodded gently as she listened into my chest.

"Do you still have chest pains?" she asked, her eyes locking with mine before moving the stethoscope to the valley between my breasts.

I nodded again, the silence seeming to soothe my racing thoughts and my shaking limbs.

"Okay," she said, stepping back from me and placing the stethoscope around her neck. "You're in shock, my love. There isn't much we can do to fix the pain in your chest since there isn't anything physically wrong. There's no medication to fix a hurting heart."

"Thank you," I whispered, moving into a sitting position on the bed.

"You can stay in here as long as you need to. If you start feeling faint, let me know so we can reassess you. Okay?" She smiled.

I gave her a small smile and nodded my head tightly. I just wanted to get to Tate. I needed to get to Tate. The nurse left the room, leaving the door open behind her. Moments later Jace walked through the door, the door frame tiny in comparison to his large build.

"How are you feeling, babe?" he asked, moving into the room and taking a seat on the edge of the bed.

"I… I," I stuttered. I grumbled before spitting out what I was trying to say. "I'm fine. I need to get to Tate."

"They're still setting him up in ICU. Do you want to get some coffee while we wait?" he asked tentatively.

My stomach rolled at the thought.

"I don't think I could stomach it."

"You're going to have to try and eat something, even if it's a small piece of the double chocolate cupcake I've been drooling over in the canteen." He smiled, clearly trying to lift my mood. But there was no amount of chocolate or coffee in the world that would settle my racing thoughts and churning stomach.

"I might vomit if I put any of those near my lips." I sighed, pausing for a moment before asking the question I couldn't get out of my mind. "What happened to my father?"

His gaze drifted to the open door, staring out into the corridor before finally answering my question.

"Tate called the cops. Your dad fired, Tate jumped and took the bullet. The cops came running in the minute the shot rang out. They witnessed your father shooting Tate, the Glock was still smoking when they arrested him," he said, never once taking his eyes off the corridor.

"You and I both know he'll get off," I whispered, the words weighing heavy on my chest. "He always does."

"Something tells me he isn't going to get off lightly this time, babe." His eyes shifted over to mine, glossy and glazed over. I couldn't read Jace. I never could and right then, I had no idea what the whole glossy eyes meant. Something told me I didn't want to.

For the first time since we had met all those years ago, there was an awkward silence, as if he wasn't telling me everything. I, not knowingly, yearned to know. Secrets are a two way street: you speak one aloud while simultaneously hiding one within your own mind. We all have secrets, every last one of us. Secrets are sugarcoated lies, hidden within our own mind. Just because you don't speak it doesn't mean you don't feel it.

The truth doesn't cost anything, but a lie could cost you everything.

I've lied, cheated, manipulated and deceived: holding back secrets, producing half-truths to try and rid the guilt about what the whole truth meant.

I am Willow Knoxx, master of deception, secrets and lies. I am Low Parker, the girl just wanting to break free of her past. A nameless face with multiple personalities. One's a liar, a cheat, a fraud. The other? A fraud, but one who wanted to be caught.

I had no doubt a therapist would have a field day with me.

"Come on, I can smell that damn cupcake from here and it's got my name written all over it." Jace smiled, throwing my clothes at me. I dressed quickly before he grabbed me by the wrist and pulled me out of the room and down the corridor with so much speed I couldn't keep up.

"Jesus, Jace. Slow down!" I laughed, quickly regretting it as it slipped from my lips.

Guilt gripped me. How could I laugh when the man I loved was lying in a bed? The man who was shot because of me, because of my lies? I stopped in my tracks, pulling against Jace's grip.

His eyes found mine, silently questioning me. "I feel so guilty."

Tears formed and built as I stood in the middle of the corridor, hugging myself as I felt the guilt wash over me.

"You tried to protect him, Willow. We tried to protect everyone, but guess what? You can't protect the heart: it wants what it wants." He shrugged, placing his hand in mine. "Come on, babe. I need to feed you."

Nodding slightly, I closed my hand around his and let him all but drag me to the canteen where he sat with the biggest smile on his face as he devoured the cupcake.

"Do you need a bib? A napkin… something?" I smirked, swallowing down a laugh as I noticed chocolate frosting on his top lip.

"Fon't fate, Fillow."

"Sorry, what? I can't understand a word you're saying with all…" I waved my hand in front of his mouth. "… that going on. Seriously! Bite. Chew. Swallow. Is it so hard to eat like a normal person?"

He swallowed, smirking as he wiped his hands. "Don't hate. Chocolate is a man's best friend too, you know."

"Or his worst enemy, in your case. What happened to getting ready for your next fight?"

He eyes drifted to the crumbs on the table. "You know we can't go back to that."

Huh?

"What do you mean?"

"I mean things are going to start changing."

"Stop talking cryptic and tell me what you're talking about," I said, irritated with the run around he was giving me.

"I received a call an hour ago," he said, bringing his eyes back to mine. "I can't go back, Willow."

I blinked, trying to wrap my head around what he was telling me. He slid his coffee towards me, an action I was so used to doing with him over the last couple of weeks. It felt like a peace offering. I didn't like it.

"I've been summoned. I can't ignore it now," he whispered.

He had been summoned by his family, his own mafia family. Holy shit.

"Do they know? I mean, do they know where you've been all this time?" I gulped, hoping that what we'd done had been kept hidden from the Rowe family.

"Yes. Yes, they know." He sighed. "Listen, I'm going to do everything I can to keep you from that table, Willow. You know as well as I do, even if your father is prosecuted and does time for what he did, he'll still get out eventually. He has connections, ones that could completely tear apart everything we have tried to build."

My world crumbled for the second time that day. I couldn't do it. I wouldn't do it.

"Jace, there is no way in hell. I'm not stepping foot anywhere near that manor."

"I know you don't want to, but if your father is inside, you'll have to take the chair," he mumbled. "Look, you could always take the chair and vote someone in as lead. You don't have to be the head of the family, Willow. You have a choice."

"Kill or be killed."

Story of my life.

"I'll kill whoever stands in your way, Willow. Never forget that."

That's what I was afraid of.

Chapter Twenty-Two

Tears spilled from my eyes as I stared at the man who had completely stolen my heart, the man who looked nothing like the one I had fallen for. Machines surrounded him, beeping intermittently, reading his vitals. The doctor said he was stable. Stable? This is what they called stable?

He looked as though he was sleeping, but the color from his beautiful olive face had completely disappeared. I watched, watched in absolute agony as a nurse checked his vitals, moving around the room without a care in the world.

"It's okay, sweetie. Come and take a seat," the nurse cooed at me.

My eyes were trained on Tate, so unmoving, so still. I hadn't noticed Jace's hands on my shoulders until I felt my knees giving out from beneath me as he walked us towards Tate's bedside.

"It's okay, babe. I've got you," Jace whispered into my ear, the sound registering but no longer filling me with the hope it used to.

Maybe hoping was just naïve.

I could feel my body shaking as Jace all but put me into the chair, my hands fisting within my lap.

"He's fully sedated, but he can hear you," the nurse said as she handed me a small cup of water. "I'm Julianne. I will be part of the six nurse team that's looking after your young man."

My eyes widened as I finally registered her voice. It wasn't a voice I recognized but it was helping me feel calm amongst the chaos, like a soothing song in a world of white noise.

"Dr. Carter is one of two doctors who will be taking care of Tate. We're just about to do a shift change, but someone will come and check in with you soon." She smiled softly, placing a reassuring hand on my shoulder before nodding towards Jace and leaving the room.

"He looks so… lifeless," I whispered after a beat. I didn't know if it was aimed at Jace, Tate or myself. It was intended as a statement, but sounded like a question.

"He's strong, babe. He's already proved that, but his body needs rest. We can all fight the bullet if needed, but the body can't fight against exhaustion. He'll be okay." He paused, his gaze landing on Tate's pale skin on his face. "I'll get you some coffee."

I hadn't even noticed Jace leaving the room. The room was silent except for the sounds of the machines beeping and Tate's ventilator breathing for him. A wave of emotions suddenly hit me like a sledgehammer. Pain, grief, guilt. So much guilt. This was all my fault, I had gotten too close, too tangledin Tate, that I ultimately put him at risk, no matter how much I tried to stop it.

Tears rolled painfully down my face as I reached out for his right hand. It was warm, so warm. Taking his hand in both of mine, I leaned forward, pressing my soaking cheek against his warm flesh and closing my eyes.

"You need to wake up soon, baby. I know you're tired but I need you to get better and wake up."

Turning my cheek, I ran my nose up and down the skin on the back of his hand, inhaling as he would do to my skin. He smelt like summer: warm days and sunshine. My heart fluttered from his scent. Even in the state he was in, he could still make me feel.

"I'm so sorry I lied." I sniffed, feeling the hot, wet tears mar his beautifully warm skin. "I lied so much to try and protect you, and you were still hurt. I'm so sorry."

"None of this is your fault, Low."

Logan's voice cut deep within my gut, the whisper of my alias stinging like a knife running through my throat.

"Logan," I ground out. I was angry: angry with myself, angry with others for not stopping me from lying. I was being irrational. How were they to know about my lies, my past, the deceit? "Do you know who I am?"

I felt his footsteps before I could hear them against the floor. He took a seat in the only other chair in the room, the one opposite mine.

"You're Low Parker, my best friend's girl, and this..." he said, pointing at an immobile Tate, "isn't your fault."

I closed my eyes tight as I moved my face away from Tate's warmth, turning my head towards Logan.

"No, Logan. I'm Willow Knoxx. My father is Jaxson Knoxx, the son of a bitch who shot your best friend. He shot your best friend because his daughter wouldn't sit at the top of the family table."

I stood, my hand leaving Tate's, my body instantly missing the contact. My gaze was hard as I watched the shock hit Logan's face. It was subtle, but it was there.

"I'm a killer and a liar, and a damn good one at that. Don't sugarcoat this shit, Logan. You're not Willy fucking Wonka. This can't be fixed like Neva, you can't nurture this shit. I was born into a mafia family. My father is one of the biggest mob bosses within the US. I've been lying. The man you know as Ace? That's an alias. His name is Jace Rowe, son to Julias Rowe, the mob boss. Lies, Logan. All fucking lies."

"Are you done with your self-pity, *Low?*" he asked, raising his brow as he stood in front of me. He was at least a foot taller than me, but it wasn't intimidating. "Because to be honest, I don't think anyone gives a shit about who you were. You're not the same person anymore, Low. You refused to be that person. Jace already filled us in on what happened with your father. He also told us exactly who you are and who he is. Your past doesn't define you. I will tell you, and I'll tell Neva until the moon shines out of my god damn ass. Never let your past define who you are. The past has gone, the future's a mystery, but the present is a gift. So open your fucking gift, maybe you'll find peace in the present inside it."

Suddenly I was gripped into a tight hold, Logan's arms wrapped around my small frame like a blanket. His warmth catapulted into my cold bones, helping warm the shell I had been hiding in for years. The mask, the façade, the hidden girl that was screaming to be released broke the barrier. The fractures had completely burst open, spilling its contents for all to see. I was no longer in hiding, no longer holding back secrets. I no longer had reasons to lie.

Tears formed again, building in intensity as Logan held me tighter. All of a sudden, I was crying. Hard, ugly tears escaped me as I held on for a dear life. Every single tear represented all the lies, deceit, and hurt I had caused, and what I had been through to protect someone who had ultimately seen through the lies from the very beginning and fell in love with the girl who had been in hiding for so long.

"This isn't your fault, Low," he whispered over and over as he rocked me gently, soothing the painful ache in my chest.

"He could die, Logan." I sniffed, the tears still coming hard.

"I know, darlin'," he whispered on a shaky breath. "But his love for you will help him fight. I promise."

Logan held me until the tears stopped flowing and only the ragged sound of my hiccups echoed around the room. My body was drained. Only Logan holding me upright. I was quickly bundled into the cove of Logan's chest as he sat down with me on his lap, and like a small child I closed my eyes, and prayed silently.

Please let him live.

As Logan lulled me into exhausted sleep, the room filled with friends and family. The painful ache in my chest making it harder to breathe with every person who entered, the guilt eating at my heart. Everyone was in the room within minutes: Neva, Jace, Colt, Zane and Lorena. All of them congregating around myself and Tate's bed.

My eyes fluttered open for long enough to catch Lorena's hand on my hair, stroking it as if soothing me while Neva held onto Logan's free hand. It was then I realized I wasn't blamed for what happened to Tate; instead, they were helping me through the pain of what happened. Fresh tears appeared from their kindness, kindness I didn't deserve.

Darkness surrounded me as I fell into a disturbed sleep in the warm alcove of Logan's chest, holding onto hope that Tate was strong enough to pull through all of this.

Chapter Twenty-Three

Three days.

Three long and painful days since Tate was taken off his sedation and his ventilator was removed, and he still hadn't woken up. The doctors were reassuring us that his body just needed time to rest. Every minute that ticked by felt like a god damn eternity. I missed the sound of his voice, the way he would yawn with a husky whisper in the morning, the way his gravelly laugh would fill my stomach with butterflies. I missed him. I wanted him back.

The chair at his bedside had become my new home, only getting out of it when my bladder would scream out at me to pee. Friends and family would come in and out, staying an hour here and there, bringing me food and spare clothes. But I didn't care for eating; my stomach was still in knots with every minute that ticked by unchanged. And just getting changed into clean clothes felt too challenging. I only wanted to be by his side, to lead a normal life with the man I loved.

Tate's doctor, Dr. Carter, had dropped by early that morning, checking the wound on Tate's stomach. He said he was healing well and there had been no complications. He was positive Tate would pull through and would be back on his feet in no time. It was just a waiting game – not a game I wanted to play.

I slowly ran my fingers over the soft skin of Tate's palm. I missed his touch. I missed the way he would be so alpha, yet so caring, I missed the way he would hold me, care for me, thrill me. That thought filled me with happiness and so much sorrow as I placed my right hand in Tate's.

"Any change?"

Jace's voice pulled me out of my thoughts. I turned to Jace; my eyes widened as I noticed my suitcase in his right hand, the one I had packed the day my father's men had taken us.

"How did you get that?" I asked, eyeing the case.

"The police released it from evidence this morning. You know they're going to want to talk to you about what happened?" he asked, placing the small case next to my chair beside my feet.

"What's the point? He's going to get off scot free like he always does," I said, tears building in my eyes. "What am I going to do if he comes for me again? It's not just me anymore, Jace. I won't leave him again."

His dark chocolate eyes locked with mine as he walked around Tate's bed and took a seat in a chair. "He isn't going to get out," he stated flatly. "The police placed him on remand until they complete witness testimonies."

"Let me guess, there were no other witnesses besides us?" I asked. I don't know why I asked; I knew there wouldn't be.

"No. But he isn't getting out, babe," he said surely.

How the hell could he be so sure he wouldn't get out? I didn't understand.

"What aren't you telling me, Jace?"

"They found him dead this morning."

A large gasp escaped my lips as Jace's words penetrated my mind, my heart breaking. I didn't understand. I didn't understand why I felt pain ripping through my chest at his words. Why would I feel some sort of remorse for the man who threatened to kill me? Why would I have any form of emotions to the man who shot the love of my life?

I suppose my want for a normal life, a normal family overshadowed the feelings I should have had towards my father. Hatred, pain, disdain – I felt none of those. Instead, I felt the need to try to love the man who ruined my future by fathering me.

"I'm so fucking confused," I whispered. "What happened?"

"I did something I'm not proud of," Jace said, his eyes hollow.

"Oh, Jace. What have you done?"

"I sacrificed one life for another, and that's all I'm going to tell you," he said, standing from the chair and making his way over to me. Standing before me, he placed the softest kiss against my forehead. "I love you, Little Willow. Don't you ever forget that."

Those were his only parting words as he left the room and, unbeknown to me, walked right out of my life.

With a heavy sigh, I slowly opened my suitcase beside my chair, my right hand still holding on tight to Tate's as I did.

Sitting front and center in my case was my jar of hearts, my mason jar of lies. I lifted my hand from Tate's. Picking up the mason jar with both hands, I studied every single lie that sat within the prison of glass.

"So many lies," I whispered.

With shaky hands, I unscrewed the lid. For a moment I thought if I removed the lid, it would somehow release my sins and wipe the slate clean of all my lies. But, in truth, I knew it would never heal the hurt I had caused.

"How's my man doing?"

I startled slightly at the sound of Jenna's voice, Tate's regular nurse who'd taken a shinning to him. The first time we had met her, she told us that Tate was the most handsome patient she was looking after. I think I would've been offended hadn't she been in her late fifties.

"Still the same." I sighed.

"Well, let's see if we can wake sleeping beauty, huh, handsome?"

Placing on her latex gloves, she placed a clenched fist against his chest and rubbed gently before checking his eyes with her pen torch. Sighing, she pulled off her gloves.

"Well, I hope you're full of beans when you wake up, young man. I want to see those beautiful eyes," Jenna said, grabbing Tate's chart.

"Jenna?" I said timidly.

Her gaze locked with mine, a flash of sadness washing over her features. "Yes, love?"

"Um, do you have some paper and a black marker?" I asked.

"I'm sure I can dig one out for you." She smiled before exiting the room.

Ten minutes later, Jenna walked back into the room, bringing a piece of paper and a black marker like I had asked. Placing Tate's chart back on his bed, she smiled warmly before quietly leaving the room again.

With a deep sigh, I started tearing up the paper into small uneven squares. I made sure each individual square wasn't the same. No lie is ever the same. Why kid yourself into thinking they are?

I drew nineteen little lies, all of which representing everything I hated. The lies about my father, the lies about who I was, who Jace was. There were no amount of jars, no amount of tiny black hearts I could draw that would change any of that.

Two hundred and one little lies sat in my jar of hearts.

Two hundred and one reasons to believe that eventually the truth will prevail.

Holding onto my jar in my left hand, I assumed the position I had been in for the past couple of days: my hand in Tate's, holding on as I prayed for him to wake up.

Chapter Twenty-Four

My mind was in a dream, faceless people stood all around me, staring as if they knew all of my secrets. It was terrifying yet liberating all at the same time. The room was blanketed in darkness, only a slither of light penetrated the room, masking the faces of my dream in a deep shadow. As the first man stepped out of the shadows, I broke down in tears.

"Stop your crying." he snapped.

"I can't do this, please don't make me do this," I begged, pleaded.

"You need to learn, Little Willow. It's just the cleaner, no one will miss him," he stated flatly, as if the Glock in my hand and what he was forcing me to do were regular daily occurrences.

"I… I can't," I stuttered.

He stepped behind me, his entire body flush with my back. I cringed. His right arm came over my shoulder, placing his hand over my shaking one. The blindfolded man cried softly on the chair, his hands and feet restrained with ropes as he prayed to be released.

My stomach rolled. I was going to vomit.

"Get yourself together, girl!" he yelled, his grip around my hand tightening painfully. "Place your finger on the trigger."

My body wasn't responding. Before his presence would make me tremble. Now he was physically touching me and all I could do was shrink like a child.

"Do it, or I'll shoot you instead," he growled into my ear.

Slowly, and with hands shaking beyond natural tremors, I placed my finger around the trigger. The cries of the man getting louder as my father moved my body into the position he thought was best to get a clear, clean shot.

Without warning, a shot rang out.

I screamed.

I sobbed.

I broke.

My eyes were closed so tight and I prayed I could turn myself blind from it. I didn't want to open them. I didn't want to see what I had done at the hands of my father. Then his hands moved to my head, forcing me forward, forcing me to see.

"Open your eyes, Little Willow."

Pressure in my right hand caused my body to jump, a pressure I hadn't felt in so long. Slowly my eyes flickered open, as I started to move my aching muscles. Groggy from sleep, I turned to Tate. Color had started to slowly come to his cheeks with a rosy tint, finally coloring the grey we had been seeing since he was shot.

Suddenly, I felt the pressure again that had woken me from my sleep. I gasped as my eyes locked on Tate's hand, entwined with my own. Squeeze. Release. Squeeze. Release.

It couldn't be… could it?

My eyes moved to Tate's eyes, which were still tightly sealed. Closing my eyes, I waited to see if it wasn't just his reflexes. Sure enough, seconds later, it happened again.

Squeeze. Release. Squeeze. Release.

"My god," I whispered in awe, my eyes trained on our entwined hands. "Baby, if you can hear me, please, please squeeze my hand again."

As if on cue, and with a little more pressure, Tate squeezed my hand three times.

Tears built, my heart quickened against my chest, and the flood gates opened. Tears streamed down my face like a never ending waterfall as I watched Tate's hand squeeze mine.

With his hand still in mine, I leaned over and pressed the call button on the wall, hoping Jenna would get here quickly to see exactly what I was seeing.

"Hey, hon. You called?" Jenna's cheery voice quickly wavered the moment her eyes locked onto mine. "Tell me what's going on, sweetie," she said as she made her way to my side.

"Watch," I whispered.

"Tate. Baby, squeeze my hand if you can hear my voice," I said in a collected voice.

Just like that, Tate squeezed my hand with a little more pressure than before. My eyes darted to Jenna as I noticed her wiping away a stray tear from her eye.

"I'll get Dr. Carter," she whispered gently as she scurried out of the room.

The room fell silent as my eyes never left Tate's face, soaking in his features, which had softened this morning. He was looking more normal, more like he really was just sleeping and not healing from a gunshot wound to his torso.

I watched as goosebumps covered the smooth skin of his hand. Instinctively I ran my nose over each and every little goose pimple, inhaling as I went along.

A soft moan escaped Tate's dry lips as I placed a tender kiss against the palm of his hand, the machine that read his heart rate beeping faster. My heart fluttered at his natural reaction, so I did it again. I placed soft and tender kisses over every inch of skin on his palm, basking in the sound of his heart rate raising with every kiss.

"Low." He groaned, his voice gravelly and cracking as he tried to repeat my name.

"I'm here, baby," I whispered, squeezing his hand. I smiled as I felt him squeeze my hand back.

"I believe we had some movement?" Dr. Carter's voice rang out into the room.

Smiling softly, I nodded, never taking my eyes off Tate.

"Let's take a look, shall we?" he said, moving over to Tate's bedside, checking his vitals. "Tate, I'm Dr. Carter, you're in hospital. I'm just going to shine a light into your eyes, okay, buddy?"

A deep and husky groan fell from Tate's lips the minute the light hit his eye, the pressure of his hand becoming stronger as he squeezed.

"Sorry, Tate," Dr. Carter apologized softly. "Everything looks good." He turned to me, continuing. "He could be like this for a few hours, maybe a couple of days. He just needs time to wake from the sedation, I have no doubt he'll drop in and out, so don't worry if he suddenly stops squeezing your hand. He's making good progress."

With a smile and Tate's chart, Jenna and Dr. Carter left the room; in their place was Tate's mom and Neva.

"What's wrong?" Lorena asked, her face filled with panic.

"There's nothing wrong." I smiled. "He's waking up."

"Oh god!" Neva cried, running to my side and pulling me into a hug.

"Here," I said, grasping Neva's hand and placing it within her brothers. "Talk to him, he can hear you. He was squeezing my hand."

"Tate? Tate, it's me, Neva. Can you hear me?" she asked, leaning in close to her brother. "Oh… wow," she whispered after a beat, staring at his hand. "He squeezed my hand, he can hear us!"

My gaze drifted back to Lorena, who stood in utter shock, her body unmoving, I couldn't tell if she was even breathing. The only indication was her bottom lip. It trembled like a child's as she tried to hold in the emotion.

"It's okay," I whispered, standing from the confines of the chair and walking over to Tate's mom. "He's going to be fine."

I tried to sound reassuring, although I wasn't sure I did. I was so wrapped up in Tate, so wrapped up in hiding all of my lies that what Tate's mom was going through didn't even flutter through my mind. My god, this woman had been through it all. From her husband being ripped away from her far too soon to her daughter's PTSD to Neva being taken by the man who had claimed to love her. Not to mention the rocky relationship she shared with her son since any of us could remember. How she wasn't a crumbling mess right now was beyond me. She was tough. Tate was more like his mother than he would care to admit.

She nodded slightly, wiping her face roughly with the back of her hand. "Thank you, Low," she whispered, a small smile gracing her lips towards me and her daughter before she slowly exited the room. She needed time to compose herself, something I completely understood.

The way Lorena had thanked me softly stayed with me well into the evening. Colt, Zane, Logan and Neva stayed in the room with me for a good few hours, all wanting to be there when he finally woke. There were moments when I panicked, thinking something happened when Tate would no longer respond to my voice. Neva quickly reminded me what the doctor had said and I soon felt calmer as the evening rolled on.

"We should throw him a party when he wakes up," Colt piped up after a while.

The room had been silent for around thirty minutes, all of us sitting in a comfortable silence as we just waited.

"He's going to be exhausted for a while, dude. But when he's back on his feet and at home, we could always throw one then," Logan replied, tightening his hold on a soundly sleeping Neva, who'd made herself comfortable on his lap.

"I think he'd like that," I replied, smiling at Colt for making a sensible suggestion for a change.

"Think about all the women he would attract to the party with his battle scar!" Colt added.

I sighed hard. I knew saying the word 'sensible' and 'Colt' in the same sentence wasn't a good idea.

"Is that all you really think about?" Zane fired at his twin, shaking his head.

"Vag? Yeah, pretty much." Colt laughed softly.

"Baby, please stop the pig from talking about vagina. I'm trying to sleep," Neva whispered to Logan.

I chuckled softly at Neva's sleepy comment, but quickly laughed louder as I noticed Colt's eyes gleam.

"Dude, she said vagina. There is a god." Colt winked at me.

I knew what he was doing, he was trying to deviate the subject from Tate, knowing it was a little more than we all could handle right now. We had no idea when he was going to wake up, only he was going to within the next couple of days. Colt's distraction was just what we needed.

"I'm going to grab some coffee," Zane said as he stood from his chair, stretching his arms above his head, releasing a sleepy groan. His shirt rode up a couple of inches, gracing us all with some serious abs.

Well, who knew? "Anyone want any?"

"I need a really greasy burger right about now. I'm so freaking hungry," Colt said, standing and joining his twin.

"I'm going to take Neva home, she's wiped out," Logan said as he stood from his chair, bundling Neva tighter to his chest.

"Do you want me to get you anything, Low?" Zane asked as he pulled me into a tight hug.

I wasn't expecting the personal contact from Zane. To be honest, the twins were never really around much. They were pretty much friends with anyone and everyone, always jumping from group to group. I couldn't blame anyone though. They were funny and didn't really congregate around drama and were pretty much lone rangers.

"Um, no. No, I'm good," I said as Zane squeezed me a little tighter before letting me go. That was… well, that was odd.

With that the room started to empty, the last person leaving was Logan. Neva was completely out of it, softly snoring against Logan's chest as he turned to me.

"Will you call me if there is any change?" he asked quietly, trying not to wake Neva.

"Of course," I replied, giving him a small smile.

"Get some sleep, Low. You look like hell."

Then Logan did something completely unexpected: stepping towards me, he placed a soft kiss against my forehead. I sat down, in total shock, in the chair besides Tate's bed, my hand slipping into his as I drifted off into another bout restless sleep.

Chapter Twenty-Five

I peeled my eyes open for the third time, my eyes stung from the lack of sleep and the shitty overhead lamp. I was restless. I had no idea what had woken me this time, but I knew I wasn't going to fall back to sleep.

Pulling out my phone, I checked the time. 3am. Great. Throwing my phone in my pocket, I stretched my body, my mid-back cracking at the movement. I stood from the really uncomfortable chair and stretched some more. Looking around the room I spotted my glass jar sitting beside my suitcase. Out of habit, I picked it up and took it back to my spot beside Tate.

Holding up my jar of hearts, I let the light from the overhead lamp shine through the glass, producing a rainbow of color inside. Each and every lie stared back at me as I watched the colors illuminating the jar. I sighed deep before placing my right hand in Tate's once again, still studying my jar of hearts.

"Low."

My head whipped around so quick I thought it might roll off my shoulders. I gasped as I watched Tate's eyes flicker open and closed, my name a whisper on his lips.

"I'm here, baby," I whispered, placing a soft kiss on his palm.

"Low." He groaned out, his eyes flickering more. "Don't shoot her."

Warmth filled my body at the mention of my name, but the dread completely over took my body when I realized the truth. He remembers… he remembers. Oh god. What if he remembers absolutely everything? My betrayal, my lies, the deceit. What if he remembers everything and can't forgive me for the things I've done? I'm the reason Tate is lying in a hospital bed with a serious wound in his abdomen. I did this to him and I have no idea if he'll ever forgive me.

"I'm here," I repeated.

The instant my voice left the confines of my lips, Tate's hand squeezed mine harder than he had over the last couple of days. My heart leapt and soared at the newfound strength he found, but, at the same time, filled me with so much fear of what might happen when he eventually came to.

I watched in awe as Tate's eyes no longer fluttered in limbo. No, they were wide open. Glazed over, but fully alert.

"What. Ah." He paused, wincing as he tried to speak. "Water."

The crackly whisper that escaped his lips brought tears to my eyes. Tate was staring straight at the white ceiling above him, seemingly still in his own sedated little world.

"I'll get you some water, baby," I whispered, standing from my chair and moving to the table on the opposite side of his bed.

His eyes never moved from the ceiling above him as I poured out a small glass of water. The only indication he even knew I was in the room was the flexing in his right hand—it was if it was searching for my touch.

Stepping to his bedside, I placed my left hand upon the warm flesh of his cheek as I brought the cup to his lips.

"Slow, small sips, baby," I whispered gently as Tate sipped from the cup.

He closed his eyes as if savoring the flavorless water within his mouth before opening them and staring at the ceiling once more. My heart fractured within the confines of my chest as he just stared, not saying a single word, not even glancing towards me. He wasn't even acknowledging my existence, and I could feel the fear building in my gut.

"I'll get the doctor," I said, slipping out of the room without a backward glance in his direction.

The minute his door clicked closed behind me, I sagged against the hard wood, the tears that had built behind my eyes breaking the barrier. The tears flowed down the flesh of my cheeks, dripping slowly down to the tiled floor I was staring at.

"Low?" Jenna's usually cheery voice was laced with concern as she stepped towards me. Placing her hands on my shoulders, she spoke with a hushed whisper. "What's wrong, sweetie?"

"He's fully awake," I replied, the pain on my face clearly evident as I looked into her grey eyes.

"That's a good thing, sweetie. So why are you crying?" she asked.

I couldn't tell her I was the reason Tate was lying in that bed in the first place.

"I don't know. It's probably the lack of sleep," I said on a fake laugh.

"Oh, sweetie." She sighed, a small smile gracing her lips. "I'll buzz Dr. Carter and let him know he's woken up."

With another beaming smile, walked down the corridor out of sight as she went to buzz the doctor. I had no idea what I would do if I stepped back into Tate's room. Would he tell me to get out? I would. Would he tell me he never wants to speak to me again? Why wouldn't he?

Gulping back the foul taste of fear that had coated my tongue, I turned and opened the door to Tate's room. A small gasp escaped my lips as I watched a single tear fall from his eye as he stared up at the ceiling.

"Baby," I whispered, walking to his bedside. "What's wrong?"

My heart broke as a sob escaped his lips, his eyes still staring at the ceiling. I wanted to scream, I wanted to scream at him to just look at me, see me for what I am: the woman who loves him.

"What happened?" he rasped, his voice gravelly from sleep.

"I..." Shit, what do I tell him? The truth, I'll tell him the truth. "You... you were shot, baby."

His eyes closed for a fraction of a second before opening again, his eyes no longer glazed over. No, this time his was fully alert, the realization of what happened clearly taking its effect on Tate's sleepy mind.

"What do you remember?"

"You. Holding a gun…" He paused, swallowing hard. "To my head."

Chapter Twenty-Six

Tate

My head really fucking hurt. It hurt so much I could barely tolerate the throb that radiated through every crevice of my body. Dammit, everything hurt. My stomach, my head, and now my god damn heart as I stared at the one woman who could hurt me like no fucking other.

"What do you remember?" she asked, her face blotchy from tears.

"You. Holding a gun…" I paused, swallowing hard. Fuck, even my damn throat hurt. "To my head."

I felt the gasp before I heard it, my body instantly coming to life as it recognized the fear in that one tiny little sound. That one sound, the one of fear, did things to me I couldn't explain. It made me want to throw my body out from the bed and roar like a fucking lion. The sound of fear and pain spiked my adrenaline every time it roughly rolled over my skin, pushing me to shuddering heights where I couldn't think straight.

My eyes felt glazed, as if I had been staring for too long without blinking. I was still lost somewhere between slumber and being fully awake. But the painful sob that ripped from Low's lips had me more awake than I've ever been. My head snapped to the left. My head screamed in protest as I did. Fuck, that hurt! I groaned out in agony as I watched the woman I loved crumble to the ground beside my bed.

"Low," I croaked. God damn it, I could barely talk and I was becoming more and more frustrated every time I tried to swallow.

I could feel, rather than hear, her sobs becoming stronger and it weighed heavy on my heart. I still couldn't get the fucking fog to clear from my damn head. For the most part, I knew I was in a hospital, I knew I was in a bed, and I knew that I was injured… somewhere. Where? I had no fucking clue, but right then it felt like the only thing that was injured was my heart, and yet I still had no clue as to why it did.

"Low," I tried again, my voice not sounding so croaky but still hurting like a bitch. "Please. Low."

I felt the smooth, soft skin of her palm within mine, a feeling that was so familiar but yet so foreign. The gentle caress of her fingers against the very center of my palm was so soothing it almost washed away the sickening feeling that appeared in my gut. Almost.

"What happened?" I whispered, the action relieving the pain against my throat.

"You can't remember anything after I…" she trailed off.

I tried to focus on her but all I could see was a mass of blonde hair. She looked like a god damn angel, a glowing silhouette behind her, but something in the back of my painful mind told me she was nothing like an angel.

I felt the guilt seeping out of her, as if she was bleeding it out right in front of me. Why did she feel so damn guilty? Because she held a gun against my head? My mind was a mess of memories, dreams and things I didn't know if they were damn real. I groaned as I tried to remember what the hell happened to me, but coming up absolutely blank. Nothing. Fucking nothing other than a suffering scream at the back of mind.

"I can't remember."

My face was wet, why was my face wet? Fuck, I hadn't felt so god damn vulnerable in all of my life. I couldn't move my aching body, exhaustion seemingly taking over every fucking limb. I couldn't move my god damn head without a thundering pain slicing right through me. I was fucking vulnerable and it wasn't sitting well with me. At all.

"Why can't I fucking remember?" I growled, wilting back as the pain in my throat became too much.

"Baby, you've been through a lot."

Low's soothing voice wasn't putting me at ease like it normally would. No, right now I wanted nothing other than to get out of this god damn bed and walk right out of this suffocating room. She said I had been through a lot. Go figure. I wouldn't be here if I hadn't been through a lot. The problem was I had no fucking clue what it was. No fucking clue. Nothing. Not. A. Thing.

The wetness on my face was getting on my last nerve, it was getting worse. Was I bleeding or some shit? What the fuck? I tried to move my hand to wipe whatever the hell it was from my skin, but yet again, I was stuck to a motherfucking bed.

"Tell me, Low," I said, defeated.

She paused and I growled. Get the fuck on with it already. Wait, why was I feeling so much rage towards the woman I've loved for years? This was the woman who had been at the center of my world for so long and now it felt like she had just dropped off the face of it.

"Tate, you were shot by…" She suddenly paused, uncontrollable sobs leaving her perfectly sculptured lips.

Then it hit me. It hit me full fucking force as memories fleeted through my mind like a movie. It was as if I was there but watching as an outsider.

Guns.

Men.

Pain, so much fucking pain.

Mafia.

Low. Protecting what was mine.

Suddenly noises erupted around the room, drowning out Low, drowning out everything. What was that noise? It took me only moments to realize that damn awful noise was coming from my own fucking mouth, as if the shock and the pain were filtering straight from my foggy mind, right out into the room around us.

I tried to hold it back. I tried so god damn hard to gulp back the noise that just kept on coming. I could feel myself crumbling like a vulnerable child, like the vulnerable child I was all those years ago. My mind was still sifting through memories, years of memories that stayed with me but only now decided to show all their true colors.

Memories of my mother weeping uncontrollably on her knees in her bedroom, the bed still made as if she hadn't slept in it for weeks. The vulnerability of my younger self filled my entire body with dread as the memories just kept on coming.

Empty vodka bottle.

Pills on the floor.

A broken heart.

She was so limp, her body only focusing her energy in pouring out the grief through her tears, through the loud screams that broke the barrier of her lips. My former innocent self couldn't comprehend what he was seeing, as if it was one of those nightmares my sister couldn't control. Her tears kept on coming as she lay on the floor in a heap, the woman who was once always made up, always happy and cheery was gone. In her place was someone I didn't recognize, someone defeated, someone who had given up all hope.

I stood frozen on the spot as I concentrated on counting every single pill that lay within the fibers of the thick blue carpet.

Nineteen.

Twenty.

Twenty-one.

I knew exactly how many pills were in that tiny bottle. Exactly. I had been giving them to my mom for the first couple of weeks after my father was killed. They were pills to help her sleep, to help her ease the pain. Tears had already leaked out of my eyes, coating my skin in a fine sheen. I tried to focus through the blur, still counting those little white pills on the floor.

Twenty-seven.

Twenty-eight.

A sigh of relief escaped my lips as it finally registered that she hadn't taken any, twenty-eight pills were all there and accounted for. I quietly started to pick up the pills, counting each one as I went along, just to be sure.

I placed the pill bottle on the bedside cabinet once the pills were back in their rightful place, my focus now solely on the woman who was a quivering wreck on the floor.

"Momma," I whispered.

"Tate, go downstairs to your sister, baby. I just need to clean up the room." She sniffed, her body covered in goosebumps.

Suddenly, my body and heart were filled with rage. How dare she?

"No," I ground out, my voice and childlike self no longer innocent, only tainted. "You're going to get up and clean yourself up. Get in the shower."

"Do as you're told, Tate!" she cried.

With sure steps, I grabbed her by her shoulders, using all of my strength to get her body to her feet. I pulled as she protested, all but dragging her into the bathroom. I pretty much threw her down onto the toilet seat as I went to work on turning the shower on, grabbing towels from the bathroom closet as I waited for the water to heat.

She cried softly to herself as I pulled her back up and pushed her into the shower fully clothed. I had no idea if what I was doing was right, but in that moment I was past giving her sympathy. She had lost her husband, we had lost our father. I wasn't about to let her tumble down a road we wouldn't bring her back from.

I left the room as she wailed on the floor of the shower, slamming the door hard behind me. I stomped across the hallway, my anger boiling as I pushed open the door to my mom's bedroom. I grabbed the pills, running back out to the hallway and into the bathroom.

My mother suddenly stopped her crying as she watched me pour every single last white pill down the toilet before flushing them away. Turning, our eyes locked.

"What would've happened if it was Neva who walked in on that? What if she would've been too late?" I said, shaking my head in utter disbelief. "Get dressed. Go downstairs."

"I'm sorry," she breathed, standing on shaky legs as she turned off the shower.

"From now on…" I gulped. "Don't look me in the eye."

With that, I turned on my heel and left her in the bathroom.

"Coward," I whispered as I walked into my bedroom and slumped into a heap on my bed.

I cried myself to sleep that night… and every night after that as my mother did exactly as I asked.

She never looked me in the eye again.

My eyes blinked open against the harsh light in the hospital room. I hadn't even realized I had closed my eyes. The noise previously pouring from my lips had stopped, the only sounds audible were the hiccups coming simultaneously from Low and me.

My gaze dropped onto Low, who was still crumpled on the floor, holding onto my hand for dear life. Her head was bowed, her shoulders slouched. She looked defeated, exhausted but still so fucking beautiful. She's my calm before the storm, my own slice of heaven, my best friend, my lover… one day, my wife.

"Baby," I whispered, squeezing the tiny hand that was cradled in my own.

Her gaze lifted, locking with mine. Her eyes were puffy, the soft flesh of her cheeks were blotchy and the tears she had cried blended with her flushed skin. She was a mess, but yet so stunningly beautiful that she could still take my breath away.

My beauty hiding beneath the chaos.

"Baby, come here," I whispered, my voice still husky.

Without a single hesitation, she leapt to her feet, wrapping her arms around me gently.

"I'm so sorry," she sobbed into my neck.

Her scent surrounded me, encasing me and trapping me. Like always, like it always had. I consoled her as she wept, her sobs now completely uncontrollable as I held on to her. Tears built behind my eyes as I stroked the mass of blonde hair. One more gut-wrenching sob from her and I was right there with her.

We held onto each other for a lifetime, holding on as we poured our pain, grief and love into the room. Suddenly, my hand was moving of its own accord, my body fighting against the sheer exhaustion that had taken over my body. My hand stilled as it grazed the soft flesh of Low's waist, since her top had ridden up some. I was hesitant. Closing my eyes, I stopped over-thinking and gently placed my hand on the warm heat of her silky flesh, over her heart. I wanted her to know I remembered, that I could beat myself for ever forgetting.

How could I ever forget about the woman who stole my heart? She stole my heart, encasing her own inside it before placing it back deep in my chest, but instead of one heart slowly beating… there were two.

Chapter Twenty-Seven

Low

I could feel Tate's fresh tears running into my own as we both broke open, bleeding out together. We just held each other as if our lives depended on it, his hand softly running lazy circles on the skin of my waist, as if trying to soothe me.

Our moment was suddenly interrupted by someone clearing their throat. I turned my head, noticing Dr. Carter standing in the threshold of the door with a smile on his face.

"I'm so sorry to disturb you, but I need to check Tate out," he said, walking to Tate's bedside and smiling down at him. "I'm Dr. Carter. Welcome back."

"Thank you," Tate replied warmly. There was something about Dr. Carter that made you feel at ease.

"Well, your vitals look good. How are you feeling? Any pain?"

"My body aches, and I have some pain," Tate said with a wince. Some pain, my ass; more like a lot of pain. "I'm really thirty too."

"Okay, buddy. We'll get you some more water and some pain meds, but first I need to see how your wound is doing. That okay with you?"

Tate nodded, his hand moving from my chest only to fall into my palm. Squeezing gently, kept his gaze on me as Dr. Carter went to work removing the bandage over Tate's stomach. My gaze momentarily moved over to where Dr. Carter was now examining Tate's stitches. I counted twenty-two, but I had no doubt there was internal dissolvable ones too. That's a lot of stitches. Guilt quickly surrounded the air as I tried to breathe.

"You're looking good, Tate. Your stitches are doing well, and if your vitals stay steady, I see no reason for you not to go home in a couple of days." Dr. Carter smiled. "Now, you've been through a lot, your body is going to need time to heal properly, so I would say no strenuous activity for six weeks until we know you're fully healed."

"Thank you." Tate yawned, exhaustion taking over his strong features.

"Get some rest, buddy. Tomorrow we can see how you deal with being on your feet. I'm sure you'd prefer your catheter out as soon as possible." Dr. Carter smiled before taking Tate's notes and leaving the room.

The minute the door closed behind him, Tate's gaze shifted to me.

"There's a fucking catheter… down there?" he groaned, his eyebrows pinching together. "Baby, please tell me he's joking."

"Baby, you've been out for nearly a week."

"Nurses have been looking at my junk, haven't they?" he groaned again, this time a little less dramatic than before.

"Yes, but I made sure I was there every time they did," I whispered.

Tate's eyes fluttered closed for a moment as he nodded; he was exhausted. He yawned and, before I knew it, he was snoring gently. Out like a light. I took the moment and made it ours, holding onto his hand, which had slackened within my grasp.

The warmth of his skin warmed every piece of my flesh, my muscles, my nerves. Everything that was once cold deep inside me from the years of lies was awakened in that moment. The moment where I realized every little lie I placed within the glass confines of my jar of hearts was completely inconsequential. I had spent the last six years focusing on the consequences of my actions, my thoughts, my feelings. For the first time in a long time, I stopped thinking about what would happen, what could happen. For the first time, I was ready to live my life in the moment and share that moment with the people who have stood by me, who knew me for the girl I so desperately wanted to be.

Because, as someone once said, *love conquers all.*

But could I really give up the habits of a lifetime? Could I really give up the feeling of fear with every breath I took, with every step I took? My jar of hearts was the only constant thing in my life: it was the only thing that didn't judge me. My jar didn't discriminate: it didn't care who I was when I placed each little heart inside it. It didn't care whether I was Low Parker or Willow Knoxx.

Could I really break the bond stopping me from moving forward?

As my gaze rolled over Tate's sleeping body, I reached for the jar I had hidden in my suitcase. My shaking hand left Tate's as I unscrewed the lid on the jar, the action in itself filling me with fear.

Gulping back the lump that had quickly formed in my throat, my hand pushed through the threshold of the glass, my fingers brushing against every little lie I had told in the last six years. Tears filled my eyes as I gently cupped some of them within the palm of my hand, holding on for seconds before letting them slip slowly between my fingers.

"What's this?" Tate's groggy voice pulled me out of my thoughts, my hand instantly stilling inside the glass jar.

"I... I..." I stuttered, unable to form the words I never thought I would have to say.

"Baby?" he whispered.

I jumped slightly as his palm came to my face. He had regained some of his strength and I couldn't help but lean into his soft touch.

"Tell me," he urged, his eyes landing on my hand still completely frozen inside the jar.

I swore I wouldn't lie anymore, I swore I wouldn't keep anything from him anymore. But did I want to tell him about this? Did I want to show him all of the bad, even if it didn't come with much good?

Pushing back my thoughts, I finally locked eyes with him. Even if it was going to destroy us, even if he was going to see me for all of my flaws, he had a right to know.

"Six years ago, Jace saved me and my mother from the hands of my father, from the hands of the mafia. I had just witnessed my father and his men brutally beat a young woman right in front of my eyes. She begged and pleaded for her life, only her cries went unanswered. She had exposed a small portion of my father's business to the police, and even though the police were all pretty much in my father's pocket, she still broke the code of the family.

"I didn't see that poor girl again. I turned on my heel as I heard a blood-curdling scream leave her lips and went in search of my mother who was somewhere inside the large manor. I found her in her room, crying softly into her pillow on her bed. She had heard the poor girl's screams from the opposite side of the house. It only took a gentle coaxing to convince her to leave with me. She had already lost her son to the hands of my father, and she wasn't about to lose me to it too."

With a deep sigh, I paused as the girl's scream became louder in my head. "That night, as the full moon filled the night, we left through my bedroom window while the guards were doing a shift change, the dark night cloaking us. We made it to a small motel just outside of town. We had nowhere else to go. My mother had fallen in love with a mafia boss, her parents had disowned her years before, and you couldn't have friends – never have friends outside the mafia.

"We stayed in the rundown motel room for just a couple of hours, trying to regenerate the energy it had taken to escape before we rented a car – using cash – and drove for miles. After five hours of driving, we pulled up at another motel. Using cash again, we checked in and instantly fell asleep in the shabby room. We stayed there for two weeks while we worked out our next steps. Then, one night, I heard a creaking along the hardwood flooring outside our motel room. It was Jace. He had heard of our escape through his family and decided to do the same: some of us just were not cut out for that life. Two days later, we all had an alias. Jace had gotten us and himself a place to live; he had enrolled us both in high school, and life sorta just carried on."

I stopped, watching as Tate tried to take in every detail of my account. His eyes flashed to mine as he nodded for me to carry on.

"Once we had gotten into a routine, we ensured we embraced a 'normal' life, only looking over our shoulders when no one else was watching. Then, three weeks later, a news article caught my eye. The girl my father had beaten in the manor was found brutally beaten and murdered. I recognized her eyes, ones that held so much fear and remorse. It was right then I decided to place every little lie I made from that day forward into the jar. It was a reminder that every step, every action, every word had consequences."

I stopped talking, trying to gauge Tate's reaction. He was silent. My god. He was silent for so long I almost thought I'd lost him. Not just to his injuries, but also his heart. I could feel my world crumbling around me as he stared blankly over my shoulder. I turned, hoping there was someone stood behind us, hoping what he was staring at wasn't just flashes of our future, flashes of the mafia daughter trying to live a normal life, and failing miserably.

My gaze drifted over my shoulder. A gasp of relief leaving my lips as I stared at Lorena, Tate's mother. Their relationship had never been easy; she could never look her son in the eyes and in turn their relationship was completely broken.

But right then, right in that moment, she was finally staring at Tate, finally looking him right in the eyes. A solemn smile graced his lips as he nodded gently towards his mother. She nodded in return, turning on her heel as she left the room, clicking the door closed behind her.

Suddenly, without warning, Tate emptied the contents of the mason jar onto my lap. Two hundred and one paper hearts stared back at me as I tried to study Tate's face for some kind of answer.

"I don't understand," I whispered, a small tear escaping.

"All you need to understand is," he paused, collecting the single tear with the pad of his thumb before tasting the salty moisture with his lips, "I fell in love with this."

His hand splayed across my chest, above my very own thundering heart.

"All of these little hearts are insignificant. The only heart I'm interested in is yours."

I stared at him in bewilderment as he reached over to the table at his bedside, picking up a blank square of paper and drawing one large black heart with a black marker, placing it in the glass jar that stood upright on my lap.

"Now you can carry my heart wherever you go: that little heart represents my love, adoration, desire and need for you." He paused, screwing the lid on tight. "You own me, baby. You own my heart and I never want you to let it go."

"Tate." I gasped, the breath leaving my lungs so fast I was dizzy.

"Low, I love you for who you are. You're caring, passionate, and selfless. In the face of what you've been through, your only thought was to protect us, to keep that ugly side locked away. But that ugly side is what makes you so fucking special, sweetheart. That side only illuminates the purity of your heart, the heart that stole mine all those years ago and never gave it back. I love you for you, Low. Not who you think you should be. God, I love you, baby."

"I love you too," I whispered, leaning into his touch as his palm rested against my cheek once more. Tears fell from my eyes, but were quickly wiped away by Tate.

"Don't cry, baby. I can't take it seeing you cry and being able to nothing about it to stop those tears."

"I'm sorry." I sniffed.

"Never, ever be sorry for finally letting me see you feel, baby," he said, wiping away the tears that just kept on falling.

Holding back the sob that was about to pour from my lips, I dropped my mouth to his. Taking his mouth like I always wanted, showing him just how much I loved him. How much he made me feel. The deep groan that escaped his lips was swallowed as I plunged my tongue into his mouth, fighting against his to give him that little piece of me I was always holding back.

"I paper heart you, Low," he whispered into my mouth, taking my heart to new heights as he showed me just how much he paper hearted me with his tongue.

Chapter Twenty-Eight

It had been three days since Tate poured my lies out of my jar. Three days since he replaced all of my lies with a single drawn heart. Three days of watching him get out from his bed as he winced back the pain.

I watched in awe as he took his first tentative steps three days ago, his catheter out and all of his machines unhooked. He walked like a toddler, his steps unsure and weak as he tried to move further into his room. Exhaustion overcame him though, and I felt as defeated as he did as the physiotherapist helped him back into bed.

"Why doesn't my body understand that my head wants me to fucking walk?" he growled, adjusting his pillows on his bed as he slowly sat up, leaning against his makeshift back support.

"It will soon, baby. Just give it time," I whispered gently, holding onto his hand again.

"I just want to hold you without the pain," he admitted, breaking my heart as he squeezed my hand gently.

"Maybe we can," I whispered.

Surely I could get into his bed without hurting him. If I got onto his good side, maybe it wouldn't hurt him too much. And that's exactly what I did.

Taking off my Chucks, I pulled back the sheet that covered the lower half of Tate's body, his abdomen completely on display as I slid in gently beside him. A small smile crept across his lips as I lay my head in the crook of his shoulder, my hand resting on his pec.

A sigh of contentment left his lips as his nose brushed against my hair, inhaling as he breathed.

"I've missed this," he muttered, "I've missed you. I paper heart you, baby."

"I paper heart you too," I whispered, my gaze locking on the jar that stood proud on Tate's bedside table for all to see.

It was no longer my jar of lies, no longer my little jar of broken hearts.

It was the jar that held my past, my present and now my future. The memories of my lies would always be with me as long as I had that jar, but my present and future would always tell me the beauty behind those lies would always outshine the ugly.

I woke with a jolt three hours later, Tate flat out beside me. We must have drifted off. As my eyes adjusted to the harsh light, I looked around the room to try and understand what had woken me from my sleep. Realizing it was my cell, I slowly pulled myself from Tate's warm body and off the bed. Reaching into my pocket, I pulled out my cell: it was Jace.

I hadn't heard from him since the day he gave me my suitcase before walking right out of the room.

Sliding my finger across the screen, I answered the call.

"Hello," I whispered.

"I believe he's awake," Jace's voice rang into my ear.

"Yeah, he's still recovering but he's awake. He should be allowed home soon."

"That's good." He paused, silence taking over the line as I waited to hear what was going on.

"Willow." He sighed. "You're safe."

His words penetrated my heart in a series of pins and needles. What did he mean? Before I could ask, he answered for me.

"You have been removed from the table."

"I don't understand."

"You will, soon enough."

"Jace, what does that even mean?" I demanded.

"It means… it means I'm sorry."

Then the call ended, shattering my heart. I knew what he had done. I knew what was going on but I didn't want to admit it. I didn't want to hear myself say it. Then my brain over took my heart.

Jace Rowe was now head of the Rowe family.

I was never going to have to take the chair at my table.

Suddenly, my cell pinged in my hands, alerting me to a text message. Sliding my finger across the screen, I was hit with a series of newspaper article headlines.

Julius Rowe found dead.

Jace Rowe rumored to have taken his place.

Twelve bodies recovered from the Knoxx family manor.

Has the Knoxx family been wiped out?

Jace saved me. Jace saved Tate. He saved all of us.

I owed him my life.

Chapter Twenty-Nine

Six weeks later…

I watched in total fascination as Tate walked effortlessly across the kitchen of our new home, his abdomen completely exposed as he sauntered his way towards me shirtless, only wearing a pair of low slung jeans. My mouth watered as he moved with slow and sure steps, completely barefoot. He had come a long way since the incident, since he was shot. He walked with a slight limp now, but it only added to the mysterious hotness that is Tate James.

The minute he was released from hospital, he made it his business to find a perfect home for his family, for us. Using our collected savings, we managed to pick out a small two-bedroom home only twenty minutes away from campus.

"What are you doing, baby?" I whispered from my seat on the sofa.

I watched as his eyes turned from intense to smoldering in an instant, the act in itself doing things to my body I don't think I'd ever come to understand.

"I have a present for you," he said as he stepped between my legs.

Reaching out his hand, he nodded with a small smile as I tentatively placed mine within his. It was an act that still brings tears to my eyes even now. Even through the foggy memories of sedation, the thing he truly remembered first was my touch, my hand within his.

"What sort of present?" I asked breathlessly as he walked us in the direction of our bedroom.

"You'll see." He winked.

We walked towards our door, his steps slower than they used to be. His hand rested on the handle, pausing for a moment before looking back at me.

"What's going on, Tate?" I asked, pulling back on his hand.

I had no idea what he was doing, what he had on the other side of that room.

Tate's eyes locked with mine as he tried to assess my features, trying to gauge how I'm going to react to his present. His hands cupped my face and his lips grazed against mine in a sweetly torturous kiss.

"Trust me," he breathed as he pulled his lips from mine.

My body trembled in response.

"Okay."

Tate flung open the door to the bedroom and I was suddenly frozen to the spot as I took in everything I was seeing.

The walls were no longer bare. Instead they were now painted a duck egg blue. Instead of hardwood flooring, there was now thick soft carpet. To the right stood the most beautiful white wood-framed bed I had ever seen, complete with matching blue bedding. On the left against the wall was a dresser made in the same white wood as the bed. But what I saw next brought tears to my eyes. Sitting on a side unit was a small jar: my mason jar.

With a gulp of courage, I stepped inside the room, my toes loving the soft carpet against the bare flesh. With shaky steps, I walked towards the side unit. My eyes locked onto the mason jar. Inside the glass prison was a single paper heart, hanging from the tiniest piece of string I had ever seen. I picked up the jar and unscrewed the cap. Lifting, I watched as the paper heart attached to the string left the confines of the glass. It was attached to the lid.

"Do you like it?" Tate asked tentatively from the doorway.

The tears had long since fell. I didn't think I could've loved this man any more than I already did, but in that moment, my heart swelled for the man I loved.

"I love it, baby," I whispered as I placed the lid back on the jar, screwing it back in place before putting it back on the unit.

I turned, wiping my face in the process and watched as a beautiful smile took over Tate's face. I was quickly moving, the feel of the carpet between my toes forgotten as my body ached to touch the man who had captured me mind, body and soul.

Without a second thought, I crashed my lips to his, melting into the warm heat of his body as his hands encircled my waist, pulling me against him. I whimpered as his arms wrapped around me, encasing me in his scent and warm heat.

"I paper heart you," he whispered against my mouth before plunging his tongue between my lips.

It had been just over seven weeks since he'd touched me, since I intimately felt the warmth of his bare skin against my own. The kiss quickly turned from sweet and loving to fast, hard and wanting. I wanted him to pull me onto his hips and carry me to the bed, but it was too soon for that. He was still recovering: we were still recovering.

I moaned into his mouth as my hands slid into his hair, gripping on for dear life as he devoured my mouth with his tongue. He hissed as I gripped hard, pulling him closer to my body.

"Shit, baby," he groaned as he walked us towards our bed, our lips locked in a battle of losing restraint.

"Tate," I moaned into his mouth.

Before I knew what had happened, I felt the hard surface of our bed against the back of my knees. I froze instantly. He wasn't ready for this. He was still healing.

"Baby I—"

I was swiftly cut off as I felt my body falling against the soft mattress, gasping as Tate quickly pressed his solid body above mine.

"Don't," he growled as he flexed his hips against my jean-covered center. "Don't stop this, baby. I haven't touched you in so damn long."

He flexed his hips once more and all rational thought went right out the window as I moaned his name.

"That's it. Can you feel that, baby? Can you feel what you do to me every time I look at you?" he whispered, peppering kisses against the soft flesh of my neck. "My beauty beneath the chaos."

"Oh god. Tate," I groaned, the desperation thick in my voice.

"Let me make love to you," he whispered.

Placing a soft and gentle kiss on my stomach, he smoothly glided his nose against the skin of my abdomen, moving his way up to the swell of my breasts, encased in their lace prison. My breasts were heaving with every breath. They were heaving so much I could barely stand it the minute his fingers glided beneath my bra and found the aching peaks beneath.

Tate's fingers worked my nipples, which didn't need much coaxing to respond, rolling them between his finger and thumb, spiking pleasure straight to my core. Within seconds, my tank top was quickly peeled away from my feverish skin, my bra along with it. I was bare from the waist up, matching him.

Sitting up on the bed, my hands moved to his sides. His scar stood out against his tanned and toned abdomen. Fear clinched my heart as I took in the injury I had caused, tears burning the back of my eyes.

Tate's fingers grasped my chin, lifting my face to his eye line.

"I wear my scars just like you do, baby. With fucking pride," he whispered.

I nodded, pushing back the tears before bravely leaning forward. His fingers left my face, but his eyes bore holes into me as I placed one soft kiss at the center of his scar: a silent apology, a silent plea of my love for him.

He hissed as I placed another kiss on the very edge of his scar. Gazing up through my lashes, I watched his reaction, trying to read him even with his eyes closed. I placed one last kiss on the opposite end of the scar, lingering as I swiped my tongue right down the middle of it.

"Shit," he growled, his eyes flying open.

The minute my tongue left his searing skin, I was right back where I started. On my back, beneath him. His hands went straight to my jeans, popping the button before pulling them roughly from my legs. There was a new intensity to his pace, as if he couldn't get the barriers between us away quick enough. The panties I had in place under my jeans? Yeah, gone. Completely ripped apart by the animalistic Tate panting hard above me.

I was bare, and I quickly realized I wasn't the only one. In his moment of fierce want, he stripped the rest of his clothes, leaving me with a perfect view of his delicious body. From head to toe, he was a picture of the perfect man. Dark hair: just long enough to pull on. Dark searing eyes that could have you feeling completely vulnerable. Shoulder muscles. Pec. Abs: a freaking sea of never ending abs. That deep set V that was every woman's wet dream. The happy trail your eyes couldn't help but follow right down to his hard length. But he wasn't just hard.

My, god. He was painfully hard. Painfully beautiful.

"Tate," I whispered, trying to pull him out of the trance-like state he had gotten himself into. He was just starting at me, drinking me in. "Tate," I repeated.

That seemed to get his attention as I heard a deep growl leave his lips before he was back above me, his mouth crashing against mine. His tongue delved into the deep, dark depth of my mouth as his hand moved between us, his fingers brushing against my core, making me quiver with throbbing need.

"I'm going to make you feel, baby," he groaned as he slipped a finger easily inside me.

I moaned out from the sudden invasion. The delirious high that flooded my mind took my breath away.

"I always feel with you, Tate," I moaned as his finger moved at a leisurely pace inside of me.

"I can't think straight when you moan like that, baby. I want you so bad, but I want to make love to you, not fuck you to oblivion. You deserve to be loved, every day."

I moaned as his words took me to new heady heights, his fingers slowing almost to a stop, giving me new sensations I had never experienced before.

"Make love to me, Tate," I whispered, my hand moving between us and gripping his thick, hard length in my palm.

He hissed as I squeezed with enough pressure to send his head dizzy with lust before guiding him to my entrance, stopping the moment his tip slipped inside. I moved my other hand above my head, seeking out his other hand, I placed it within mine. Always holding on, always in the moment.

Tate's hand moved from between us, grabbing onto my hip as he slowly took me, inch by inch until he was fully seated inside me.

"Christ, you feel so good," he growled.

I was growing impatient. My need for him overtaking any logical thought I might have had. Flexing my hips, I grinded against him, trying to find that delicious friction. Tate quickly got the hint as he started moving oh so slowly inside of me.

Tears stung my eyes as his penetrated mine, watching every move, every emotion, every moan that coated my skin as he slowly made love to me. He moved at such a slowly delicious pace it didn't take long for the orgasm to build. His grip on my hand tightened as he placed soft sensual kisses upon my lips, his other hand still holding on for dear life to my hip.

His tongue probed my mouth as I panted against him, trying to fight back the impending orgasm as his pace quickened, his movements becoming less synchronized as he pounded inside me relentlessly. Within moments, completely without warning, Tate's name was a whisper upon my lips as my orgasm ripped through me so fast that I was sure I was free falling.

"I paper heart you, Low," he growled as he tumbled down into his own delirious bliss.

Panting and blissfully relaxed, Tate dropped his weight against me. I couldn't deny I missed the heavy feeling of him above me.

"I paper heart you too, Tate," I whispered breathlessly.

I felt him smile against my neck before he rolled on to his side, taking me along with him, still fully seated inside me.

"I have another present for you, baby."

Pulling out of me slowly, he walked over to our dresser, completely naked. My mouth salivated at the sight of him. Well, until he held up what I presumed was my present, a huge smile on his face.

Hanging on two of his fingers was the most delicate silver chain I had ever laid eyes on. My eyes roamed every inch of silver. It seemed to go on forever until my gaze locked on the tiny pendent that hung beautifully from the chain. It was a miniature glass jar, so small I had to gaze hard to really take in its beauty.

With sure steps, Tate walked towards me, crouching beside the bed and holding up the necklace. It was only then I realized what was in the miniature jar. It was one tiny paper heart that dangled from delicate string, attached to the lid of the sealed jar.

"Now you don't have to carry around that big jar. Now you can carry my heart with you wherever you go," he whispered, moving my mass of blonde hair resting on my shoulder.

I closed my eyes as the light weight of the chain hit my neck, the chill from the silver chain licking against the flesh of my chest. I opened my eyes, looking down at the beautiful gift he had given me.

My heart was full.

My soul content.

My life complete.

No one could take away the feeling of pure bliss that washed over me in the moment. Not my father, not the mafia, not my lies or any of my past. Nothing. No one. Because it didn't matter where you came from or the ugliness of your past: as long as you knew where you were going, the ugliness would truly make the beauty shine.

Epilogue

Four months later

"I still can't get over it." I smiled, chewing on the best piece of pasta I had ever tasted. "You can cook."

Logan smiled warmly at me, his arm snaking around Neva's shoulder as he sat back and enjoyed having his ego stroked by me.

"I'm fatter than I should be, I swear," Neva groaned, rubbing her protruding stomach. "I'm twice the size of other moms at the prenatal checks."

"I love you like this." Logan smiled, placing his hand on Neva's stomach. "There's more of you to feast on."

"Again with the euphemisms," Tate groaned, placing his fork on the plate. "I don't want those pictures tainting my delicate mind."

I laughed softly as I watched my friends interact around our table. Logan, Neva, Colt and Zane bantered like usual, Colt driving most of us nuts. There was one person missing though. One person I still couldn't get off my mind.

Jace.

I had been checking the newspapers relentlessly to try and find out how he was doing. No phone calls. No letters. Nothing. It hurt my heart daily, knowing he had put himself into that position to save something he thought he could never have. A normal life.

Things had changed, like he said they would. I was still in college, Tate was still recovering, Neva was now four months pregnant, Logan was now working for a modern architecture company. Everything around us was changing. I had gotten myself a job at the coffee house alongside Jared, who was still pining over the loss of Preston, who left to take care of his sick mom.

Neva still worked at Bones, but only playing her set which Dex now pays her for. Dex and Trix: that is a whole new chapter of its own. Trix was still pissed at Dex, Dex was still hopelessly in love with the woman who couldn't separate love from paid sex.

Lorena and Tate's relationship was better. Not great, but better. He finally opened up to me, telling me what happened the day he walked into his mom's bedroom. He never planned on telling Neva something so heartbreaking, not after everything she had been through, but she overheard us talking. Learning that her mother had planned to take her own life to be with her father broke her heart, but it was clear she understood.

Neva was still seeing her therapist on a weekly basis. She still had her moments when her PTSD was overwhelming, but she was making good progress.

Everything was falling into place.

Except for Jace.

"You okay, baby?" Tate asked, taking my empty plate from in front of me and placing in on the kitchen counter.

"Yeah, I just… I just wonder what he's doing," I admitted.

All eyes turned to me. They knew who I was talking about: the man who had saved us all, if unknowingly to the rest of my friends.

"I miss his stupid ass too." Neva sniffed, drying her eyes. "God, ignore me. Stupid hormones."

I chuckled lightly, watching as every one of my friends looked at me solemnly. They all knew the truth. I hadn't kept any part of my and Jace's life before we moved here a secret. I was done with secrets, lies and deceit. I was under the impression that spilling those secrets, those lies, would make me weak, make me vulnerable. But they didn't. They only made me stronger.

"I swear, if he knocks at the door, I'm not here."

All eyes moved to the front door, where Trix had let herself in, following her as she stepped into our bathroom and locked the door behind her. Jesus, here we go again.

Seconds later, in walked a pretty pissed off Dex.

"She's in the bathroom again, isn't she?" He sighed, defeated.

"I'll talk to her," I said, standing from the table.

"No. I'm done. I'm so done there isn't a damn word for it!" he yelled, turning to the bathroom door. "You hear that, Trix?! I'm fucking done!"

With an apologetic glance towards me, he stormed right out of the house, slamming the door shut behind him.

"So… I'm just going to see if she's okay." Colt smiled, standing from his seat at the table.

"Don't you fucking dare," I hissed, pointing at his waist. "Now's not the time to think with your dick, Colt. You're not touching her: if you do, I will shoot you myself."

Not everything had changed. I still kept my Glock under my pillow and my secondary attached to my ankle. You know, just in case.

Baby steps. Tiny baby steps.

The End

Finding Forever

Angel's story

Coming late 2014

Drink. Ink. Drink. Ink. Maybe sleep.

It's been two years – two years since I started with my new life.

Two years since I walked out of that bar and drove as far away from that town as I could.

Two years since the bottle became my best friend.

Two years since my father landed himself back in jail; two years since my mother disowned me.

I'm a tattoo artist, working ink into the skin of people who have no idea of the man I am. Just the man who I pretend to be.

Vile. Disgusting. Evil.

I can feel myself spiraling out of control. Most days I don't even know my own name, never mind those of the faceless women who are wrapped around my naked body every night.

I can't flush her out. She's in my dreams, my nightmares, my damn thoughts all day, every day.

Her screams. Her pain. Her heart broken.

It's my fault.

Now I'm paying the price of taking away the chance of finally finding my own forever.

Dear Reader,

Thank you so much for taking the time out of your life to read this book! I hope you were thoroughly entertained and enjoyed reading it as much as I enjoyed writing it.

If you have any extra time, PLEASE leave a review on Amazon or Goodreads, alternatively you can send me an email (s.k.hartley@-hotmail.co.uk) so I can personally thank you.

I'm forever grateful for each and every one of you who read the words I put down on the page, and I hope to be re-invited to your bookshelf with my next release.

Dream big, aim high.

Much love,
S.K.

Acknowledgements

To my husband and Little Dude – Thank you so much for your continued support and encouragement, even when I was locked away in the writing cave, you still stood by me and pushed me to turn my dream into a reality. I love you.

To my editor, Jenn (who is no doubt reading this right now) – Thank you for putting up with my stupid tense issues, my overuse of commas, and my ridiculous addiction for over-expressive adjectives. Thank you for being a friend and my awesome editor.

To Judi, Kiki and Crystal, my team of publicist's – thank you for being so amazingly awesome, especially during a crisis. You're awesome at what you do and I'm so happy to be working alongside you.

To Cami, my beta reader – I love that you don't put up with my shit and that you're honest when something doesn't work. If it wasn't for you, *Finding Us* wouldn't be what it is today. I look forward to working with you with my future works.

To Ena, my awesome promo expert! – Thank you so much for everything that you do for me as an author and a friend. Your organization skills are second to none and no matter what the question, maybe you always answer me honestly. I love you!

To Emma Hart and Kendall Ryan, some of the best writers I know – Thank you for your support and friendship, I've loved every second of getting to know you guys and I can honestly say that I can't wait to meet you both!

To some of the most awesome people, some of who I've had the pleasure of meeting and others I am yet to meet but love like crazy – JB Salsbury; K. Bromberg; Katy Evans; Tijan; Jay McLean; Rachel Van Dyken; Michelle Valentine; Kirsty Moseley; Chelle Bliss; Kitty French; Erin Noelle; Ilsa Madden-Mills; Megan Noelle; T.A. McKay; K.

Langston… You all inspire me every day, inspire me to be a better writer and an all-round better person.

To the blogs that work tirelessly to promote their authors – Eyecandy Book Store; Swoon Worthy Books; Romance Addiction; Books, Coffee & Wine; Panty Dropping Book Blog; 50 Shades of Fictional Men and so many more! Thank you for the work that you do, you're all rockstars!

To my Heartbreakers – Thank you for supporting me. Your belief and support mean the absolute world. Thank you for being so awesome!

About the Author

S.K. Hartley is a wife, mother and author of The Bad Boy Series.

Based in the not so sunny North West of England you can find her either glued to her computer desk, in the public library (Yes, they still exist!) or floating around her favorite author's books signings.

S.K. Hartley has an unhealthy obsession with coffee, chocolate and retro computer games and a healthy obsession of stalking indie authors.

Follow S.K. Hartley!

www.facebook.com/RestrainedLove
www.twitter.com/S_K_Hartley
www.skhartleyauthor.com
www.goodreads.com/author/show/7020553.S_K_Hartley

30771448R00127

Made in the USA
Charleston, SC
26 June 2014